TERROR NOVA
WRITERS RETREAT

Published in Canada by Engen Books, St. John's, NL.

Library and Archives Canada Cataloguing in Publication

Title: Terror nova. Writers retreat, an anthology of Newfoundland inspired horror.
Names: Hickey, Mike, 1984- editor.
Description: Short stories written by several authors and selected by Mike Hickey.
Identifiers: Canadiana (print) 20210264977 | Canadiana (ebook) 20210265043 | ISBN 9781774780572
   (softcover) | ISBN 9781774780589 (PDF)
Subjects: CSH: Horror tales, Canadian (English)—Newfoundland and Labrador. | CSH: Short stories,
   Canadian (English)—Newfoundland and Labrador. | CSH: Canadian fiction (English)—21st century.
Classification: LCC PS8323.H67 T48 2020 | DDC C813/.0873808971809052—dc23

Distributed by:
Engen Books
www.engenbooks.com
submissions@engenbooks.com

First mass market paperback printing: December 2021
Cover Image: Mike Hickey

TERROR NOVA
WRITERS RETREAT

ENGEN
BOOKS

TERROR NOVA
WRITERS RETREAT

ENGEN
BOOKS

To Hayward Dobbin, Uncle of Jon Dobbin.

An educator, an inspiration, and a friend.
He lived his life to the fullest.

FOREWORD

I find myself writing the foreword of this book, *Terror Nova: Writers Retreat*, before finishing writing the book itself for one very specific reason—I need to qualify the name of the lead character.

Months before the first *Terror Nova* was released, my publisher, Matt LeDrew, and I began discussing the possibility of a follow-up and how we would set it up differently. He suggested we go meta; have it set at a launch event of a book called Terror Nova. I loved the idea of making the book a part of the story but as I started to write I drifted a bit from the plan and found myself fighting with one major element: the character of the author of *Terror Nova*.

There are a lot of people who came together to make *Terror Nova* a thing; from Matt & his team at Engen to the incredible stable of authors who contributed, to the support we received once the book got out there, so to use my name as a character was instantly a big nope from me. I tried to start referring to the character who helmed the fictional version of the anthology as "The Author," but the problem then became that the framing narrative is set at a writers' retreat, and a chunk of the other characters are authors, so I started quickly running out of synonyms for "author" when trying to write around them.

It turned out that this was becoming a bit of a bigger problem than you'd expect and was leading me to a block as I was trying to navigate the weekend of the titular retreat while constantly coming up against the wall of the protagonist's name.

So, as a bit of an homage to some recently read books, I've settled on naming "The Author" Malcolm Hennessy.

Sharing initials with me is a bit of a compromise.

Mike Hickey
Summer 2021

"Stories are relics, part of an undiscovered pre-existing world. The writer's job is to use the tools in his or her toolbox to get as much of each one out of the ground as intact as possible."

- Stephen King

1

The sound of the changing terrain from craggy black top to gravel was welcomed by Malcolm Hennessy and even more welcomed by his stomach as he turned off the two lanes that he felt he'd been travelling on forever, despite it only being an hour or so to this point.

A flash of inspiration struck, and he used a voice command function of the phone paired to his car's entertainment system to take a memo.

"The faded asphalt splayed out in the distance as far as I could see, neatly bisected by the solid yellow line that seemed brightly defiant to the age of the road and the neglect shown to its infrastructure."

He stopped as he said it, curled his lips in disgust, and poked an eager finger at the trashcan icon showing on screen and then threw the car into park.

"Neglect shown to its infrastructure? Be better," he said out loud to himself in the empty car before grabbing the caramel-coloured satchel from the passenger seat and throwing the door open.

The waning afternoon sun threw his shadow far across the parking lot as he moved to the building reading "NAN & POP'S" in bright red block lettering over cracked and peeling white painted plywood, centered between two soft drink logos of equal levels of decay. Below it, the pink faded vinyl flag that once touted "24 & More!" flavours of ice cream now flapped flaccid and illegible in the breeze.

As he opened the door, a buzzer rang, and he could see from what appeared to be a living room behind the counter an older couple turn from watching *The Price Is Right* and pull themselves from their his & hers armchairs to waddle toward him.

He knew instantly that the food in this place was going to be amazing.

"'Ows ya doin', skipper?" the old fella, presumably the titular "Pop," asked as he cocked his head to the side.

"Alright, b'y, yourself?" Normally, Malcolm didn't have much of an accent, something often met with disappointment by expectant mainlanders he had business dealings with, but he always found himself slipping into the vernacular when around those he considered "heartier" Newfoundlanders.

"Dissisit" Pop shot back.

"Is anywhere fine?" asked Hennessy, looking to the half dozen empty tables lined around the space.

"Yes, my love," answered the presumed "Nan" appearing around the counter while tying a server's apron around her waist, "anywhere you'd like."

He shot her a gracious smile as he picked a table in the corner by a window and crossed to it, barely getting a chance to retrieve his laptop from the satchel before Nan was to him with a laminated menu and a glass of ice water.

"Today we 'as pea soup on," but his nose had already provided this information as soon as he'd set foot in the place, "and we got our fish & chips on speeshawl."

"Oh! A two-piece, please," he said, passing her back the

menu instantly.

"Dressing and gravy?"

"'Magine. Just on the fries, though." He winked at her and cocked his head the same way Pop did when he first entered the place. "Could I get a cup of coffee too, please?"

"Of course." She scribbled on her pad and walked back to Pop who was waiting in the commercial kitchen, next to the makeshift living room.

Malcolm smiled and took in the place. He had always loved finding these little greasy spoons on road trips, so much so that he had bypassed several reliable chains along the Trans Canada Highway and banked on a spot like this being nestled somewhere along this slightly desolate road. They reminded him of his childhood haunts, the ice cream parlours and take-outs from road trips or hot summer days when no one wanted to be in kitchen, and then, later, the late nights trekking home from whatever bar he had drank too much at.

This place specifically reminded him of a spot from his first summer away from home. He hadn't honed his culinary skills at that point and decided that, as far as meals went, it was more cost effective to get the $2 burgers & $7 chicken finger platters from the diner on the corner than to take public transit *all the way* to a grocery store and back. Taking in this quaint space, he realized just how similar they were; the pale cream walls covered in menu updates and what appeared to be grandchildren's artwork, the off-white tiles trodden with uncleanable salt stains, the Formica tables, and mismatched hard plastic chairs...

Back to work though. He unlocked the laptop's waiting screen and was instantly faced with his albatross; the manuscript for the follow-up to his modest success of a debut work, due in under a month, currently sitting at 4 pages and just under 800 words.

Before he was able to hit another key, Nan was back with a steaming cup of coffee.

"What's this 'ere? You a reporter or somet'ing?" Her tone, inquisitive and excited, almost as if she'd be proud if his answer was yes, subverted his reaction to the invasion of privacy.

"Uh, no." He was caught off guard. Normally he would have shut down to someone looking at his screen like this, but with this woman he didn't seem to mind so much. There was an ease with this Nan. "I'm an author."

"Ooh! Would we know anyt'ing you wrote?"

"I doubt it, I write genre stuff. Horror."

"My Cyril in there loves the 'orror. I'm not much for it meself. 'E got a big ol' stack of Stephen King back in the 'ouse." It was only when she said it that it clicked for him that the room next to the kitchen *was* their living room and it was a conduit to the rest of their home, adjoined to the business. "What's one of your books? I'll see if 'e knows it."

"*Terror Nova?*" He smiled awaiting the standard reaction.

"Good name. I 'aven't 'eard of it though. Lemme see about Cyril." And she disappeared into the kitchen just below a pegged menu identical to the one from the diner he used to go to. Suddenly, Pop, now known as Cyril, emerged beneath it and pulled out the chair across from him.

"Marjorie tells me you're a writer? Does 'orror books?"

"Yea, '*Terror Nova?*'"

"Good name, don't know it though."

"It's okay. Not many do," Malcolm chuckled through his self-deprecation.

"Well, if ya likes a good 'orror story, I got one." Cyril leaned back, the plastic chair creaking under his large frame, and tucked his thumbs into the suspenders he wore over his white t-shirt. "Marj is finishin' off your lunch, so while you waits…"

AN OCCURRENCE AT
THE SHIPWRECK HIDEAWAY
Alex McIntosh

This long coastal road was ravaged by rain on a cloudy evening dating back to October of 1933. Fog, thick like white smoke, swarmed that night. The quick tread of a loud trundling Ford motorcar broke foul murky puddles, as the squeaking rubber wipers tried in vain to beat away the elements.

Mr. Vincent Sullivan was behind the wheel dressed in a long raincoat and bowler hat, his suit jacket and trousers reasonably well protected despite the uninvited shower that poured down from a leak in the roof. A night to dress prim and proper it seemed not. His attempts to defog the glass with a mysterious old rag found under the seat only worsened his view of the rocky road.

A man long in the nose with damn near duck-down pillowcases under the eyes, Mr. Sullivan preferred drinking to sleeping. A most high-functioning alcoholic, he had a million things on his mind but could barely muster the courage to discuss them with his wife.

Mrs. Doris Sullivan, with her delightfully dark complexion, was as straight-faced as they came. She had made every effort to rinse water out of her tarnished hat, however she was more concerned with the briefcase on her lap that held papers to her upcoming novel.

"According to the maps we should be a little over thirteen miles away," she said.

"Thirteen miles in this titanic rainstorm might as well be sixty by the time we get to your publisher's house," Vincent retorted.

Doris was keen on making it there that evening and not missing a moment. The conditions they encountered upon exiting the front door of their cozy townhouse in St. John's were undesirable to say the least. Rain and fog were the norm in St. John's, but this torrential deluge was something else. Doris thought back to the letter she received from her Publisher. Grant's Publishing was one of the leaders in detective fiction across North America. Doris would say she "dabbled" in short stories although this was very modest. On the contrary, she was incredibly talented. Her decidedly grisly tale "The Scarecrow's Hand" had single-handedly put the *Cold Hearts and Colder Souls* anthology into the bestseller category, and publisher Andrew Grant had taken notice. Afterwards, a novel submission from Doris had resulted in the arrival of said letter:

Dear Mrs. Sullivan, I have the utmost pleasure in inviting you and your husband to stay with me at my oceanside home in Burnt Point on October 17th. I look forward to meeting you both in person.

Yours Sincerely, Andrew Grant.

Doris was thrilled although her face barely registered delight. Despite being so deadpan, she was excited for this mysterious vacation, and Andrew Grant was not somebody you could refuse a meeting with. His letter was no more an invitation than it was a polite demand. Andrew Grant was a reclusive enigma who few people claimed to have met in person. No phone calls. No personal meetings. This publishing powerhouse had assistants working under more assistants. A personal invitation to one of his many houses could only mean big business. "Doris Sullivan: bestselling novelist." It was a far cry from her past. She liked the ring to it.

"What of tonight if we can't make it to your publisher's house?" Vincent asked.

"We passed a few houses back there. I'm sure nobody will see us stuck."

"Root cellars and a few barns are hardly my idea of the Royal York. There's so much water on the road I believe a fishing vessel might pass us by any moment. Do you think they'd have any fish and chips to spare?"

"If I was presented with that, I'd probably celebrate the occasion by cracking a smile," Doris acknowledged.

While Doris specialized in the subject of murder, Vincent specialized in acuteness to murder glasses of various whiskies. He kept up with his incessant ramblings while Doris drew a wet pen and a mildly scrunched sheet of paper from the briefcase on her lap. She spoke her scribblings out loud.

"Black rubber slipped on the oozing earth. A fragrant windswept coastline etched among a torrential cataclysm of rain."

"You think you could turn this rain into whiskey while your mind works away?" Vincent asked.

"You can spare the whiskey while you're driving, Mr. Sullivan. The fish and chips are still on my mind."

Breakfast seemed so long ago. A boiled egg and two cigarettes did not really count as a solid square meal. The conversation had certainly stirred Doris' carnivorous senses. It was right then she caught a glimpse of something outside flickering in the distance.

"I see lights up ahead."

"Oh good, that'll be the nearest lighthouse telling us we're near land again." Vincent quipped.

Vincent gently cushioned the gas pedal beneath his sturdy leather boot. Behind a curtain of rain this old wooden structure made its presence known. Stood alone on the barren coast, a rickety sign danced in the elements emblazoned proudly with "The Shipwreck Hideaway." The hinges squeaked noisily even as the sea wind squealed. Vincent admired the swinging hurricane lamps illuminating this old dark house.

"You have the eyes of an albatross, I must say," Vincent complimented to his wife.

"And your driving wasn't as bad as I initially thought," Doris joked.

Their eyes locked onto this peculiar site.

"Do you think they're even open?" Vincent asked.

"There's only one way to find out. I just hope they serve food."

Doris ventured into the shower and paced towards the imposing wooden door hoping what was inside offered a better deal of comfort than the cold flurry of Newfoundland's usual conditions. The door cracked open, and the old wooden floor seemed to groan under the weight of Doris' black hiking boots. Vincent followed with curiosity as their eyes darted about the place. Here was a large, spacious dining room with only three small oak tables laid out, each with comfortable captain's chairs and solitary candles that gently flared. The shadows danced and made the room seem busier than it was. In truth, it was ghostly. The walls were made up of reclaimed wood obviously taken from a few boats and were decorated majestically with nautical memorabilia.

"Let me hang your coat, Doris," Vincent offered.

"Thank you," Doris replied, hypnotized. She took off her wet coat and cloche hat and observed the surroundings as if the place were a museum of curiosities.

Vincent racked their outdoor garments along the wall on what looked like large iron fishhooks. To the left of this, Vincent's eyes widened at something on the wall. He took a step back to marvel at it.

A painting with the title "Poseidon's Touch." No artist listed. A painting of the sea god himself standing muscular in the ocean with a potent expression upon his handsome profile. Vincent had an all too familiar feeling deep down in the pit of his stomach. Secretive. Taunted. All he could do was stare.

Doris herself was stood transfixed on another painting in the room entitled "Siren's Lair." No artist was listed for this one either, although a look at the styles dictated it to be the same person. This one featured numerous mermaids posing together sensually, their arms draped around each other in a beastly embrace. Doris felt pent up inside. Depression was very real to her, but she knew how to hide it.

"I wonder if the proprietor was expecting anybody to show up in this weather?" Vincent asked.

"The nautical themes do this place justice; it's just like the Marie Celeste," she said.

Doris locked eyes with her husband after a quick glance at the Poseidon painting that caught his eye. Realization dawned on her, and she felt a comfort being there with Vincent. Their companionship forged the foundation of their whole relationship. They mistook it for love early on. Who knows, in a way maybe it was. Doris was about to say something until she saw a look of alarm sweep across his face. There was somebody else in the room.

A man stood there, a Tattered shirt rolled up to the elbows. He was almost skeletal, with flared nostrils, bulging eyes, and slick white hair as if cleaned in sardine oil.

"How do you do?" the man asked.

"How do you do?" Doris and Vincent in unison.

"I'm the owner of this establishment," he said quietly yet sternly. "My name is Phillips. Mr. Phillips is fine."

Not to appear rude, Vincent sold himself as best he could.

"My name is Mr. Vincent Sullivan, and this is my wife, Mrs. Doris Sullivan."

Doris applied a wry smile toward the gaunt figure of their new host.

"How do you do? I apologise for acting rather stiff; however, we are *not* open for business yet. I had set up for a small personal gathering, but they could not make it due to the inclement weather."

Doris, hungry enough as to look past the awkwardness of the situation, chimed in.

"Is the kitchen not open then? The tables do look very inviting."

Mr. Phillips had warmed slightly.

"Why, thank you. Sadly not. However, we will indeed be opening in the future."

He walked towards them with open hands to usher them out, a knowing grin etched on his wrinkled face.

"Well, we're sorry to impose on you, Mr. Phillips," Vincent said.

"No harm done. It was my fault the door was not locked. Terribly sorry for the mix up. Anyway, I shall hopefully see you lovely people when we do open some day down the road!"

"Mr. Phillips?" Doris was polite to exclaim. "Just before we leave, I don't suppose you'd be so kind as to spare something from your kitchen? Just for us to eat during the drive. Really anything is fine. We've been on the road for some time and haven't eaten since this morning."

He stood quietly to ponder, his fingernails black with grime about to touch his dry lips out of habit, his quirks on full display. He moved his head in an indecipherable manner which Doris could not make head nor tail of. Unusual for her. Vincent concurred with his wife's previous question.

"We'll happily reimburse you for your trouble, of course. If you had something already prepared, we would happily put that to good use."

"On the contrary, it isn't the money. I'm just trying to think," Mr. Phillips replied while gnawing on his nails.

Doris completely empathised with her husband's puzzled expression.

"You know what? How would *you* both feel about this now? Well, I've been trying to glamorize the menu in time for opening and I have a few dishes in mind I'd planned on presenting this evening for my other guests. How would you both feel about sitting as my guests here now for a meal?"

"You'd be happy to do that?" Doris asked with a secret unease.

"On the contrary, I'd be delighted!" he said vehemently. "You'll be doing me a favour with your criticism. This is all complimentary too. I insist."

They both thanked Mr. Phillips and watched him pull one solitary table to the centre of the room and move two captain's chairs opposite to each other. The screeching sound made waves through the whole dining space.

"Please, sit," he gestured, "may I get you something to

drink? I shall propose a toast to this little experiment. Mrs. Sullivan, would you like a glass of white wine? It will accompany the seafood rather tastefully."

Doris loved seafood. After making herself comfortable in the perfectly framed chair, she most graciously accepted the wine offer despite the dicey vibes. Vincent remained standing just to allow his eye muscles to gauge the surroundings: a maritime theme of mostly broken ship ornaments of yesteryear and landscape drawings of wrecked boats. The dark history of the place was foreboding and gave the couple chills to match the chateau wine.

Clink.

Mr. Phillips retrieved the large bottle from behind the bar and poured up a flute glass rather shakily. His hand trembled so much when pouring that Doris immediately took notice. Vincent didn't notice; his nostrils only perked at the smell of alcohol.

"Mr. Phillips, would you happen to have any whiskey by any chance?" he asked.

"Indeed, I do. Any particular kind you are fond of?"

"Anything that can sting my nostrils and mellow when it goes down."

Mr. Phillips corked the wine and placed it back into a cool storage behind the makeshift bar area. It was complete with an old white oak barrel and some crooked shelves that mysteriously managed to hold all the bottles perfectly upright. He grabbed hold of a small brown bottle and healthily poured two glasses, handing one to Vincent.

"I got this one from a passing ship five years ago. It is from the Islay region of Scotland. To your health, Mr. Sullivan."

Right there and then, Mr. Phillips swigged the glass clean

in a noisy slurp. The way his tongue flicked the bottom of the glass was rather ghastly. Still, Doris wore her stern expression with a faux blanket masking her unease. Vincent returned the toast out of politeness.

"To yours, Mr. Phillips."

"Now if you will excuse me, I will be back with your first course in a few moments."

In a flash, he charged through a back door off into God knows where. Vincent strolled over to the bar area and helped himself to another glass of wonderfully complex single malt before he engaged in conversation.

"Peculiar fellow. You should write about this place in one of your mystery novels," he suggested.

"It's too bad I left my stationery in the car. Everything about this place is worth writing about. Just our luck to stumble across it on a cold and rainy night."

Vincent acknowledged the same and sipped gently from the crystal glass. Despite the eccentricity, he was beginning to warm up. He figured it was certainly better than driving in the dark practically without headlights feeling the trickle of ice-cold water pouring down his neck.

Doris was considerably less snug. A question that sprang to mind was made open to her husband.

"Do you think he's making the food *himself*?"

"I assumed as much. Now what made you think to question that?" Vincent asked.

Doris could not shake off the feeling there was more than just Mr. Phillips in the kitchen. Her intuition was rarely wrong. Vincent too knew this.

Doris hadn't always been a writer. Just a few years before, she waitressed in downtown St. John's at a pub by the waterfront called Farrell's Tavern. It was away from the central bustle of popular George Street and for good reason. Farrell's was mostly frequented by criminals of both the organized and disorganized nature. Doris was handy to the owners in more ways than just filling cups with overpriced grog. She grew up in a small fishing community on the east coast. Around some of these outport towns where men liked to spin yarns of old—or just plain fabricate information—Doris could tell a lie from a mile away and became quite the bloodhound. Such she was at analyzing people just by looking into their eyes, she could quickly read when an ugly situation was about to turn volatile. Doris was kept reasonably safe by the landlord and landlady, Mr. and Mrs. Murphy, which meant she could carry a concealed pistol. The Murphys, very short in stature with the thickest glasses covering their squinty eyes, were likely to quote scripture to teach a lesson and yet had no quarrels in disposing of several dead bodies during one nasty evening's bloodshed. They loved Doris to pieces.

The porcelain plates clashed the back door loudly when Mr. Phillips hurried into the dining room. The relieved couple watched with open gaze to see the treats beautifully presented on the dishes.

"Here is your first course," Mr. Phillips grandly proclaimed, now sweating rather profusely, gesturing to admire the carefully prepared yet mysterious seafood medley. "The first dish is fresh salt and pepper oysters accompanied by a dried fig and sesame cucumber garnish. The oysters were shucked less than two minutes ago. Enjoy!"

Doris recognized the host taking a moment at this time to stare awkwardly and look for approval.

"My goodness, it sounds lovely. I'll go ahead," she said to break the ice.

A great sport, she took the shell lightly and allowed it to rest between her dark fingernails for a second, then swallowed the oyster. Her taste buds ignited at the sensation. Without hesitation, she tucked into the salad flaked next to the exotic morsels.

"This is just incredible. The flavours are so dominant. Excuse me," she said, her mouth full.

Mr. Phillips grinned and looked to Vincent, who followed suit.

"My word, this is wonderful stuff."

It was nearly as good as the whiskey.

Mr. Phillips could hardly contain himself. His whole body shook giddily as if ice cold. It would have alarmed the diners had they seen it.

"Excellent! I am *so* happy. Please excuse me and I will make sure the main course is nearly ready. It shan't take long."

He ventured off again.

Downstairs.

Doris had been careful to observe Mr. Phillips leave the room just from a quick glance and noticed the echo. This place had another level like the proprietor's own personality. She sat silent, her plate bare.

"Whatever the main course is I'd say we are both in for a treat. This first course was exquisite," Vincent said.

Doris' hunger was eased ever so slightly but not enough to prevent a hearty anticipation over the main course. Vincent was correct in his assessment of the appetizer. He enjoyed his salad while Doris sat cordially baring concerns on the tip of her tongue; it had everything to do with their eventual destination out of the weather.

"Vincent, I want to talk to you about this meeting at my publisher's."

"What about it?" Vincent asked. His eyes never moved from the plate.

"If all goes well with this meeting with Mr. Grant, do you know what my next step would be?"

"I remember. You still want to move away to Toronto," Vincent said with sobriety; it was fresh in his mind. "What more is there to say? You want to move, and I do not blame you. You feel this is a chance to become a successful novelist who will wine and dine with the literature greats in a bigger jungle, and that's fine."

Doris knew Vincent was stubborn, but to pretend he was fine with her moving away was an insult to her perception. Vincent did not mention it this time, but in a previous moment of bitter debate at home Vincent had volunteered to stay in St. John's while Doris go alone to her publisher's retreat this very night. Doris had collated a great source of writing inspiration from her time at Farrell's, all buried secrets among hoodlums and felons, murderers, and cutthroats. The oldest city in North America would forever remind her of her previous life buried in bloody history. She wanted a fresh start, to take advantage of publicity tours, seek new inspiration, meet new people. But she was also selfless enough to want the same for her husband.

Vincent Sullivan was the youngest of thirteen children. Unlucky for him. Born into a wealthy policeman's family, his mother died of pneumonia when he was only six. The tragedy hit him hard. His father never cared for him growing up; he was different from the rest of his siblings. During his teenage years especially, Vincent felt a deep-rooted anxiety shift inside him. He tried to keep his feelings a secret, and he did so well since his father could barely make eye contact with him during the day. Eventually, the subject of marriage came up in discussion between he and his father.

"When are you going to man up and find yourself a wife?"

This was to be the regular interrogation that drove Vincent to drink. So much pent-up frustration Vincent felt he simply could not bring to his father's attention for fear of consequences. The options were clear. Explain to his strict God-fearing disciplinarian father that he was not interested in marriage or members of the opposite sex? Or hope the downtown pubs could provide enough liquid suppression to crush the shame he felt his entire life? The latter seemed easier.

"Doris, if you want to move to Toronto, I'm not stopping you," Vincent offered stubbornly. "Just don't think I'm going to give up a steady job and throw myself into a new environment like that. I'm not as brave as you and I certainly can't write like you."

"I'll bet you could write anything you put your mind to," she replied supportively.

"On the contrary, I tried my hand at writing once before. I wrote a piece of correspondence once detailing the personal struggles of a young man. It received a poor review. The critic called it a waste of *his* time, *my* time, and *everybody's* time."

"Why, that's horrible. Who in the world would give you a

review like that?"

"My father," Vincent said with a repressed anger before his eyes drifted to the Poseidon painting. Again, Doris could empathise.

CLANK

Two piping hot plates recklessly made their place onto the table.

"I present to you the main course! Any more drinks? Another wine, Mrs. Sullivan?" Mr. Phillips barked.

Doris graciously accepted the offer and held the pretense that she was perfectly fine with Mr. Phillips' unusual mannerisms, despite noticing him gawking at her uncomfortably. He poured the wine with that same giddiness as before. Still, Doris' attention was focused on the next round of delicacies: an oddly colorful mashed potato concoction with a small pie. The aroma that emanated sang a delightful tune inside her, while echoes of a demonic London barber came to mind.

"You appeared to enjoy the starter. Now I ask that you taste this one first *before* I tell you what it is!" Mr. Phillips insisted.

Doris held her expression but laughed somewhat nervously. The little horror story was already playing out in her mind like a theatrical piece. Poison pies? Perhaps pies made using the corpses of some unlucky previous guests? It felt a bit extreme, but then Doris' life had never been straightforward.

Farrell's Tavern was about to close one foggy Saturday evening. The smell of saltwater from the harbor piqued the air. During that week, Doris had held her pistol closer than normal. She believed she was being stalked. At first glance the person appeared to be within a crew of regulars, but his glare cut through the seams of everybody in the bar. An oily brown jacket, a scarf wrapped around his face, and a tattered seal-skin hat painted a most grim picture. His eyes never blinked. They just watched Doris' every move.

Doris had dealt strongly with all sorts of controvertible people. She had been spat at, punched, kicked, and grabbed more times than anybody had in their right mind could imagine. The indescribable dirt of men's hands had become so familiarly dug into her skin that the scolding hot water of many washes could not rinse the feeling from her. She was as tough as cowhide leather, but this unknown patron terrified her.

Saturday evening before closing, with one lonely patron tucked away in the corner finishing his fifth glass of whiskey, the door swung open. At the entrance, a set of piercing eyes watched Doris as she picked up glasses with her back turned. A gloved hand holding a fishing blade moved toward her with intent. Whether it was an act of bravery brought on by festering anger, frustration, or old-fashioned Dutch courage, the lonely patron saw the blade glimmer in the lamplight and decided to intervene.

Doris startled when she heard the struggle and turned around quickly. Chairs thudded on the floor as the two men wrestled. Doris took a step back and saw those familiar burning eyes look to her. With the lonely patron shoved to the ground, this devil was free to carry out whatever ghastly scene he had in mind.

"He has a knife!" a slurred voice from the floor called out.

She was fast. A swift hand to her hidden holster and it was all over. She shot him dead right there on the spot. The patron looked on, his eyes blurry as he tried to make sense of everything.

"Thank you," Doris said with her stony expression but with relief too.

The patron lay slumped on the floor, not in any hurry to get up and probably too drunk to assemble the strength. He heard her voice ask:

"Who are you?"

"Sullivan," he replied. "And you are?"

Vincent looked down at the meal upon his plate so lavishly put. His sense of smell was invigorated by the pie.

"I'll go first this time, Doris. You really have me intrigued now, Mr. Phillips. Pie and mash is a favourite dish of mine."

Mr. Phillips watched on with relish to near arousal in his expression. Vincent sank a fork into the delicate pastry and scooped a portion of the hot substance inside. It looked like nothing familiar, and Mr. Phillips salivated as he watched. Vincent took a mouthful and posted an interested expression.

"My *word*, this is incredible."

Doris followed suit and received the same splendor.

"Absolutely the best pie I've ever tasted." She continued to dig in.

Mr. Phillips, practically giggling with a stale aroma off-putting to most, could not wait to inform them of what they were feasting on.

"What you're dining on this very moment is a roasted seal and octopus tentacle puff pastry pie served with a jellyfish and basil mashed potato."

Both wife and husband stopped at the news. A look of repulsion from Vincent. A look of intrigue from Doris.

"I didn't know you could even *eat* those creatures?" Vincent mused.

"It's a far cry away from mutton and carrots," Doris said.

"Everything in the sea is edible as long as you have the correct tools and recipes to prepare it. We are proud to bring the very best of both here," Mr. Phillips exclaimed.

There it was. That *we*. Doris was pleased that Mr. Phillips had confirmed her suspicions for he meant he was not alone in this establishment. Whether an open admission or a slip of the tongue, she was keen to continue her dig for more information related to the silent partner of the Shipwreck Hideaway.

"Your Chef knows a great deal about seafood then?" she asked pleasantly.

Mr. Phillips' expression had turned from pride to the look of a toddler caught with their hands in the candy jar. It appeared to Doris that he had indeed been caught out.

"Yes. If you will excuse me, Mrs. Sullivan, I must see if they need any help with the dessert."

Mr. Phillips shot her with a scornful expression on the way out. His eyes burned like ice. The light draft from his very loose clothes along with the strong scent gave her goosebumps. The door squeaked loudly and exacerbated the sinking feeling Doris felt, that she had seen eyes like that before. Vincent was quick to pick up on her discomfort this time.

"My dear, whatever is the matter?"

Doris stared into nothingness until her eyes diverted to the mermaid painting once more. Vincent had grown used to her poker face over the years. So much so he knew when she appeared lost.

"I'm sorry?" she asked.

"What ever is the matter? You look as though you saw the *Titanic* sink. You know it might be the first time your face has changed expression this whole evening."

"He just gave me a look, that's all. It seems silly but it frightened me."

"How so?"

"The way Mr. Phillips looked at me reminded me of the man from the tavern."

Vincent knew the uncertainty in her voice. She was no longer comfortable here. Her fork eased off the rest of her meal and her hunger had given way to a bout of mild post-trauma. To an onlooker she just looked perfectly normal, but her husband knew the difference. They had both cemented a full marriage built on trust, loyalty, and ardent friendship. Vincent knew her well enough to know she had a devil resurface in her mind.

"It's perfectly normal to still feel things. I wished I'd have killed him myself. It would have spared you the endless grief of what you had to do."

Vincent's words were true, and they were a comfort to her. Just him being there made things a little easier. Their complex puzzle of a marriage was one that only they understood. Doris had no interest in personal displays of affection or the goings on behind closed doors. She knew this early on in her life. It wasn't just the being surrounded by men her entire working life ogling and objectifying her. That moment had firmly shut the door on any attempt at her, in the words of her mother, "being normal."

"Vincent, if you were not there that evening, I would not be sharing this feast with you."

"At the very least I wouldn't be driving through thick mud and rain. And if it is any consolation, I don't believe Mr. Phillips to be the Devil. Just a very strange man with a great chef helping him in the basement."

The basement, he said.

Doris admired this observation on the part of her best friend. The couple now actively listened for the door and were careful to chatter in delicate whispers.

"What kind of *company* was he expecting? Who is the chef?" he asked her.

"A wanted criminal?" Doris suggested.

"That makes more sense than what I had in mind."

"What did you make of it?"

"Vampires," Vincent said theatrically.

"You fool," Doris laughed, her deadpan expression finally broken.

"He does look a tad like Varney the Vampire, doesn't he?"

Doris had yearned for this kind of banter. Ever since the discussion of moving away, Vincent was clearly put out. It was a joy to share time with him, despite the strange locale.

"I'm just glad we didn't assume a murder plot involving poisoning or we'd definitely be in for it," Vincent said.

"It would be a shame to leave our fat old cadavers slumped here on the table," Doris smiled.

CRASH.

Both jumped at the noise from behind the door. It was loud enough to wake the dead, all broken pottery and heavy cutlery. Both anticipated the door to swing open any second until finally Mr. Phillips barged in, his head covered in an oily dripping resembling a thick sweat, with an incensed rage about him.

"I'm afraid the final course is off!"

Spit flew from his blistered lips. He clutched onto his arm, his spindly fingers wrapped around it like snakes. Doris saw the blood right away.

"Mr. Phillips, your arm?"

He looked down and wore a distressed tone as well as many other mixed emotions. The blood was dripping loudly on the floor; each droplet seemed to thud against the dusty old wood.

"Nasty. How very nasty," he said too calmly.

"Are you certain everything is all right?" Doris asked.

"Just a minor accident with some cutlery. I feel rather embarrassed, but you both must leave right now. I'm closing up for the night."

Vincent's eyes focused firmly on their coats and the front door. A small galivant to their car and they would be right on the final stretch of their journey. Vincent fetched from his pocket a black leather wallet and flicked out a bill which he offered to Mr. Phillips.

"Please might you kindly pass this along. Tonight's offerings were most exceptional."

"Yes. Your culinary delights are worth writing about. Take care, Mr. Phillips," Doris said.

Mr. Phillips' indignant demeanor appeared happily relieved.

"You are both too kind. On behalf of the Shipwreck Hideaway, your custom is dearly appreciated. I hope the light guides you well to your destination this evening!"

Vincent held the weighty door open. The rain rushed in from the high wind. Both left urgently with their faces down to block out the elements.

Vincent allowed his fingers to rest on the steering wheel for one moment. Doris saw he was alleviated to get out of there. Never a fan of new experiences, she realized he would add this to his list of reasons *not* to listen to her. If they were to remain together of course. She knew he would not be pleased with her next suggestion.

"I say we go back inside and check out that basement."

Right then, in Vincent's eyes, Doris was damn near shocked by what she saw—gameness.

"Normally I'd say you were quite mad; however, you *are* certain about this?"

"I'm telling you, Vincent, if Mr. Phillips was hiding some-body downstairs my intuition is telling me he might have mur-dered them just now," she said, both eyes locked on the dark building.

"Shan't we fetch the police?"

"No. I know the whole incident will be long cleaned up by then. Any evidence will have been destroyed."

Vincent trusted Doris was correct. God knows how many cleanups Doris had been personally involved with.

"Do you still have that pistol?" he asked.

Doris reached inside the glovebox and took hold of her trusty firearm. Despite leaving her old past behind her, she felt safer with it. Old habits die hard. At least she had a chance to put something right here this evening.

Vincent was quite bewildered that Mr. Phillips *still* had not locked the front door. His business downstairs was clearly eat-ing up his time. Doris coolly followed with her weapon hidden but ready to take on all comers if necessary. The dining room hadn't been touched and their half-eaten main course was still fresh on the table. The door to the basement lay open by a crack. No noise, no shouting. It was time to act.

A wide stone stairway presented itself behind the small

wooden backdoor. It was cold, very much like a castle in a gothic horror picture, lit by the oscillation of several flame sconces bouncing in the draft. There was a small landing with a large oak door at the bottom. They gently walked down, their footsteps so tender only a bat would hear them. There was shouting coming from inside the room and a small crack in the splintered door gave a small viewing window. Vincent leaned in.

With limited view, he saw some old pots and pans, cutlery, and an old pot-boiler stove with a bent chimney. The shadows on the wall presented what looked like two persons. Vincent heard a door open from within and then slam shut again. The battering rain and howling winds outside practically screamed.

"I believe they just left," Vincent whispered.

"*They*? If either one sees the car parked outside, they'll be looking for *us* next," Doris replied.

"I'm going to check it out," Vincent said. "You take the gun and just aim it through this split and make sure nothing happens to me. I shan't be too long, and you're a much better shot than I am."

Vincent barely gave time to argue. He knew she would volunteer to do the same and he could not allow that. She *was* the better shot, and this was something he knew he had to do. Vincent slipped in neatly through the door, no going back. Doris was at a loss for words. She just set up her position and held the grip tightly, a watchful eye kept over proceedings. She had the same limited view of the room and prayed Vincent would not leave her line of sight.

"My word," Vincent said to himself.

Inside this oversized room was a tidal pool sweeping right underneath the building. Anything from the ocean next to the building's backbone could come right in like a boathouse. A large table with kitchen utensils and two plates was positioned at the pool's edge. Vincent noticed the plates, and then a shift in the water. A shape moved in the pool.

SPLASH.

A thunderous rush tore up from the murky void. Vincent regained his senses just enough to duck and hide behind a table as a large figure emerged from the pool. A ferocious humanoid covered in slick brown scales and webbing, devoid of human characteristics with apparent arms shackled in rusty chains.

Vincent, still with a belly full of rich seafood but more importantly grit, peaked out to see what the thing was doing. He saw its slimy fingers place a handful of tiny molluscs on the two plates and faultlessly prepare them. A nauseated feeling came over Vincent when he concluded that this was the chef.

Mr. Phillips stormed in through the outside door soaked to the bone, his clothes flushed with rainwater and blood. Vincent's heart pumped mercilessly, but he kept himself hidden.

"It was foolish of me to think that this would be a good idea! If it weren't for me, you would have been exploited across the world in some carnival sideshow by now! And you repay me with my own blood, *biting* the very hand that feeds you?! You've left me little choice but to do away with you completely!"

Across the room Mr. Phillips grabbed a hefty meat cleaver from a butcher's block. The creature kept its eyes curiously on him before it saw the blade then expeditiously retreated into the black water below.

"Stay down there, my beauty! You will have to pop up for air soon enough," Mr. Phillips said with a vainglorious air.

He admired the ardent design of the metal cutter—even more so the shine that offered reflection on prying eyes spying on him in the room.

"*You* can come up for air now too, Mr. Sullivan," he said.

Vincent sprang to his feet and kept focus on the blade. His befuddlement at the situation had taken a backseat to the immediate danger he faced. His peripheral vision tried to spot the portion of the room where Doris might have a clear shot. Mr. Phillips with all the attentiveness of a hawk paced over to block his exit to the door.

"Stand still, Mr. Sullivan."

"I will do whatever you say. You're the one with the knife," Vincent said with noticeable nervousness.

"Knife? Why this isn't a knife, Mr. Sullivan." Mr. Phillips seemed to take great joy in handling it.

"Oh no?"

"No. This is a cleaver. A meat cleaver is much more versatile than just a knife. Stronger too. Designed to hammer right through cartilage and bone with enough repetition. You would normally use it on cows or pigs. However, as you can tell, we're happy to use it on seafood, amongst other things."

Vincent planted his feet; his heart fired on all cylinders and the sweat from his brow rolled down to his pencil mustache. He knew his next move would have to be quick.

"You plan on murdering me?" Vincent asked.

"On the contrary, I plan on murdering all of you at this moment. Where exactly is your lovely wife?"

"She's outside in the car."

"You're lying!"

"I think not."

"Well, no matter. She will find you soon enough. I assume you both wanted to meet the chef?"

Vincent was repulsed at the admission.

"That thing in there?" he inquired.

"*Thing!?* A mermaid, dear fellow! She is a mermaid. Such a beautiful and extraordinary find of mine."

"I have an idea to run by you—why don't you let me go, and we shall never speak of this to anybody?"

Mr. Phillips' eyes had ostensibly grown bigger when they glared sinfully at Vincent.

"And do you really think me to be a fool?"

"Even if we do tell, who is going to believe our story? What kind of sane human being would?"

Vincent, ever the salesman.

"You muster a valid point. However, it's going to be so much easier just to dispose of you both. The pool here connects right to the ocean. Peace of mind, and no loose ends."

Mr. Phillips raised his hand. Vincent took a sharp step back and called out.

"Doris!"

Mr. Phillips took a swipe and missed by a caplin's eye while Vincent tumbled backwards over a small table. Within the same timeframe, Doris barged into the room. With no hesitation or second guessing, she fired two rounds at Mr. Phillips. Teeth clenched, he dropped the cleaver and took hold of his paining wounds. Her fierce eyes looked stoically at him. After a short stumble he sank to the floor. Doris paced over to Vincent to help him up. Mr. Phillips was dead.

"Are you alright, my dear?" she asked him collectedly. Her deceptive strength eased him up from the ground.

A sudden wake swelled in the water. Vincent grabbed Doris instinctively and watched motionless in his expression. Mr. Phillips' body twitched and then began to slide across the floor, grabbed by one leg and pulled slowly into the pool. His expression seemed to beg for help as his lifeless body entered the void of the pool. Doris' hand gripped tightly like a vice as she was met with the remarkable sight of the mermaid taking its attempted murderer away.

"What on Earth?!"

If Doris' face were a stonewall, it had just been cracked to pieces at the sight. Vincent could not help but laugh at the indescribability of the whole thing.

"Yes, I respectfully have to tell you that your guess on the situation here was very much incorrect," he said.

"Who was that woman in the water?" she asked.

"*Woman*?" Vincent asked, taken aback.

SPLASH.

Water erupted from the pool in a surge, and the creature met with Vincent face on. He laid his eyes right on the thing as it hissed in his direction, baring a row of sharp translucent teeth from its crescent-shaped mouth, its gargantuan eyes beaming like a lighthouse.

"We should get going immediately! Come on!" he shouted.

Vincent wore the assumption that Doris followed him out, however this was not to be the case. Doris had not moved from where she stood. She was in awe. This woman was the most alluring and beauteous person she had ever seen, and she was locked mesmerized on her. Hair flowed red just like fire down her back, a shapely figure that fell into a shine of scales from the waist down; her bewitching eyes were like diamonds reflecting in an elegant pool, and they had ground Doris to pay close attention. This was undeniably that siren of the sea only heard of in folk tales, a true Mermaid! Vincent did not see this, nay, *could* not see this. A woman enslaved against her will; Doris could not let this be.

"You were imprisoned here?" Doris asked.

The woman cupped her hands and rattled the iron shackles, blood and scratches evident on her soft skin. The mermaid, eyes mysteriously commanding, pointed to the wall behind Doris where a set of keys rested on a protruding nail.

"I see them."

Wasting no time, she took the keys and unlocked the chains from the maiden's delicate hands. The Mermaid smiled cravingly while Doris stared back in a trance. As soon as the chains fell and broke the surface of the black saltwater pool, the mermaid wrapped her suddenly elongated fingers around Doris' arms.

"Doris!"

Vincent shouted from the entrance. She regained her senses almost immediately and scrambled for her pistol. The mermaid screamed at the top of its lungs a most frightening wail that would wake the dead from their watery grave. She quickly submerged allowing Doris to turn and hurry out. Vincent was equally keen to get back in the car and head as far away from this godforsaken hideaway as possible.

They were short of breath, sweating, nerves turned to excitement, dirty, soaked to their skin, but comforted by their familiar metal chariot, as well as each other.

"She had some sort of spell over me, Vincent," Doris said, her hands instinctively grabbing her briefcase.

"Well, we're both alive. Which reminds me." Vincent looked at her face with a gentle smile. "When *do* we leave for Toronto?"

Doris smiled back, completely out of her trance. Erasing it from her face would be impossible.

2

Marjorie placed the plate of food in front of Hennessy, who glanced down at the two pieces of battered cod glistening from the fry and instantly wished he had opted for the soup.

"Well, I'll leave you to it," said Cyril, now revelling in his audience's wariness to dig into the seafood in front of him. Pushing back his chair, Pop joined Nan in their living room and left Malcolm to close his laptop and push around the food with his fork.

Finally, he chuckled, impressed with the old man's ability to throw him, a "bestselling horror author," off his game. He muttered "Well done, Pop," and began wolfing down the food.

He was right in his earlier assessment of the place; the food was amazing.

He finished his meal, argued with Marjorie over his need to try a twirled soft serve cone before he left (he assured her he was full, she assured him he had to try it), and settled up then headed to his car with a full stomach and rivulets of vanilla & chocolate melting over his hand.

His guts rumbled from the massive helping of greasy fish, and he looked back to the place trying to decide whether or not to head back into their washroom before getting back on the road. Nan and Pop had been gracious hosts, but he was worried the bathroom would have been in their living quarters and decided to take his chances on getting to his destination before the situation became dire.

He plopped into the driver's seat, started the car, pulled back on to the narrow road lined with changing leaves, and cruised toward what he had originally hoped would be a relaxing weekend. Other plans forced him to cancel heading out for Friday, and now he was running late.

In the time since the book came out, he had been hustling. That was what he understood as being required of him. He had taken every interview, signing, and event that had been put in front of him. He was tired, but this would be the last thing he had to deal with before a three-week break between Halloween and the Christmas markets. In those three weeks, sleep and television binges would be caught up on. But until tomorrow, he was still on.

He was struggling with the follow-up and it was nagging at his mind, making the recuperation this retreat was supposed to give him all the harder to achieve, even though it also presented a great opportunity for inspiration; after all, it's not every day that horror authors get invited to start-up writing festivals that happen in two-hundred-year-old estates over Halloween—it seemed too good to be true.

He craned his neck to look up at the towering lodge poking out from the treeline. Hints of turrets and windowed peaks appeared through the boreal canopy, which rapidly receded to reveal Cantwell House, a massive home built by the merchant family during the earlier part of the nineteenth century. There had been diversification, but the family's main business had always been fish, and following the moratorium they fell on times as hard as anyone with two centuries of accumulated wealth could suffer. The ruling generation had finally settled a decades-long debate to convert the family estate into an inn just in time for a pandemic to bring global travel to a halt.

They had limped through a year and a half of "staycations" and now the whole property seemed to yearn for the weekend retreat that would fill up its dozen guest rooms over the course of a weekend that would be in their slow season, had the last eighteen months not been a whole different kind of slow season.

He leaned forward as he rolled the car to a stop, looking at the building, even grander up close. He suddenly became aware of the slack-jawed reflection staring back at him in the windshield and fell back in his seat, hoping none of the other visitors milling around the grounds saw him act so embarrassingly touristy.

Suddenly, there was a knock on his driver's side window. Hennessy lurched forward, startled, and nearly choked himself on the seatbelt. A teenaged bellhop stood outside the car, eagerly pressing his face into the glass.

"Hello!" the bellhop shouted through the window, which didn't actually muffle any of the sound. Malcolm rolled it down anyway.

"Hi," he said, apprehensive of the zeal.

"I'm Jacob, can I get your bags?"

"Uh, sure," Malcolm replied, leaning forward to pull the trunk latch. "It's just the one."

"Weekender for the weekend!" Jacob cheerily called as he rushed from the back of the car with the small leather bag.

"Yea, a little on the nose, I guess. I'm Mal—"

"Oh, I know who you are. I follow you on Twitter! Loved

the book."

Hennessy was taken aback. He was more used to the reaction from the restaurant and honestly, appreciated Jacob's excitement a bit more now. This seemed like a young man with a good head on his shoulders. He knows what he likes. You've got to respect that.

"Thank you…" before he could finish, the teenager pulled a copy of the book from his uniform jacket with a pen.

"Would you mind?"

"Of course not." And he honestly didn't mind. He had been kind of hoping for this sort of interaction since he wrote the book, but all of the signings he had done were sort of forced and to have an actual fan thrust his work at him felt, well, it felt pretty nice. He took it and stared at the title page, trying to think of a heartfelt inscription to match the sincerity Jacob was bestowing on him and after a long pause of no ideas he wrote the same thing he did on every other book, complete with the doodled jack-o'-lantern.

"I really liked it! I had no idea there were so many other authors in Newfoundland writing horror!" Jacob chimed as he hovered, watching every pen stroke.

"Other authors? You're a writer, Jacob?"

"Hope to be. I've been at it since I was a kid but haven't really known how to get going."

"Well, I guess this weekend is a big one for you. Do you do genre stuff?"

"Yea, started with fantasy. I used to have this regular D&D campaign. I was the Dungeon Master, but two of the guys in our guild were brothers and they moved away and whole thing sort of fizzled. Then I just started writing the campaigns as short stories to send to them, and it started just getting darker and darker, and before I knew it, I had stopped sending the stories to the guys and was pretty much just writing horror." Jacob's excitement was infectious, and Hennessy didn't realize that they were now inside the lobby, lined up behind other guests with the lone bellhop chewing his ear off. As the woman in line ahead of him got her keys and left the counter he realized that this exchange had the potential to hold up the line.

"Sorry, I've got to get checked in."

"Of course."

"It's just the one bag, I can take it. There must be someone else around who needs more help than me." He felt rude. He wasn't trying to shake the kid but was legitimately trying to free him up for the other guests. In what he could only describe as a fit of panic, he over-corrected: "If you've got something you want me to check out, get my number from the desk and drop it by the room later."

"You mean it?" Jacob was already shaking off the initial hurt and transitioning back to excitement as he threw Malcolm's bag back to him.

"Yeah, just find out which ro—"

"I already know! Everything was prebooked!" And he took off down a dark hallway.

Malcolm turned to the desk.

"Jacob's a good kid." The manager smiled, sliding a room key across the front desk. Malcolm glanced at her nametag: MAGGIE. "A bit over the top, but weren't we all at that age?"

When he opened the door to Room 8, the Nathaniel Suite, Malcolm's foot didn't land on the plush, gold and forest green carpet he saw stretched across the room; it landed on a small stack of freshly printed paper, held together with a folding clip in the top corner…

IF YOU STAY
Phil Goodridge

I sat down directly across from her. I could've puked it was so awkward. I don't know why I had agreed to do this other than the fact that it seemed like the right thing, like what a decent person would do. And I occasionally liked to think I was a decent person. So, I took a deep breath to stall the vomit. Good thing too—this was clearly the Good Room. That room some people have in the house that was always neat as a goddam pin, which your mother said never to go into. "That room is for when we have company." But on the rare occasion that company came it still wasn't used. The only thing missing in here was plastic on the furniture. The air in the Good Room was thicker, unused, and the silence was overbearing.

Finally, she spoke.

"Would you...like anything?"

"Whiskey?" I asked.

"Oh...I... could see if..." she began, unsure.

"No, sorry, no, I'm...that was just a joke. I'm fine". My attempt to cut the tension resulted in more tension. Awesome.

She fixed a stern gaze on me. "I'd like you to tell me everything. Everything that happened that night."

I swallowed. "Well...you really already know..."

"I know what the police told me. But I want to know what happened before. Leading up to it."

"Are you sure you…"

"I'm sure." Her face was hardened. *"You owe me at least that."*

I resisted the urge to say, "hey lady I don't owe you shit." Because I didn't. But I was just being super defensive. I may not have owed her, but, honestly, telling her what really happened was the least I could do. What a decent person would do. So, this was going to be agonizing. But I started.

I saw his headlights coming down through the trees on the snowy dirt driveway. I warned him it wasn't plowed, and he might not spot the turn off in the dark, but he said he didn't mind taking a chance. Moment of truth. Did he actually look like his picture or was that taken like ten years ago and filtered up just to entice me? Oh well, adds a bit of anticipation, I thought, and besides I never really care as long as the real thing is at least a reasonable facsimile of what was presented. His RawR profile was faceless, which I hate, and I never meet a guy from online without a pic. I was very firm about that. No pic, no dick—specifically a face pic, a name, some details, and a way to look you up and see who you really are. I don't care how horny you are; if you don't like my rules then see ya. I'm sure there's plenty of other faceless randos who'll take you sight unseen. Me, I like to know who I'm meeting, and I like to have a little insurance.

His name was Harold, 53, 5'10, stocky, lived nearby. "Nearby" could've been a lot of places but judging by his location on the RawR app it was most likely Carbonear or somewhere close to it. There was no social media to creep (most likely closeted), but he gave me his phone number and he did send a picture. And Harold was hot. Salt and pepper beard, buzzed head, beefy. I like older men. Who am I kidding, I just like men in general. But older rugged dudes get a pass to the front of the line. His chats were pretty sweet too. Awkward but charming, and occasionally kind of filthy. Harold seemed like a great way to spend a Saturday night in the woods.

His truck skidded coming down the end of the driveway and I thought he was about to total my car when he got the rights of it back under control. Wouldn't THAT have been a great way to start our magical hook up. I'd get LOTS of Harold's info then. He parked between my car and the shed and hopped out. He was too far away for the porch lights to expose his details, so I sauntered away from the window and awaited the big reveal. I mean it would've been pretty fuckin awkward if he walked up to the house to see me just staring out the window at him. Great first impression, weirdo.

I surveyed the cottage. Cottage is a loose term in this scenario. That's what the website called it but building a straight-up regular house deep in the woods doesn't make it a cottage. Generic modern furnishings, kitschy trinkets lying around, Newfoundland landscapes hung on the well, seashells in a bowl. How clever. But really though, it was a sweet little place and I'm not too picky about my getaway accommodations as long as it's clean, cozy, and a stone's throw from civilization. My only real bone of contention was the lettering stencilled on to the wall above the fireplace. "Live. Laugh. Love." Honestly. I would not get along with these people.

I heard Harold's heavy booted feet come up the porch steps as I flicked on the fireplace with the remote. Thank god these people didn't expect me to build a fire on my own. I opened the door just before he could knock, which scared the shit out of him. Jumpy fella.

"Sorry! Didn't mean to spook ya. Come on in and get

warm." He was definitely nervous.

"Oh, it's, uh…it's no odds." His voice was deep and rich. "So, I'm Harold. Disappointed er wha?"

Wow, straight out the gate with the low self esteem. In actual fact he had nothing to be worried about.

"Harold, ya look hot as fuck," I said, "better than your picture, which is rare. I'm Tom, nice to meet you. What about me, am I up to snuff?"

He smiled timidly, avoiding my eyes. This was a big dude, a dude you could mistake for being the head of a biker gang (maybe he *was* the head of a biker gang, I dunno) and to see him shift and shuffle in his puffy camouflage jacket was honestly friggin adorable.

"No, you're great, you look great, really nice."

"Take your coat off and stay awhile," I said, channeling my Nan and instantly feeling like an utter tool for saying it. He complied, hung his jacket on one of the hooks by the door.

"My, lovely spot," he said in a quiet gravelly tone. He had a really sexy voice. "Oh that's really nice, isn't it?" He was pointing to the words above the fireplace. Oh Harold. Lucky you're cute. He definitely seemed out of his element as he shifted his weight from side to side.

"You want anything to drink?" Let's move this along.

"Naw I'm driving."

"I'm getting a drink. Have a seat".

Our dialogue was clunky. This was going to take some finessing. No big. I've dealt with uneasy fellas before and I'm pretty good at sussing out when to make the first move. I came back from the kitchen with my wine and sat down jauntily beside him. I was about to break the silence with something cute and clever when he clumsily blurted: "I don't do this a lot…"

Most of the time that's a lie, of course, but I kind of assumed the big guy was telling the truth.

"Well, I do, so I'll guide you through it," I said lightly.

"Oh…well, I…"

"Sorry. That was a joke. Well. Kind of, haha, I guess. I believe in free love as long as everyone's safe and on the same page." Why lie? Sex is great.

"I guess that makes sense," he said, a little more at ease. "What brings ya out here to the middle of nowhere anyways?"

"My buddy was supposed to come with me but had to cancel. But there's no refunds so I figured I'd come out here and see what might happen. And congrats, Harold, you're what happened." I raised my glass to him. That got a flustered little laugh out of him. Good. Then he got an inquisitive look.

"Your buddy? Like your boyfriend?"

"Hell no. I mean he's nice enough but I'm not in the market. My last guy was…it ended really shitty. And it complicated a lot of things. This is…less complicated."

He looked at me curiously. He definitely didn't do this a lot.

"I have a few friends I get extracurricular with," I chuckled, "occasional hook ups from RawR or whatever. But I don't like to just bang and bail. I'm in it for the company too. That's why I made ya jump through a few hoops hahah with your face pic, name and all that, I like to know who I'm meeting." He nodded. "Plus now your deets are on my phone, I've got evidence of you so if you murder me you won't get away with."

Harold looked at me like a deer in headlights. Guess that was a bad way to set the tone of the evening. I tried to rescue myself from the moment.

"That…was another joke."

"You're not very funny," he said dryly.

Ok, honestly, that freaked me out. He didn't laugh off the murder joke and so immediately my mind spiralled into him being twice my size and I am NOT a fast runner, and my keys were in my coat in the bedroom and—

And then he belted out what can only be described as a hearty chortle. The man's laugh was a big joyful boom and I immediately fell back into comfort with him.

"Guess I won't start my stand-up career just yet," I stammered. He leaned in close to me.

"Can I kiss you?" he asked with a deep grumble. What a gentleman. Dammit, I was putty in his hands.

"You can. In fact, I recommend it."

He reached his big bear paw of a hand up to my face, drew me in, and—

"Jesus Christ" she snipped, ripping me out of one of my only good memories from that night, honestly one of the hottest moments I've ever—

"I don't need to hear that, any of that," she said tersely.

I took a breath.

"You said you wanted to know everything." I truly hoped I didn't sound sarcastic. Honestly, sometimes I just sound that way, which is problematic, but I was just trying to adhere to her wishes.

"You don't need to tell me…that."

"Ok. Gotcha. Sorry…So…just the relevant stuff or…"

"Just…everything that pertains to…what happened."

"Ok." I kind of felt like an idiot. Of course, she wouldn't want to hear about us having sex. For the record, it was amazing, but yeah, I should've been smart enough to maybe skip those bits while here in her

company. I readjusted both my body and my brain.

"Well…we did…that…stuff."

She rolled her eyes so hard they almost flew out of her head on to the floor behind her. Lady, you asked for this story so…

I woke up in darkness. Which I knew was wrong. I was groggy but I remembered for sure leaving the living room lights on, so I should've been able to see the light from the hallway through the bedroom door at the other end of the room. Or the green alarm clock digits, they should've been making a hazy little goblin halo by the bed. Nothing. There was a breath of moonlight coming in from the window, and I could just make out the bathroom doorway. Harold was snoring like chainsaw through concrete but that's not what woke me. Outside the wind was attacking the walls, beating against the house trying to rip it from its foundation and flick it out into the woods. The storm. The power must be out. I sat up, surrounded by a fog of sound closing in on me. I swiped about the bed and the end table to find my phone, get a light source, when I looked up.

Something moved. Over there, in the bathroom doorway, movement, slight, subtle, but something was in there. I stopped breathing. I thrust myself back against the headboard without thinking. Harold didn't stir. My mind sped through the things it could be, the logical explanations, a towel hung on the door, a bend of the light, something. I reached over to turn on the lamp and remembered, fuck, the power, and then the thing, whatever it was, swooped in a blur from the bathroom door and ran out into the hall.

"JESUS FUCK!"

That jolted Harold. He bolted upright.

"What happened?!"

"There's someone in the house!" My voice cracked and shredded as I yelled. My throat had gripped itself tight, but the adrenaline demanded the sounds come of out me.

"GET OUT!" I screamed, more shrill, more torn. Harold immediately leaped out of bed and hurriedly began to dress. This baffled me so much that I was able to ground myself in the situation. Here I was afraid of being murdered and he was afraid of, what, being caught naked? In a surprising show of bravery and rage I grabbed the lamp, yanked it out of the wall, and stormed naked into the living room.

"I will fucking mess you up!!!" I trampled into the room brandishing the lamp as a club in one hand and the cord like a whip in the other. It was like someone had hired a stunt double for me in the movie of my life. I was not this guy. But then I'd never been in this situation. I guess I'm a little badass. And a little reckless. Harold stumbled in, fully dressed except for his socks in his hand.

"Where is he?" he growled. He had his wits about him now and even though there was panic in his eyes he was ready for action.

"Check the kitchen, the back door," I ordered. He sped off in the other direction and I marched to the front door. Still locked. No wet foot prints on the floor. I looked out the window. It was a massive swirl of white. The porch lights were out but in the moonlight I could still make out our vehicles—just our vehicles, no one else's. No one would be out here on foot, there's no way, and there were no other cabins nearby. Harold came back.

"Nobody. And the door's locked."

"The bathroom. In the bedroom."

He ran in to check. My eyes darted around the room, my

weapons at the ready. He came back in.

"Bathroom's empty. And the bedroom window is…locked." Everything was locked. There was no sign of anyone, anything. But I had seen something.

"You're…um…" Harold paused, staring at me.

"What?!" I snapped.

After a moment of tense silence Harold tried to stifle a laugh. Bless him, he was trying hard to keep it in but here I was stark naked, glaring wildly, and brandishing housewares like a gladiator.

"Someone was here," I said, losing some of my firmness.

Harold lost his battle with the laughter and doubled over. Ok, I understood the humour of the moment and the evidence was against me.

"There was something…" there was a giggle in my voice though I had tried to suppress it. Harold caught his breath.

"Well, I'm sure if there is something here, you'll protect me." And then the chortle erupted again, tears filled his eyes, and he fell on the couch.

I had never "seen things" before. Is that really what a trick of light can do? Or being half awake? I was so goddam sure. I got dressed and came back out, plopped myself next to Harold on the couch, his fits beginning to subside. He smiled at me.

"There's no way anyone got in," he said gently. He pulled me into his body with one big arm. Cozy. Happily caught in his tight lock I suddenly became nervous. It could be him. He could've planned something. Maybe got his pals or someone to…but that made even less sense. Why do what we did only to do something like that? And his face when I said I saw someone, how fast he reached for his clothes. That was a man who did NOT want to be caught with another man. I relaxed into him.

"Geez," he said softly "didn't know we was callin' for weather."

"I don't think we were," I said sleepily.

"Won't be able to see me hand in front of me face out there."

I could see where this was going.

"Well, Harold, what're you gonna do?"

"Oh b'y I can drive real slow, no one out in this so I allow I'd be alright"

"You could wait and see if it clears up."

"Could I s'pose. If that's alright"

I was done teasing him. And it would be a comfort having a big brute in the house.

"Or you could just stay the night. You could have a drink then too." I liked Harold. I probably would've suggested the slumber party even if I hadn't seen anything. He gave me a squeeze.

"Well, I got nowhere to be tonight." He tried to hide his happiness, but he failed, much to my delight.

"Excellent. Settled. Now, let's see what we can do here." Having something to do, something to focus on, always calmed me down. I turned on the fireplace. That still worked without electricity, thank God. It was the only source of light right now and I hadn't realized how cold it had gotten with the heat off. I grabbed my phone and shined my way through the drawers and cupboards. No flashlight. No lighter. No candles. The Wi-Fi was down and there was no cell service in this deep snowy forest bowl. A perfect storm.

The shed. There might be something in the shed.

"You make yourself a drink," I said. "I'm gonna dart out to

the shed, see if they've got anything, batteries and stuff." Harold gave me a dirty smirk.

"Batteries, hey? What did you bring that needs batteries?" Harold was getting ideas and I liked it.

"Ok, seriously?" She huffed.

"Sorry, sorry, but I mean that's what happened, that's why I went out to the shed. Batteries for a radio. There was a tiny stereo but no power."

"A radio?"

"That's what you're supposed to do right? Light candles, turn on the radio. We couldn't use our phones to get an update or anything, ya know, if there was some emergency or news or something, get a camp stove, I mean we couldn't cook anything so what if this storm was gonna last and—"

"Jesus Christ, ok, so you went to the shed."

"This is really fucking hard, ok?" I snipped at her. Reliving it was getting to me. "I'm sorry. I know that this is…for you, it's… horrible." I couldn't look her in the eye.

After a moment, she softened.

"It is. Extremely. For both of us." She took a deep breath. "If you want to stop…"

"You deserve to know the truth."

So. I went to the shed. It sounds counterintuitive after what I'd just been through, seeing or not seeing whatever it was or wasn't, but honestly I was just trying to convince myself I was brave. Ya know, like, "of course that was nothing and to prove to myself it was nothing I'll do this seemingly scary thing like run out to the shed in a snowstorm because everything is totally fine." I could've sent the handsome tough but I was starting to feel like I'd been an idiot so this would be my personal redemption. Harold offered because he's a sweetheart, but I was proud. And stubborn. I threw on my coat and opened the front door, only to be pounded in the face by the bluster. I immediately regretted volunteering for this task. The shed was only fifty feet away, but it was like marching through the friggin' arctic to get to it, the flashlight on my phone offering exactly zero guidance. All it did was make the white wind whiter. At one point I swear it nearly lifted me off my feet, but I eventually forced my way to the door and flung myself in, falling to the floor as I yanked it shut behind me. I started to think maybe candles and batteries were not as important as I had led myself to believe. I stumbled around not really know what anything was. The beam from the phone was mostly just picking up the dust floating through the air. There were cupboards, shelves, random shit lying around, nails, planks, an old bike, and I think what might've been a deflated boat. The sporadic rhythm of that blizzard shook this little room too; tiny things were clanging, thumping, shaking around me. I didn't find anything useful so I turned to go… only…I couldn't find the door. It was a small space but so full of crap and debris and trinkets that I actually got disoriented. Which way did I even come in?

Then all the sounds fell away. The rattling of items, the brazen wind, all sucked away leaving an emptiness. And a new sound came. A rasp, so faint, like it was miles away, far outside the confines of the shed, but it was the only thing needling my ear. It was…almost human.

"Ehhhhhhhhhhhh…….. ehhhhhh sssssssssssssssssssssss"

I was about to throw up I was that panicked. I started swiping my hands around looking for the wall. Find the wall, find the door. The rasp was slowly making its way to me, closing this impossible gap.

"Ffffffffffffsssssssssstttttaaaaaaaaaaaaaahhhhhhhhhhhh"

"Who's there?" I demanded. I very seriously considered that I might be having some kind of breakdown. Is this what it feels like? I mean I really had no point of reference; this could well be it. I was drowning in the darkness, but I kept swinging around, reaching, flinging the light around every corner to find the way out. The voice sped closer now, its drawn out wheeze closing in right behind me.

"Ehhhhhhhhhhffffffffffffffsssssssssss"

I spun around to catch it in the light of my phone. A hand. Just…a hand…floating in front of me. Reaching for me. It was wet…no…not wet…but dripping, like it was made of flesh coloured mercury, oozing, and morphing but forming very clearly a clawed hand. From where there should've been a wrist, exposed veins and muscle threaded their way into the darkness, attached to nothing, drifting into a vapour the colour of blood. I screamed, I screamed so fucking hard, a scream that should've shattered ear drums, but my scream made no sound. All I could hear was that rasp…now directly in my ear. The hand floated toward me. I turned, I banged silently against the walls. I groped desperately for the doorknob, found it, and thrust it open. The frozen blasts of wind returned and the rasp was enveloped in it. I fell hard into the snow. I flipped over, looking at the open shed door. Just darkness. But this time I know I saw what I saw. I ran back towards the house, my throat raw and dry from the cry that never actually came. My body was trying so hard to get me the fuck out of there that my limbs moved faster than my brain. I tripped over myself and fell in the snow. When I got up,

I realized I was running blind. The blizzard was worse now. I couldn't even tell where the house was.

The glow! I could see the glow of the fireplace through the front window. I wasn't far off track. I ran towards it imaging how I would explain this to Harold, what I would have to say to convince him we had to go. Not the truth, obviously. Maybe that I was hurt, needed a doctor, needed to brave the storm. And if he wouldn't go with me then fuck it. I tripped up on to the porch, threw myself at the door and burst in.

"Harold, we—"

But instead of Harold greeting me I saw…someone…a thing…in the middle of the living room. It was turned away from me, slight frame, dark hair drifting down its back, the ends like coils of smoke. It wore a pale green dress that seemed to float, undulating closely to its body. It began to turn. Slowly. Achingly slow. But I was frozen, hypnotized. It didn't turn all at once. The legs started, but the torso began to drift around a few seconds later, like it had forgotten it was all one body. The head…the head waited a little longer, but then listlessly began its journey around. There was no face at first. Not really. Instead, there was a shifting mass, shapes pulling apart in different directions. Like the hand, it dripped, morphed…flesh seemed to drift upwards, sideways. Features started to form, flowing in and out of place, eyes growing too large then too small, a nose sloughing up towards the forehead, its ears at impossible angles, no mouth. Yet. The face eventually drew itself together, still fluid, but now more…human…if you can call her that. And where no mouth had been, a tiny hole began to open. And it grew. It grew to the size of a mouth but then this opening began to stretch wider. I began to hear it again. The rasping.

Even at this her reaction didn't change.

"She was there. That's what I saw," I said, indignantly.

"Ok," came her smooth reply.

"Well, I didn't tell the police that. Obviously."

"Obviously." She stared at me, curious.

"Look I don't care if you don't believe me, it happened and I—"

"I believe you. Completely. I know you're telling the truth."

I mean I was...but...

"But how do you—"

"Finish the story."

"If you stayyyyyyyyyy..." Like before, the rasp came from some unknown distant space, but this time I could make out the words. It sounded like a hoarse whisper, but I realized it was a scream. A scream lost in some far away ether.

"Iffffff youuuuu"

Harold casually strolled in from the kitchen.

"Find anything?"

I looked at him, unable to make a sound, unable to move, then looked back at the thing, waiting for him to see. I must've looked how I felt.

"Jesus, Tom, what happened?"

I finally managed to squeeze out a word.

"There."

He looked at it. At her. Then back at me.

"What, Tom, what is it? The fireplace?"

I thought "there for fuck's sake, Harold, the fucking ghost or demon or whatever the fuck it is, there, she's RIGHT THERE" but I just stood there, trembling. The Lamp Gladiator in me was nowhere to be found, and I was reduced to a shivering husk. Her head turned slowly like molasses to look at him. The eyes, still shifting slightly, opened inhumanly wide. She oozed towards him, starting with her torso. It pulled forward in a curve, the head and legs still attached but stretching away behind it. The head began to follow next, then the legs slimed their way across the floor until her whole body was back to its full form right next to Harold. Her face staring at his face, him staring at me.

"Tom, buddy, you should lie down."

Her body was unstable again, limbs, features, protruding and pulling out then in, and the opening that was meant to be a mouth began to drop open even more, the jaw sliding slowly all the way down to her chest, then the flowing body pulled itself back to a relatively human shape, but the mouth still gaped wide. I heard a thin, light, piercing high-pitched sound, air squeezing out of a tight balloon. It was her. It was her scream calling out form that far away dark place. Then the jaw snapped shut. She shot her gaze at me, the torso and legs turning just after to face me. Her misshapen mouth was shouting out the words to me, but I still couldn't hear it all..."If you stay"... something else... "if you stay, you"... she kept repeating it, this muffled scream, and I just wanted her to get it the fuck over with.

"IF YOU STAY YOU DIE."

In an instant her face was in mine. The scream blasted into the room, burning my ears. I fell back on to the floor. Harold ran to me. His body passed right through hers. He knelt down, reached for me.

"Tom, whaddya need, whaddya want me to do?!"

I looked over his shoulder. She hovered there still, now

pointing at Harold with her hand, the hand I saw in the shed. Her knobby finger stretched closer to him. This time it wasn't a scream but a trembling, raging voice.

"If… you stayyyyyyy… you…diiiiiiiiie."

I looked into Harold's eyes.

"Do you see her?! Do you even fucking hear her?!"

"There's nobody here!"

"We have to go!" I scrambled to my feet and I was not having this shit anymore. Survival kicked in. "We're leaving."

"There's no way. Sure, we'll be killed out there, and there's nothing here!"

"JUST FUCKING CHRIST TRUST ME OK?!"

He took a step back. I scared him. Good. He should be scared. She was still there, hovering. Her mouth began to twist itself into a smile, a vile jack o' lantern grin. She shook her head. It lazily glided from side to side.

"Hiiiiiiiiiiiiiiiiiiiiiiimmmmmmmmmmmmmmmmmmmmmm."

My mind cracked open and the possibilities started to overflow. Him? Was this thing here to hurt us? Just to scare us? To kill us? Were we both in danger here? Or was she telling me something else? Was she telling me… that Harold was here to hurt me? Or worse? This could've been his whole plan, stay the night, have his way, chop me up, evidence be damned. And how would she know? Who the fuck is she? A victim? A curse? Or was I actually going insane? Did Harold slip me something, was this some messed up high? Instinct snapped into place and I realized every possibility boiled down to one solution. Getting the hell out of there. She saw me come to that conclusion. She thrust her whole body through Harold, lunged at me, and this incredible force like a moving brick wall hit my body and slammed me, body and bones, out the door.

"FUCK THIS" I screamed, got up, and ran for my car.

Harold called out to me from the doorway, clearly shaken up. Sorry buddy, you're on your own. I tried. My keys, thank God, were still in my coat pocket. I didn't give a shit about any of my stuff—

"So, you just left him there?" Her words were coated thick with judgement. I looked at her dead in the eyes. Did this asshole not hear a goddam word I've been saying?

"Go to hell." I got up to leave.

"After what you saw you just left him there, with that?" she called after me.

"Fuck you," I snapped from the porch.

"Come back! PLEASE!" She sounded like she was on the brink of tears. She pleaded quietly from the Good Room. "Please. I'm sorry. This is... this is..."

I walked back in.

"I was scared. Get it? I'm sorry but I was scared. More than scared. There isn't a word for what I felt. This...woman tormenting me...and him... I didn't know him...I didn't know...anything. I was in real fucking serious danger, that's what I knew. And what would you have done? In my position? If he wasn't your—"

"You've made your point," she said softly, "please finish."

At least this would all be over soon.

Harold called out to me from the house. I looked back to make sure neither he nor this thing were following me. He stood in the door yelling my name but I kept going, the storm raging harder now than ever, tossing me around like a doll in a dryer.

I got into the freezing car and turned the key. I didn't know if I'd even be able to get up out of the driveway or how far I'd get before getting stuck but dammit I was gonna try. It started up right away. I took one last look towards the cabin. I could see the glow from the living room. And two silhouettes looking out. I had no choice. I slammed down on the gas and swerved around in the snow. I could barely tell where the driveway went up through the trees, but luck was on my side, I thought, and I started up. My tires couldn't find much traction and I started to slide back. Not this goddamn night. I turned the wheel sharply, hoping to catch a break and suddenly I sped forward. YES, I thought, as long as I can get up, I'm outta here. Then I heard her again, that shrill cry echoing in the darkness…and I slammed directly into a tree.

I woke up God knows how long later with a splitting headache. For a second I had forgotten what I was running from, disoriented, thinking "why am I in my car? Oh. Right. Fuck." The storm had passed, the forest was still and calm. I thought it must be dawn. There was an orange glow coming in against the dashboard. But I looked out the windshield up at the sky. Still pitch black. I got out. The car wasn't gonna get me anywhere now, and as soon as I did I looked back and saw what caused that orange glow. The cottage was engulfed in flame, swallowed whole. Harold's truck was still by the shed. Even before the investigation and all that, I knew he was gone. And I knew she was too.

I took a deep breath.
"So. That's it. I walked until I got service and called 911 and—"
"I know the rest." She looked down at the coffee table. I shifted

awkwardly in the fancy chair. I wasn't sure what to do next. I was about to get up and say I should go.

"It was a fetch," she said. "What you saw...it's called a fetch."

I looked at her, baffled. She continued.

"It means different things in different places but...when someone is in their last moments they can...send their spirit...leave a final message for someone."

That cleared up nothing. That didn't sound like what I experienced. She started to dig through her purse and said: "My grandmother appeared to me...late one night at the foot of my bed when I was seven. She told me she was leaving, that she was calm, and that she would always be with me..." She pulled out her phone, brought something up on it, and handed it to me.

My stomach dropped and a lump caught in my throat as I looked at the picture on the screen.

"This...is the thing...the woman. I mean...it looked different sometimes but this...this is her."

"That's my mother." Harold's daughter stared into my eyes, waiting for me to make the connection. "That night you spent with my dad...my mom passed away too, here in town. I lost both my parents that night."

My hands went weak. I dropped her phone, fell back into the chair.

"He never said he was married." My voice quivered.

"Divorced. She didn't take his being gay very well." That hung in the room for a moment.

"Ya know," I said awkwardly, trying to comfort her, "when people come out later in life— "

"Please don't do that," she said firmly. "What I mean is...I'm fine. We were fine. I wasn't mad at him for being gay. I was just... mad. Mom was too. But he and I...after some time...we were great...

we were great." This stern, cool, collected woman I had been talking to couldn't hold it together anymore. I let her cry. She needed deep and heavy tears right now. I don't think she'd allowed herself that necessity since it happened. I just sat with her. After some time, she took a deep breath.

"Mom got sick a few years after they broke up. She didn't…she couldn't…reconcile…I wish…she would've tried. I was with her the night she died. She was in and out, never lucid, mumbling things, angry things. I couldn't reach her." She paused. Her face took on a shade of bitterness. "And instead of appearing to me, or my sister, or anyone else who loved her, sending anyone a final goodbye, words of comfort…she sent her fetch to you."

I felt like absolute shit. This wasn't my fault, and I knew that, but this felt like absolute shit.

"So maybe…" I offered, "maybe she came to us to warn us. Ya know? Tried to get us out? Maybe she knew the place would catch fire, that the propane would—"

"She appeared to you. A stranger. Not to him," she said plainly. "Maybe she started the fire herself. And was giving you an out. If she wanted to spare him, she would've—"

"Maybe…maybe not…I…" I had nothing, no solace for her, nothing. "When your grandmother…came to you… did she look…"

"Nothing like that. She looked…like the most beautiful version of herself. It felt warm. But my mother…" She couldn't finish. She caught the next set of tears before they erupted and gave me a hard stare. She couldn't be that much younger than me and already she'd lost more than I could even understand.

"I'm not mad at you," she stated. She was back to her old self. "But I'm left knowing that's the choice she made. She chose that… instead of us." Neither of us moved for a few moments. Then with a "Thank you for your time," she concluded the proceedings.

I saw myself out of her home on to Gower Street and decided to stroll around downtown St. John's in the light dusk snowfall. Well. I thought I was messed up after the fire. This was an entirely new level of mind fuckery that I never in all my years could've planned for. A mess. A dark, hollow, all consuming mess.

I had been spared. I stopped on the sidewalk and cried. Just…stood there and cried. Not even really sure which part I was crying about.

I was scared, empty, lost. I texted my buddy. Told him I really needed him. He texted back in seconds: "I'm on my way <3"

3

Jacob couldn't believe that Malcolm Hennessy, the author of *Terror Nova*, was actually willing to read his work. This was huge. The whole reason he had taken this job was because the hotel held the writers' retreat and he was hoping to sneak in some networking while lugging bags around, but he never dreamed that the person he saw as his best chance to have a story published was willing—no, not just willing, *specifically requested*—to read something he had written.

"I get it," said Sadie, who was waitressing her way through a second gap year in the hotel's dining room. "You're excited."

She offered Jacob a drag of her cigarette and after he flagged it off, she crushed it under the toe of her Docs.

"You don't get it; this could be huge!" Jacob flew back into his excited monologue: "From what I hear they're still looking for stories for the second book! If he likes what I give him, I could actually get published!"

What story, though?

His favourite was the one he was currently working on, but it wasn't quite finished. It was about a young girl with asthma who loved Halloween, but her parents were afraid to let her trick-or-treat or any of her other favorite seasonal activities during COVID, so her father turned their house into a haunt for her. She insists on going through the makeshift haunt by herself but disappears while alone in the house. Then the story picks up a year later with her parents' relationship strained from the combination of grief and allegations. With Halloween approaching, strange things start happening around the house and they begin to expect that there might be an opportunity to undo whatever has happened to their daughter.

Only the story was far from done. Every time Jacob had opened the file over the course of the last six months the cursor blinked at him from the same point of the story: a paragraph describing a cold reunion after the father has been dragged into the local police station for another round of questioning.

Jacob felt that this story was a breakthrough for him. He had a breadth of work but felt it all lacked depth. This one had an opportunity to say something. Something about the pandemic, about race, about family dynamics, all themes he hadn't come close to touching in his previous stories. Confronted by the turning point of writing something with that kind of weight had intimidated him into writer's block.

"Look, if you think you could get close with this story, just finish it." Sadie's reasoning seemed to ignore the inconvenient reality of Jacob's job.

"I'm working, there'll be no time."

"Everyone is pretty much checked in now anyway, and I'll cover for you with Maggie where I can."

Maggie Cantwell was one of *those* Cantwells. She had been the driving force behind turning the estate into the inn and event space it now was and was the one responsible for the day-to-day, acting as the manager while her older brother was acting as an asshole. Sometimes her frustration with him boiled over to Jacob, Sadie, and the other staff, but she was mostly easy to work for. That said, she knew of Jacob's literary ambitions and already had her back up about how much time he'd be spending working versus networking during the retreat.

Jacob looked up to the sky where dark storm clouds were beginning to form and shrugged, thinking of the guests who would have to bring their own bags to their rooms while he hid out in the basement, straining his eyes over his laptop trying to finish the thing or maybe pick out another story.

He'd listen to Sadie and went for it.

Jacob watched from the edge of the door to the drawing room, looking for Maggie. Not seeing her, he snuck by the front desk to the employee cloak room to grab his backpack off the hook under his raincoat, which he was glad to have with him now that the skies had opened, and hard rain blasted against the windows. He kept his eyes on the office, so intently that as he rounded the corner he plowed into another writer and sent a flurry of pages in the air.

"Shit, I'm so sorry!" Jacob whisper-shouted. He was supposed to be helping these people, not sending their works into disarray.

He looked up and caught the eyes of Monica Weller, a writer who had racked up nominations for several prominent literary awards and took a shellacking from the local writing critics for "slumming it and descending to the world of genre pulp" with an entry in the first *Terror Nova*.

"Gah! I'm so sorry" Jacob repeated as he helped her collect the scattered pages off the floor.

"It's okay, it's my fault. I should be paperless by now," she offered, trying to laugh off the commotion.

"No, I need to be more careful." Jacob shifted the backpack

over his shoulder, trying to shield it from her in embarrassment. He was very conscious of his JanSport bag. Real authors were supposed to have supple leather messenger bags, preferably well-worn ones, not school bags from the mall. Hell, Monica Weller was walking around with a printed hardcopy of her manuscript. She would certainly judge him and not take him seriously.

"You work here?" she asked.

"Yeah."

"Would you mind doing me a huge favour?"

"Of course, I certainly owe you."

"I'm running late for a reading series in the…uh…?" Her brain, frazzled from the collision, wouldn't provide the name of the room.

"The Matthias Room," Jacob offered. He had memorized the schedule of events.

"Right! Thank you! I'm running late and I'm supposed to be reading from this," she gestured to the heap between them, "in about twenty minutes, but I have to get there for introductions and stuff. If I leave this with you, could you put the pages in order? They're all numbered."

"Definitely!" Jacob almost leapt with excitement over the confidence bestowed on him and chose to ignore that it was a relatively menial task that was also sort of his fault.

"Perfect. Thanks."

And she left him with her story.

FEBRUARY 2
Lauralana Dunne

The weak afternoon sunlight filtered through the cracks in the patio's broken blinds.

Cassie winced and opened her eyes. She didn't remember falling asleep.

Her head pounded where it rested against the couch cushions, and she placed a careful hand against the back of her skull and winced.

Coffee. She needed coffee.

Rolling to her feet with a grunt, she walked the short distance from the couch into the kitchen.

The click of the coffeemaker greeted her arrival. She grabbed the handle of the full pot and pulled it off its base. Devastation bloomed in her chest when she realized that it had already gone cold.

She sighed and flicked on the grinder as she dumped the cold coffee down the drain. Only a fresh brew was going to help with this monster of a headache.

She spooned the grounds into the last coffee filter and added water, resting her hip against the kitchen counter as the machine started to grumble with percolating noises. Cassie grabbed a black marker from the junk drawer and snagged a piece of scrap paper. The coffee would take a few minutes—

might as well write up a few items while she waited.

She slapped the paper onto the kitchen island then paused, blinking. There, next to the edge, was an already-started grocery list. She identified the slant of the handwriting as her own.

"Weird," she muttered, swiping the paper back into the drawer with a huff.

Her body ached. She stretched and felt a band of tension tug across her back as her muscles protested the action. Pulled muscles or bruises? She couldn't tell. Cassie pressed a hand to the small of her back and winced at the sensation.

A loud crash caught her attention.

Cassie jerked her head and scanned the empty hallway. She stilled, listening for the source. Geoff would be at work by now. She was the only one home.

The hairs on the back of her neck prickled in warning. Unable to ignore it, Cassie pushed herself away from the counter and waited. Her gaze fell on the knife block by the sink. The large chef knife—her go-to item for meal prep—was missing from its slot. Geoff had probably put it in the dishwasher again. She continually reminded him that the harsh detergents could ruin the blade, but he somehow always managed to forget that when it was his turn to do the dishes. Shaking off her annoyance, she padded into the hallway, her bare feet silent against the hardwood floor...

The house was quiet. The creeping light from outside cast muted half-shadows across the floor. Cassie looked around but could see nothing out of place. Even the outside was still. Nothing moved.

She felt foolish. "Get it together, Cas." Her voice seemed hollow in the tense quiet. She pressed a fingertip to her throbbing temple and turned her attention longingly back to the coffee in the kitchen.

Another loud crash caused her to jump. Cassie peered up the stairwell into the gloom of the unlit second floor but saw nothing. "Hello?" she called. "Geoff?"

No answer.

She rested a foot on the first carpeted stair and hesitated. She could hear scraping, as if something heavy was being dragged across a rough surface. She wracked her brain for what could be making that noise but could think of nothing that fit.

It must be coming from outside.

Frowning, she turned toward the large window in the front hall. It sounded like metal being dragged across asphalt. Abandoning the stairs, she stepped into the porch and grasped for the flimsy curtains next to the locked door. The light outside seemed so strange…

She felt dizzy.

Cassie rested a hand against the wall to keep her balance. Her fingers splayed over markings that were scribbled on the wall. She moved back to read the graffiti that had been scrawled next to the door in black ink.

GET OUT

Another crash, larger than the first, distracted her by shaking the house around her.

It had definitely come from the basement.

Cassie whirled, her heart sinking in her chest. The basement was underground. The only way to get in was to break one of the fixed windows.

She walked to the basement door and grasped the clunky doorknob as she listened for any indication of an intruder rummaging around downstairs. The was more scraping, and the distinct screech of metal being dragged against the concrete floor.

Cassie calmed the pounding of her heart and slowly opened the door. She was greeted by the steep wooden staircase that disappeared into the darkness of the crawl space. Reflexively, she reached up to pull the chain hanging from the bare light-bulb but stopped short when she saw the wooden support beam next to it.

Someone had written something on it in black marker.

Cassie rose to her tiptoes, stretching herself to read the message in the dim light.

RUN

The block letters had been gone over several times to thicken them.

Cassie snorted. "I'm going to kill Geoff for marking up the house," she vowed, glaring at the sharpie ink that had settled permanently into the wood grain.

Gurgling from the basement distracted her from her murderous thoughts. Forgetting about the light, she clutched the wobbly railing and slowly descended into the darkness. The pounding of her heart had slowed. Instead of fear gripping her chest, she now felt irritation tapping against the inside of her temples. Geoff's latest prank had gone too far.

The stairs creaked under her careful footsteps and she winced, but the noise was drowned out as the scraping sound continued. The spare fridge was leaning forward on its open door, biting into the floor. The door's hinge had cracked from the weight of the appliance where it had fallen.

The smell hit her and she gagged. Pressing a mouth over her nose, she looked around the room in disbelief. Broken containers and bottled food were strewn across the floor. The mixture of smells from the smashed Tupperware was enough to nauseate her.

Geoff's legs were visible from the other side of the fridge. The light from the fridge made it look like he was kneeling on the ground, but he was jerking so erratically that she couldn't figure out what he was trying to do.

"What happened?" Cassie couldn't keep the peevish note out of her voice as she strode toward him.

Geoff's legs slowed in their movement, but he didn't answer. Cassie felt her temper rise as a result.

"What are you doing down he—" Cassie slipped in an unseen puddle on the floor. The thick wetness squished between her bare toes as she slid a short distance before snagging a low-hanging wooden beam.

"Ugh!" The tacky substance pulled at Cassie's feet as she minced toward the fridge. "I better not cut myself on any broken glass.

When Geoff didn't answer, her temper flared into a full-blown rage. He rummaged in the fridge as she marched toward him. *Splat, splat, splat.* Her footsteps weren't loud, but the sensation went through her as her toes dug through the puddle to find purchase against the rough concrete underneath.

Geoff's feet stuck out beyond the fridge door. He was obstructed from her view, but he looked to be kneeling on the floor while frantically searching for something in the back of the shelves. His head tilted back to view the entire fridge at once. The noise of his rummaging had blocked her voice until now.

Cassie narrowed her eyes on the back of Geoff's bobbing head. She stomped forward, chest puffed out as she filled her lungs with the anger that she was about to throw at him.

A loud crack stopped her in her tracks. The sound went through her, sending chills across her skin while causing her stomach to roll. It wasn't the sound of breaking metal or cracking wood—it was the sound of a bone snapping.

Geoff's head tipped back. Cassie braced herself for a cry or a scream of pain, but he made no noise.

Instead, she watched in horror as his head rolled down his back and tumbled to the floor. Bile rose in her throat at the sight. It fell on its side, and Cassie would have screamed if the terror of what happened hadn't stolen the air out of her lungs.

Geoff's face was missing.

The skin had been torn from the skull. A few tatters remained attached by the hairline, but the rest had been ripped off to display the raw tissue underneath. His nose had been reduced to a bloody stump, his warm brown eyes had been removed, leaving two gaping, bloody hollows that seemed to stare right through her. His jaw was missing, as was his top lip. All that was left was his top row of teeth, forming a slash of a white smile. The slight overlap of the front teeth left no doubt in her mind that the head belonged to Geoff—a small piece of normalcy attached to the grisliest display she had ever seen.

Cassie froze with shock. Her lungs contracted in protest, sharply sucking in an intake of air as she stared at Geoff's detached head. The edges of her vision went black, and tunnel vision consumed her as her fear spiked.

She was frozen in place, hyperventilating, and she couldn't stop it. Each intake of breath pushed her closer and closer to the hysteria that was threatening to take over her brain.

A hollow silence filled the room around her breathing. A thin ribbon of fear coiled itself around Cassie's spine as she stared in dread at the open fridge. Whatever was making the noise had stilled, causing the room to go quiet.

The fridge door swung back on its hinges. The light from

inside fanned across the room, and Cassie was finally able to see the damage to the floor from all the spilled food.

Only it wasn't food. It was blood.

Revulsion punched her in the gut. It was all she could do to keep from vomiting at the feeling of blood squishing between her toes.

Geoff's body stilled. The fridge door continued to swing open, coming to a halt only when the damaged hinge cracked further when it swooped in an arc. Cassie barely noticed. Her attention wasn't fixated on the broken appliance. Instead, she held her breath as a large creature, originally hidden by the door, slowly came into view.

Large, curved talons gripped the floor where the creature crouched. Its skin was a mottled grey that appeared translucent where it stretched over the creature's thick rib cage, making it look as though it were starving despite the bulk of muscles that rippled along its forearms. Cassie's brain tried to make sense of the animal before her. It resembled the images of demons and grotesques from old oil paintings. The difference was that this one didn't have anything that resembled a devil's face. She wasn't even sure if it had a face. Instead, a large, vertical slit up the front of its triangular skull was its only defining feature.

It took a lumbering step forward. The stench of decay followed, clinging thickly to its hulking frame. Multiple slits along its body contracted with a sharp inhale, and Cassie realized that it had nostrils all over its body. The creature had heard her and was attempting to pinpoint her location.

Cassie froze, not daring to breathe as the blood-covered horror crept toward her.

It swung its angled head around, searching for her. Its tail, hidden until now, lashed across the floor, sweeping through the blood with enough speed to leave a wake in its path. The vertical split peeled open, displaying rows upon rows of razor-sharp teeth that folded open as it threw back its head and roared.

Instinctual, primal terror rooted her to the spot. Warmth crept down Cassie's legs as her bladder let loose. She backed away, slowly, holding her breath as she fought to make the least amount of noise as possible. Her heart pounded so heavily in her ears that she was convinced that the creature could hear it.

It lowered its head and sniffed again. This time it paused as it pointed its sightless face directly at her. It had caught the scent of her urine. It had found her.

All rational thought emptied from her head as pure panic set in.

Cassie lunged toward the basement steps just as the creature struck. Her toenails bit into the wood, cracking with the force from scrabbling to remain upright as her blood-slickened soles slipped across the surface.

She grabbed the rickety railing and launched herself toward the top of the stairs, falling up them in her haste to escape the basement.

The stench of decay blasted at her from behind as the creature roared with anger, its putrid breath washing over her as the sound of snapping teeth filled the air.

She could feel its hot breath on her heels from the near miss of its fangs. Cassie's heart stuttered in panic as she used her arms to throw herself onto the main floor. She'd never moved so fast in her life.

It caused her to stumble.

Her shins barked in pain against the top step before she regained her balance. She scrambled into the hallway, her mind spiraling in panic as she slid across the hardwood floor. A thick smear of red stretched behind her.

Splintering wood accompanied an angry bellow that erupted from the basement. Without thinking, Cassie turned around and slammed the door shut behind her, effectively cutting off the worst of the creature's sound.

She stood poised in front of the door. While she enjoyed the momentary relief of silencing it, she knew that closing the door was not a solution to containing it. Her mind raced to come up with an escape plan.

If she could just get to the front door...

There was a large crash, and the heavy basement door fractured as easily as she could snap a popsicle stick. Cassie leapt aside to avoid the large wooden shards that flew toward her. She was fast but not fast enough to dodge the searching claw that swiped out from the stairs.

The massive claw clipped her side and threw her backwards into the kitchen like a rag doll. She managed to miss the island by an inch and slammed onto the floor. The air rushed from her lungs and she struggled to take a breath.

The creature screamed in irritated fury. Cassidy felt it in her bones. Her blood ran cold at the sound, and her terror spurned her forward. She rolled to her feet, clutching her side where the creature had struck her.

It lunged toward her. The door frame buckled from the force but held. The creature roared as its shoulders became stuck. The slit on its massive head split open, and Cassie could see the rows of razorblade teeth extend toward her. Large strings of drool slid from its open maw and onto the floor.

It was in her way. The creature and its massive claws were between her and the front door. There was no way she could reach it without being torn to shreds.

Her terror-stricken mind focused.

The patio. She could escape from the patio.

She turned and ran just as the creature lunged again. This time the frame gave way and it spilled into the hallway, sliding into the wall in its haste to reach her.

Cassie grabbed the living room door frame and used it to swing herself into the room, keeping her momentum up in an attempt to escape from the creature.

But she hadn't realized the reach of its tail.

The sound of the patio blinds breaking was her only warning. It whipped toward her, the air whistling around it, and clipped the back of her head with enough force that her trajectory faltered and she stumbled. Stars burst into life behind her eyes, and it was all she could do to stay conscious.

She careened into the far wall. She fell to her knees from the impact but caught herself before smashing her face into the wall. A clatter caught her attention, and she looked down to see that she had struck her missing chef knife that lay next to the baseboard.

"What the f—"

The hairs on the back of her neck prickled. On instinct, Cassie grabbed the handle of the chef knife and whirled.

The creature had slipped in through the wider opening of the room. It launched at her with a snarl, lips spread wide as it aimed to clamp its mouth around her head.

On instinct, Cassie ducked and curled herself into a ball. She thrust the knife up into the air, blind, attempting to scare the creature away from her. If it backed up long enough, she would be able to get to the sliding patio door.

There was a sickening crunch, and the creature grunted.

Cassie's eyes popped open.

The long blade of the chef knife had pierced the space between its brittle ribs. The weight of its torso had snapped the ribs from the impact, driving the blade through the ribcage and into its heart.

The creature slumped against her, then staggered backwards. A thin whine filled the air as it struggled to remove the knife that was embedded in its chest. Cassie rolled to her feet and backed away while it was distracted.

The keening continued, increasing in intensity as it attempted to remove the knife from its chest. Long, curved talons shred the flesh away from its chest as it grasped for the knife handle. Cassie swallowed back bile as large chunks of flesh and bone were flung around the room. Thick, black blood sprayed across the wall with its movements.

The creature gave a wet gurgle and slumped to the floor. Cassie took a step back, placing as much distance between it and herself as the room would allow.

She held her breath, feeling the throbbing in her head where the creature's tail had struck her, and waited.

It didn't move again. Instead, to her immense surprise, it started to crackle. It sounded like a campfire. The noises confused her until one of its limbs twitched. She refused to move closer to inspect it.

The corpse continued to pop and crack. She could see large movements across its back, twitching under the skin in time to the sharp staccato sounds.

Its bones were breaking.

Cassidy watched in muted horror as the creature disintegrated in front of her. Its bones shattered into nothing. It lay on the floor in a giant pool, looking like an oil slick spread across the middle of the room, the knife still embedded where it slouched against the wall. A bubbling sound took over. The skin became brittle and pale, fizzing away into nothing as if some cosmic cleaner had removed it. The mess from the creature—the blood and gore that coated the room—followed suit and disappeared, removing any trace of the creature except for the broken blinds and Cassie's throbbing head.

She stared around in disbelief. She took a step toward the kitchen, wobbling slightly on her feet. She pressed a hand to the side of her skull and felt a lump forming where she had been struck.

Her balance faltered and she tipped to her side, falling onto the couch in her hurry. With a groan, she twisted herself so that her cheek rested on the plush arm, and the softness of the fabric caused her to close her eyes for a brief moment as it cradled her aching head.

The weak afternoon sunlight filtered through the cracks in the patio's broken blinds.

Cassie winced and opened her eyes. She didn't remember falling asleep.

Her head pounded where it rested against the couch cushions, and she placed a careful hand against the back of her skull and winced.

Coffee. She needed coffee.

Rolling to her feet with a grunt, she walked the short distance from the couch into the kitchen.

The click of the coffeemaker greeted her arrival. She grabbed the handle of the full pot and pulled it off its base. Devastation bloomed in her chest when she realized that it had already gone cold.

She sighed and flicked on the grinder as she dumped the cold coffee down the drain. Only a fresh brew was going to help with this monster of a headache.

She spooned the grounds into the last coffee filter and added water, resting her hip against the kitchen counter as the machine started to grumble with percolating noises. Cassie grabbed a black marker from the junk drawer and snagged a piece of scrap paper. The coffee would take a few minutes—ight as well write up a few items while she waited.

She slapped the paper onto the kitchen island, then paused, blinking. There, next to the edge, was an already-started grocery list. She identified the slant of the handwriting as her own.

"Weird," she muttered, swiping the paper back into the drawer with a huff.

Her body ached. She stretched and felt a band of tension tug across her back as her muscles protested the action. Pulled muscles or bruises? She couldn't tell. Cassie pressed a hand to the small of her back and winced at the sensation.

A loud crash caught her attention.

Cassie jerked her head and scanned the empty hallway. She stilled, listening for the source. Geoff would be at work by now. She was the only one home.

The hairs on the back of her neck prickled in warning. Unable to ignore it, Cassie pushed herself away from the counter and waited. Her gaze fell on the knife block by the sink. The large chef knife—her go-to item for meal prep—was missing from its slot. Geoff had probably put it in the dishwasher again. She continually reminded him that the harsh detergents could ruin the blade, but he somehow always managed to forget that when it was his turn to do the dishes. Shaking off her annoyance, she padded into the hallway, her bare feet silent against the hardwood floor...

4

"The pursuit of the heavens is a noble one. From the first time we gazed upwards, humans have always attempted to grasp what lay beyond our reach.

"So, I can appreciate anyone who sees the world around us and thinks that our time is ticking away and that pushing for a new frontier has become less about knowledge and more about survival.

"But when the pursuit is financed not by government agencies mandated with expanding our own boundaries of discovery, but by billionaire man-boys who ride shotgun in giant allegories for what a dildo they are, allegories that cost more than ending world hunger would, I can't help but feel pessimistic about their intentions and that it's not about advancing our understanding of the universe, but about a pissing contest at a children's table to see who can claim the title of 'most self-important asshat'."

"Jesus." Malcolm took off his glasses and rubbed the bridge of his nose as he muttered.

"You don't agree?"

He jumped in his seat; he didn't realize anyone was close enough to him to hear his utterance. Looking up, he saw Monica a few seats away.

"Mon! Hi!" He hadn't seen Monica Weller since the launch events for the first book a year ago, and he didn't know her that well. She had been match-made by the publisher who knew Monica and thought that her reputation as a "real writer" would elevate the book.

"I actually do agree, whole-heartedly, but at which point of decrying the most self-important asshats do you become a self-important asshat?" He shifted a seat over, closing the gap between them while still providing a few seats buffer.

"Oh, come on. You know Xander isn't that bad." She said and did the same, shifting over from her side so just a single empty seat separated them.

"Alex wasn't that bad. Xander, I'm increasingly unsure of."

"What?" She asked.

"I've known Alex Williams since high school and when he went to college, he reinvented himself as 'Xander Guillaume' and has been become a leading authority on being better than everyone ever since."

"Ah."

"So, it isn't the sentiment, it's the smugness."

"Um, Ms. Weller?" They both looked up to see Jacob, the bellhop, standing meekly behind them, holding a stack of crumpled papers that he presented triumphantly to Monica over the empty seat.

As Alex Williams' diatribe on the quest for building a stairway to the stars on the back of minimum-wage-earning warehouse workers ended, Nick Cantwell, the owner of the hotel stepped to the microphone to thank Xander for his "thought-provoking essay," then introduced the next scribe to the stage.

"Y'know, Jacob here is a writer himself," Malcolm said as Jacob handed the pages over to Monica.

"Is that right?" she inquired, but before Jacob could stammer out an answer there was a loud crack and the lights in the hotel were snuffed into blackness.

Whispers and whimpers rumbled through the crowd before Cantwell stepped to the front of the stage where the podium remained shrouded in darkness.

"Ladies and gentlemen, please excuse this disruption." Nick Cantwell had all the charm of a faith healer, loud and boisterous, slick and superficial. "We do have a back-up generator, which I'm sure we'll have up and running momentarily."

As he spoke two of the stagehands from the audio-visual company rushed out on the stage with battery powered LED panels and set up two facing toward the podium, bathing Cantwell in a cold blue light. As he blinked into the sudden brightness they dialed in a warmer temperature, bringing him to a much more humane peach tone.

"Our next writer has promised that their voice can carry well and has offered to perform a reading for you while we wait for the power to come back. So, if you wouldn't mind giving them your undivided attention…"

TAKE OR BE TAKEN
Kelley Power

Thomas Goodridge might shit his pants. Not that he lets it show, lips curved in a smile, head tilted in attention to the nonsense coming out of Jim Keenin's mouth.

"Can you believe they think *I'm* the crazy one?" Keenin says. "My whole family! No matter how many times I tell them, no matter how many times I show them the pictures. Thank you. *Thank you* for believing me."

Goodridge clenches his butt cheeks and hands the man a white business card with a 1-900 number printed on the front.

"Of course," Goodridge says, nodding. "If the vampire returns tonight, you can call this number." He squeezes his client's shoulder. "It's an afterhours line I set up for people who need help outside office appointments. There's a fee—I have to pay for the service, I'm sure you understand but this is a pivotal time for you, and you shouldn't hesitate to call."

Keenin slips the card into the breast pocket of his plaid collared shirt and snags Goodridge's left hand in both his own, pumping it so vigorously the doctor winces. "Thank you, Dr. Goodridge. It's been...I don't know how to tell you...to finally feel heard and understood. The therapists, they just didn't understand."

Goodridge withdraws his hand and nods, trying to ignore the tickle of the beads of sweat gathering at his hairline. "You're not the only one who's come to me as a last resort, Mr. Keenin."

"Jimmy," Kennin says.

Goodridge's smile deepens. "Jimmy. Call me Thomas."

Keenin continues his effusive thanks as Goodridge glances at the clock on the wall behind him. Half-past two. His next appointment is three o'clock and he needs to get to the bathroom before his next session. He guides Keenin to a door on the right side of the room with the firm pressure of his hand on the man's back.

The scuffed wooden door sticks, then creaks open when Goodridge tugs. He ushers Keenin through it as he reiterates his client's next appointment time. Goodridge waits for him to take a breath. "Looking forward to seeing you again Thursday, Jimmy. Remember," he points to the man's breast pocket, where the faint outline of the business card is visible, "call if anything comes up. My partner, Alice, has the instructions you'll need to help you if the creature returns." And to talk you out of calling the cops on the creeping peeper hanging around outside your house, if there's anyone there at all. He wishes Keenin a good day and closes the door as the man opens his mouth to speak again.

Goodridge counts to 10, knees locked together, giving Keenin time to get to the stairwell at the end of the hall, and cracks the door to peek out. The dark, dim-lit hallway is clear. He scutters across the hall and flings open the door to the bathroom and has his pants around his knees before it shuts behind him. His belt buckle hits the linoleum floor with a thud as he drops onto the toilet. The pain in his gut goes from wrenching to dull as he's finally able to evacuate himself.

The worst time yet, he thinks, breath quickened and eyes heavy as the episode subsides. More like a God damn attack, his brain counters. "Episode" is for soap operas and fainting spells; this is having phantom fingers reach inside your guts and tie your intestines into knots. He glances at the tissue with mild dread as he cleans himself up. There it is again. Bright blood amongst…the rest of it. He sighs. This is beyond Pepto Bismol; he'll have to call the doctor in the morning.

Finishing at the sink, Goodridge splashes water on his face and checks his tie. Slightly askew and loose at the neck. Approachable. He looks into the mirror, past the purple smears under his eyes, and practices his listening face. His sympathy face. His surprise face. By the end of the pantomimes, he's feeling back to himself, with a benign ache in his stomach and behind his eyes.

His watch reads 2:58.

Back in his office, he stands with his hand on the knob of the door to the small waiting room. Before turning it, he yawns hugely. The insomnia has been getting worse. Two nights in a row now with only an hour or less of sleep. He drags his free hand down over his face, stretching out the skin, and slaps himself on the cheek. When his hand falls, it grazes his front pants pocket. He pats the bump there, imagining Jim Keenin's folded twenty-dollar bills curled up next to the wad he has collected from his other clients today. Maybe he'll take a vacation soon, hit up one of those all-expenses-paid resorts. He's been working flat out for the past four months, trying to keep up with the demand for his service. The business of bilking the bat-shit crazy is booming.

Take or be taken. That was Thomas Goodridge's creed. And Tommy Goodwell's, Tom Janes', and the handful of other aliases used by the man born Tom G. Upshall. Thomas Goodridge was the latest – and if he did say so himself, greatest – in a long line of fake names and lives Upshall had taken on in his 38 years.

He knew he wasn't smart in the conventional, Nobel-prize winning sense. He didn't have one of those beautiful minds that saw something once and could spin it into a million different directions and reveal the mysteries of the universe. But if there was a prize for survival skills, he'd have his name on that trophy a hundred times over. His father used to say Tom could put an ass in a cat: fix anything, build anything. And reading people? He'd learned to do that before he got his First Holy Communion. The one thing he couldn't do was let someone else dictate his life. Not parents, not teachers. It'd be the same for any jackass he'd end up working for in a factory or on a kill floor. He'd known that at 15, as surely as he'd known a high school diploma would be useless to him. So, he dropped out and started running scams with his buddy Dion.

Every cheat was different, but they all worked the same: find the person's weakness and fertilize it with the best brand of bullshit you have until it starts to flower. The two of them started out with grifts on "Seven Deadly Sinners": the type of people who got greedy for fast money, or indiscreetly fucked around on their spouses. Tom saw more. His eye picked out the opportunities among the trusting; the generous and gullible. Dion couldn't see the possibilities there, didn't want to. Drew the line at taking advantage of what he called good, God-fearing people. Fucking Catholic. That's when they parted. Tom made sure to loot the collection box at St. Michael's, Dion's church, before he split and moved his game over to the west end.

When he ran away from the rank government-issued apartment his mother raised him in, he figured out that uncovering what people wanted most in the world was the ticket to getting whatever he liked out of them: a meal, a place to stay, favours. Best of all, money. He stayed off the streets with an abused runaway routine, taken in under the wings of kindly geriatrics — widows, widowers, old farts with kids who ignored them — and managed to wheedle their dollars away a handful at a time and still eat at their kitchen tables every night. That con worked for years. He finally gave it up after the night Marjorie Horwood rolled up on him in her wheelchair while he literally had his hand in her cookie jar — that's where she kept her cash, right there on the counter in brown a ceramic jar, the dumb cow — and went into a tirade about him being a thief and an ingrate and whatever else she could throw at him, while he stared dumbly at her, wondering how he was going to get out the door with her blocking the only way out of the place with that rickety old chair. She saved him the trouble of figuring it out by having the decency to work herself up enough to drop dead of a heart attack on the spot. He grabbed every dollar in the jar and rolled her aside until her knees came up against the cupboards with a thud and she slumped forward in the chair. That was about 20 years ago and to this day any time he saw a wheelchair he thought of Marj. She never had kids and most of her friends only saw her at the community hall on bingo night. He wondered if she had to start rotting before anyone went to the dingy apartment to check on her.

The girlfriend game came next. That kept him in warm beds and hot meals for months at a time. Find one who always begged for compliments or had a hard time looking you in the eye and he was set for a year at least. By the time they figured out his heart wasn't in it and there wouldn't be an engagement, or a marriage, and they weren't going to meet his mother, he already had the next one lined up, ready to go.

Not that he was cruel. He never beat on any of them or ran them down to their faces. A few even had kids. He never stooped to babysitting them or doing homework with them, naturally, but didn't take food out of their mouths. He even tried to teach them a thing or two about life. He taught Nathan Baker how to get his mother to keep doing his laundry and making his dinners for him long after he was old enough to do them himself. "If you screw it up enough on your own, she'll just take care of it when she gets sick of buying you new clothes and worrying about you burning down the house when you boil water." Deidra Stapleton knew how to get every guy tapping their feet to her beat after he'd taught her about hormones. "The right smile, the right touch of a hand on his arm, and he'll be steaming up his glasses, working double-time to get your homework done for you."

He was a gold-standard humanitarian.

It was because of the kids, or one kid in particular, that he hit the con jackpot.

"Mandy Chang. Time for your first appointment with Dr. Feelgood Goodridge."

He opens the waiting room door. A short heavy-set woman with straight dark hair down her back is sitting opposite, reading a tabloid. Her skin is sallow, almost grey, as if she and the sun are estranged. A good sign.

"Ms. Chang?"

The woman looks up at him and blinked rapidly. "Yes.

Hello."

She opens the large canvas satchel on her lap and stuffs the paper inside as she stands. Tom notices it's a copy of the *National Enquirer* with the headline, "2 Catholic Priests Say: Flying Saucers Are Real!".

He sticks out his hand to shake hers and she looks at it like he's offered her a dead cat. He clears his throat and turns the aborded handshake into a sweeping wave, stepping aside to usher her ahead of him. She walks with wide, determined steps. She stands in the middle of office and looks around at the yellowed wallpaper and the two framed diplomas he stuck on the wall next to his desk when he moved in. The key to faking it is not getting too ambitious; nobody would believe he'd graduated from a big-league university and gone on to do this work, in this shit-hole, so Greenwood Community College and The Institute of American Sciences stood in as his *alma maters*.

Ms. Chang is quiet after her perusal of his credentials. She turns around and moves toward the set of worn and cracked leather chairs he curated as part of his set. Those he'd picked up off a sidewalk where they'd been left with a "free 2 take" sign. His luck was amazing.

"Please, take a seat," he says. She takes a pack of wet towelettes from her purse and pulls a string of two or three out to wipe down the seat and armrests on the chair. The smell of alcohol hits his nose and he smiles inside, giddy with the possibilities. When she settles herself into the seat, he sits across from her. Rather than take on the relaxed posture he used with his other patients – leaning forward, elbows on knees, hands hanging loosely in front of him – he sits back in his chair and picks up his pen and notepad. This one will want formality, not his casual, inviting routine. She doesn't want a buddy to listen; she wants a doctor to analyze and prescribe solutions.

"You said on the phone you wanted to discuss the portal that opened up in your bedroom closet. I can review my notes, but why don't we start from the beginning, now that we're face-to-face."

Given the way 1982 started, he couldn't have dreamed the year would treat him so well. His girlfriend at the time had gotten unreasonable about his contributions to the household. Turned out emptying the six-packs of Bud she brought home into his grateful gullet and keeping the couch warm with his ass all day long weren't Tammy's idea of him being a helping hand around the apartment. Wasn't his fault the con game had gone dry for a couple of months. The news piece on his grift didn't help. How was he supposed to cold call people and hard-sell them into "investing" in Venezuela's next big gold mine when the God damn police were on TV warning people about it? All he needed was some time to get back on his feet. So what if the rent had evaporated for a month or two? Or four? Tammy got her brothers to come and turf him out after he tried a bit too eagerly to get her to give him more time. Not with his fists – he wasn't an animal – but with a little pleading here, a little reminder there that she'd skimmed a few hundred dollars out of the till at the diner where she worked, and wouldn't it be a shame if someone told her boss about it. He thought her brothers would understand if he explained how unreasonable she was being; fellowship of men and all that. Only one important lesson was learned, though: Tom came to understand that even if a man's fist isn't small enough to fit into your eye socket, it'll still feel like he's crushed your eyeball when he punches you there, and the sensation that the fist will suck that eyeball right out of your head when he pulls his fist back will make your nuts retreat right up into your guts.

He was two weeks into sleeping on his buddy Vern's air mattress when Sandra Murphy showed up. She dropped by with a box of stuff belonging to Vern's brother, who she'd just booted out because he'd been cheating on her. Tom invited her in to wait until Vern got back from buying smokes. She sat down at the kitchen table with him and before she knew what was happening, he'd charmed her into taking him to dinner and the rest was moving-in-in-a-rush history.

Her kid was Tom's gateway to the world of Dr. Thomas Goodridge.

Dusty Murphy was the biggest geek he'd ever met. A 12-year-old who spent about as much time with his mind on this planet as Tom himself spent thinking about being a monk. The walls of his bedroom were papered with posters, from the tender nerdiness of *Battlestar Galactica* and *Star Trek*, to the grittier likes of *Alien* and *The Texas Chainsaw Massacre*. He had a model of the solar system hanging off the ceiling light in his room. Tom went looking for a stash of titty magazines in the kid's room one day when Dusty and Sandra were out and all he found was a stack of a local rag called *Tales of the Weird*. He would've passed them over if it wasn't for the delicious covers: volume after volume with paintings of space ladies in silver unitards, jungle ladies in leopard-skin unitards, screaming ladies in tattered red unitards. It was a buffet of impossibly round asses and valley-deep cleavage. Way to go, Dusty.

Tom sat on the bed and leafed through an issue. The fiction stories were pulpy enough to make toilet paper. The small non-fiction section was made up of first-person accounts of people living in haunted houses, being cursed by witches, stalked by man-eating wargs. Thomas snorted and shook his head. He flicked to the last page. Large and small blocks of text butted up against one another. Personal ads, product ads. Ads asking, *Are you a victim of alien abduction? Call now.* Ads offering help to write a manuscript, publish a manuscript. Think about a manuscript. Ads for 1-900 numbers putting you in contact with psychics who could find your longest, lostest loves. Ads selling 100% authentic props from *The Amityville Horror, Soylent Green,* and some other movies he'd never heard of. A few of the ads must be legit, he figured, but the invisible hand behind many looked a lot like his own: open, grasping, waiting for some naïve mark to fall into it.

A sliver of an idea itched his grey matter. He sat on the bed flicking back and forth through the pages of the magazine. Then he picked up another. And another. By the time he'd finished with the sixth magazine, the sliver was a fully formed chunk of brilliance.

He placed his first ad in the May 1982 volume of *Tales of the Weird:*

Need a guide for your paranormal and supernatural experiences?
Call Dr. Tom Goodridge
Specializing in parapsychology and cryptozoology
709-555-6060

His first call came within the week.

"I got bit by a werewolf," the guy said. "My sister says it was just a German Shepherd. You know, one of them all black ones. But she didn't see it happen. The thing had red eyes, for Chrissakes."

"We should talk before the full moon on Friday," Goodridge

told him. "How does Tuesday sound?"

He spent his evenings getting up to speed on what his clients were likely to throw his way. His stack of library books was starting to rival his stack of *Hustler*. Endless volumes on the weird, crazy shit his clients believed in. *Encyclopedia of Monsters, Compendium of Supernatural Creatures, The Normal Paranormal, Roswell and other Tales of Extraterrestrials*. Within a month he had a menagerie tracking through the shabby rented office, all haunted, stalked, seduced, or infected in the most comical ways. In the beginning, he found it hard to keep a straight face. The closest he came to losing it was with a client who told him she had a gnome-like creature living in her muffer (she couldn't bring herself to say vagina). He'd bitten the insides of his cheeks to keep the laughter from flowing out of him like a waterfall. If she'd been better looking, he might've taken her up on her invitation to do a manual inspection.

Tom had seen two dozen clients before Archie Perry walked through his door and gave him his first case of stone-cold creeps. The guy arrived with his salt-and-pepper hair slicked back with brill cream, his long, lanky limbs clothed in a dark brown suit that bulged and creased when he walked like it was trying to hold liquid in place. His red bowtie was the weirdness cherry on top. Rather than take a seat, Perry went to the chipped wooden bookcases between the entrance and exit doors. Seeing Perry examine the titles, Thomas congratulated himself again on the time he'd taken to curate the volumes there from flea markets and charity sales. Dog-eared editions of *Dracula, Frankenstein, The Haunting of Hill House*, and other horror classics. *War of the Worlds, Starship Troopers*. Collections of real-life accounts of ghost ships, incubi, succubi, lizard people. The King James Bible. It was a multi-shelved homage to the seeds of every twisted tale people told him in this space. Perry pulled a book off the shelf and examined the blurb on the back. Thomas saw *Church of the Lamb of God* written in large red block letters across the front. Perry murmured a word as he slipped the volume back on the shelf; Thomas wasn't sure, but he thought it was, "Amateurs."

The man turned on his heel and took a seat in one of the leather chairs. It wasn't until Thomas sat down across from him that he noticed the pale blue eyes behind his black horn-rimmed glasses. He had an immediate sense of those eyes penetrating his brain and pulsing against the back of his skull. Inviting Perry to repeat what he'd told him over the phone, Tom leaned back in his seat, putting as much distance between him and Perry as he could without looking unprofessional. Perry put his elbows on the arms of his chair and laced his fingers together in front of him.

"As I mentioned, I'm head of a large group of individuals — a collective, you might say — who are interested in enlighten-ment through occult practices." The unique tenor of the man's voice was more pronounced in person than it had been over the phone. Thomas remembered thinking it was rough; in the same room with the man, it sounded like the words were being forced out of a throat lined with gravel. Perry started rubbing his laced fingers together rhythmically. "We need a certain critical mass of members to make our collective work and, unfortunately, re-cent circumstances have led to us losing several."

Tom was dying to know what those circumstances were. He looked down at the words he'd scribbled on his notepad two days ago, when Perry had briefed him during their initial phone call. *Cult, Jim Jones type.* He underlined the words three times and felt the hair prickle at the back of his neck. "I'll be honest, Mr. Perry," he said. "I took this appointment because you insisted." And on the off chance you could turn out to be a cash cow. "But my initial assessment stands: I'm not sure what I can offer you. Most people reach out to me because they need someone to talk to about their supernatural or paranormal experiences. You seem to be…" Too confident, too self-assured to be a valuable mark "…very comfortable in your dealings with the extra-usual world."

"You're right, Dr. Goodridge. I don't need your therapeutic services." His fingers stilled. "I need a recruiter and the game you're playing here creates a fruitful environment for recruitment."

Tom stared at him for a span of seconds, synapses firing. Had he given himself away, or was Perry fishing? The man's expression was opaque. No clues there. "I'm afraid you've misread me, Mr. Perry. I provide a legitimate service. My clients need a sympathetic, knowledgeable ear and I provide it."

Perry didn't break eye contact when he leaned forward. "We would pay cash," he said. "Say, forty dollars per person? Unfortunately, your clients would be unlikely to come back to see you once they joined the collective, so we would want your compensation to reflect that loss."

A second denial came to his lips, but Tom held on to it.

Recruiting cult members for a cash take? It wouldn't take much, just pass along the names of the most likely candidates out of his client list. Commission sales. He liked the ease of the transaction. There was never a guarantee a client would come back, so the deal had a certain bird-in-the-hand appeal. But it would mean losing his independence. His brain recoiled at the idea of working for someone else, even if all it meant was a few phone calls per week. Working for this man in particular made his self-preservation instincts vibrate; he didn't want to be any-where near a bunch of potential Kool-Aid drinkers.

He sighed and stood. "Mr. Perry, there's no arrangement for us to make here. I would never encourage my clients into a setting where they could be taken advantage of." His sense of humour was tickled by this particular hypocrisy, and he had to cough to cover the chuckle that rose up the back of his throat. "I'll forgive you the insult, I know my line of work isn't com-mon, but let's not prolong this session. My answer is final, so I can't imagine you have anything else to say to me."

The two men stared at one another. Thomas knew this game. Being the first to speak would be tantamount to breaking character. He had to keep his mouth shut, let the silence add weight to his indignancy. What he wasn't used to, though, was playing this game with someone who made him feel like they were plying layers off his brain as the silence dragged on. Why wouldn't the bastard look away?

Thomas couldn't help but shift from foot to foot. He didn't think it was a concession, but it made Perry smile and look down at his laced fingers; they were moving again, the long digits sliding against one another.

"I'll leave you to think about it. We'll work better together if your mind is open to it. I'll stop by some time to finish our negotiations, no need to pencil me in for another appointment." Tom's eyes followed Perry's progress as he unfolded himself from the chair and walked to the exit door. "You look tired, Mr. Upshall," he said as he opened the door. "Do try and get some sleep."

The door closed behind him and Tom exhaled a breath he hadn't known he was holding. Hearing his real name on the man's lips made his heart trip in his chest. He raked a hand through his hair and turned back to the room. A fifty-dollar bill was sitting on the seat Perry had vacated. When he picked it up and slid it into his pocket, his guts twisted in a spasm and he felt a strong urge to go to the bathroom.

For a week after Archie Perry's visit, Thomas' palms sweat every time his phone rang or he checked his answering machine. If he never heard the scrape of his voice again, he'd be golden. It wasn't only that Perry knew who he was and the scam he was running, it was the eviscerating stares; Tom couldn't shake the feeling that Perry knew *everything* about him, right down to his blood type, just by looking at him. His body lived in a state of anxious flux, sending him to the bathroom like a fat man getting repeat helpings at an all-you-can-eat buffet. He slept, but he woke up throughout the night. He stopped remembering his dreams.

When a second week passed, Tom took stock. His encounter with Perry left him feeling exposed. He needed to find cover. Come up with contingencies. The 1-900 number was born out of his conviction that if Perry himself didn't return, the cops were going to come breaking down the office door any day. A phone number was portable. Not only could he disappear into the background and reap the profits, but he could advertise it anywhere, take this baby nation-wide. It was his insurance for when the in-person con got too hot. He hit the bookstore on Jack Street and picked up every geek magazine he could find that ran ads on their back pages. *Gorror, Reading Reaper, Star Chronicles* and their cousins. For an operator, he needed someone on the end of the phone line that would reassure and comfort. He called up his old friend Alexis.

"Hi Lexi."

"You owe me three hundred bucks, you prick."

"I've got a gig for that silver tongue that will pay triple what I owe you inside of four weeks."

For once, he was true to his word. Lexi worked the phone line as his assistant, Alice, and shepherded callers through their nightmares and spectral apparitions and lonely nights to the tune of fifty cents per minute. In time, he started giving the number to his own clients, too, in the spirit of making the most hay while the sun was shiniest.

The money rolled in with the predictability of waves hitting the beach. With every lucrative week that passed, the memory of Archie Perry and the scratchy, parchment-paper sound of his fingers sliding against each other, faded. Tom hadn't abandoned the idea of closing his in-person practice, but he set the decision adrift to linger distantly on the horizon. Six weeks after he first set eyes on Perry, Tom barely thought of him. Only when he noticed the purple bruising under his sunken eyes or tightened his belt another notch because he was shitting his food out at record speed, did thoughts of the icy-eyed bastard piss all over his parade.

Tom clicks his pen and scratches it across the notepad as Mandy Chang outlines how once or twice per week in the middle of the night, her closet door swings open to reveal a horned creature the size of a 10-year-old child, white face flattened and featureless, except a narrow pink slit where the mouth would be. Dr. Thomas Goodridge utters "yes", "go on", "hmm" as appropriate, moving the pen faster where she explains how her body goes rigid and the creature scrapes its hooved feet across the floor to her bed, then pulls itself up to sit on her chest. She strains against the paralysis as its pink mouth opens, opens, and opens, jaw unhinging, revealing an empty black maw, wide enough to take her whole face in its mouth. At this point her paralysis snaps. She screams and twists in the bed, bucking the creature onto the floor. It hisses and crab walks on all fours back to the closet.

Thomas notices her tone stays the same throughout her story. Her shoulders are relaxed, hands loose on the arms of the chair. He'd be shocked if her pulse went more than a beat above normal. She's lying through her teeth. Excellent. He congratulates her on her courage coming to him. "Yours isn't the first story of this kind I've heard. Night haunting is a very common affliction." The corners of her mouth turn down as he denies her the cachet of bringing him a report he hasn't heard before. Good, good. "These types of supernatural encounters are often a gateway to more dangerous events." Her frown lifts and she nods. That's right, cook up something really disturbing to tell me next time. Keep topping yourself, Ms. Chang; I've got all kinds of time for you.

He advises her that he's here to support her and additional sessions may help her feel more comfortable with this strange reality she's experiencing. Same time next week? As he stands to take the cash, she extents to him in a Ziploc bag, he glances down at the notepad he's holding against his chest and the dollar signs he doodled there throughout her session.

He shows Ms. Chang out and locks the exit door behind her. His cloth-covered desk chair squeals as he sinks into it and tilts back, stretching his arms over his head. He pivots the chair and looks out his second-story window to watch her stride to her plain beige two-door compact. Metallic foreskin, Vern calls that colour. As she pulls out of her parking spot, a black sedan pulls into an adjacent one. Thomas frowns and leans back to check his appointment book. Nothing for the rest of the day. He stands and watches the driver's door of the sedan open. It feels like his Adam's apple lodges over his windpipe when a praying mantis of a human unfurls his lanky limbs from the car and straightens his dark suit with long fingers. The man looks up at the second floor and Tom steps back so fast he trips over his chair, cracking his head on his desk on his way to the floor. Even lying on the musty, green shag carpet, out of sight of the window, he can feel frosty shards from Archie Perry's pale blue stare stabbing into his head before his eyes roll back and he blacks out.

"You've lost weight, Mr. Upshall. That wasn't my intention."

Light filters through Tom's eyelashes as he struggles to come back to the world. Being prone on the floor in Perry's company is about as relaxing as lying next to a pit viper. Imagining the insect man leaning over him causes a river of adrenaline to flood him. His eyes flick open, and he sits up fast enough to see a sparkle of stars as the blood reorganizes itself in his body and for the aching at the back of his head to become the steady pounding of a jackhammer. Flummoxed by the sudden stimuli, his body does the only thing it can: projectile vomit yellow bile all over itself from the thighs down.

Perry tsks but stays in the desk chair he commandeered when he entered the room, looking down at the soiled man on the floor.

Tom wipes his mouth with the back of his hand. "What are you doing here?"

"You're not an unintelligent man, Mr. Upshall, so I'll chalk that question up to your head wound."

Those God damn hands are at it again. Rubbing. Rubbing. Dead, dry leaves brushing against each other. The sound of it makes Tom's stomach roil, but a firm swallow keeps what bile is left in his stomach from visiting his mouth. He touches the back of his head and finds a sticky wet spot at the base of his skull. The blood is already coagulating. He wonders how long he's been unconscious with Perry staring down at him.

"I told you I wasn't interested," Tom says, groaning the last word as he delicately leverages himself up off the floor and leans against the windowsill to put the light of the early evening behind him, out of his throbbing eyes. He can feel rivulets of puke running down the front of his pants. His position puts the sick right at Perry's eye-level, no more than a couple of feet away. The man stays in the chair.

"I know," Perry sighs and stills. "And I told you it would be better if you came around to working with us on your own. I should've been clearer: you are coming to work for me. The only choice you have is whether you benefit from it financially, or simply work to live."

"I'm not a man you want to threaten," Tom says. The con world isn't a safe one. He prides himself on using his brains to get him out of trouble most of the time, but he's had to throw a punch and click open his switchblade a few times to keep stubborn bruisers away. This slick dick in his red bowtie makes his skin crawl more than the average leech, but he'll grind the gangly fucker into the floor if he has to.

"And I'm supposed to say, 'it's not a threat, it's a promise' and on and on we go until you try to take a swing at me and realize what a pointless act it is. Let's skip all that." Perry goes on to explain his collective is skilled at conjuring a range of unpleasant effects on uncooperative people.

Tom barks a laugh. "Are you telling me you're going to put a *curse* on me if I don't do what you want, you creepy loopy fuck?"

"No, Mr. Upshall. I'm telling you I already have." Perry makes a fist with his left hand.

Tom's guts are doused in napalm. He doubles-over, hands clutching his abdomen. Air rushes out his nose as he clenches his jaw to bear down on the agony. The pressure on his intestines builds. He recognizes the sensation as the one that had dogged him over the past weeks, driving him to the bathroom again and again, causing the pounds to peel off his body as it starved itself of calories and nutrients.

In an instant, the pain vanishes. Tom looks up. Perry's left hand is open and elevated like he's waiting for a high-five.

Panting ensures Tom can't speak, even if he could think of something to say. All his brain cells are careening into each other, trying to stuff this new information into one of the familiar slots of reality that makes up his view of the world. With a closed fist, a man had just caused his body to want to turn itself inside out. He keeps telling himself it's impossible. Coincidence. Hallucination. Coincidence. Hallucination. The two ideas kept circling, like a dog chasing its tail.

"No coincidences, Mr. Upshall. No hallucinations. Although, admittedly, you are sleep deprived enough for your mind to play a few tricks on you. I'm sorry; it wasn't my intention to turn you into an insomniac. As I told you, the collective has lost some members recently. Some of our best. I had to engage our second string to work with you. Poor Nadine. Her sleep control needs work. She makes up for it in blood craft..."

A spiraling feeling of being outside his own body takes over Tom's senses, overriding Perry's words with a whooshing thrum. The red bowtie swells in vibrancy; edges of the desk and chairs come into sharp relief. The sour scent of puke fills his nostrils. His head thumps, picking up pace, keeping time with his stampeding heart. One thought plays like a skipping record and he grasps his head to try and squeeze it out: no control, no control, no control. He has lost. Perry owns him. Not because he cracked the code on his con game; because he can command Tom's body. Starve it. Sleep deprive it. Kill it. The man may as well ram a hand up his ass and operate him like a puppet.

He starts sobbing.

"It's all right, Thomas. You can't see it now, but this is going to be good for you. You'll do some of your best work with us. Your abilities have been wasted on petty scams. Although, this one brought me to you, so…" Perry places a hand on Tom's shoulder and he jumps. "You've also attracted some talent with this game. You dismiss them, but several of your clients have a very strong connection to the occult. Ms. Chang has some real potential. And Danny Parker…"

Perry lists a third of his clients and paints a picture of the grand contributions they can make to the collective. He compliments Tom on the 1-900 number. "A stroke of genius. We can recruit from all over the country now." As the master plan is described to him in detail, Tom sucks air into his lungs until the buttons on his shirt strain against their threads, then forces it out in a long, harsh hiss. In and out. His heart rate comes down and the brightness and sounds around him dial back to normal.

A dry, parchment-papery sound starts up behind him.

"It was a disappointment when so many members got it

into their heads to shortcut their enlightenment. I blame Jonestown. There are always a few, not everyone has the fortitude for life in our collective, but plastering pictures of a thousand dead people in the Guyanese jungle all over the news is like shoving the weak in the back while they're at the cliffside."

Tom rubs the tears off his face with the heels of his hands and turns to the window.

"You'll keep an eye out for signs of that kind of thing in the client names you pass on to me, Thomas."

The sun sets behind the Salvation Army thrift shop on the opposite side of the parking lot, casting the front of the long, low building in shadow. Tom imagines that if he believed in God, he'd start praying to Him now to have mercy on his soul for what he must do. But he wasn't a praying kind of man. Take or be taken. That was his religion.

5

The Matthias Room was an addition to the house added by Matthias Cantwell in 1878, long after his grandfather Nathaniel had broken ground on the estate over sixty years earlier. Matthias simply referred to it as the ballroom and it was Nick and Maggie who added the names of their ancestors to the rooms along with short history lessons about their family on plaques outside each space: "Matthias, a lifelong bachelor, revelled in throwing lavish parties, and commissioned this ballroom to be built from repurposed lumber taken from one of the family's retired vessels." It was in these special touches that Maggie and Nick took the most pride. But none of it mattered at the moment. The plaques, like the rest of the inn, and its increasingly annoyed guests, were still submerged in darkness, waiting for the generator to kick in.

Nick Cantwell walked back onstage and into the only light in the place after the assembled audience applauded the story. He graciously waved both arms to have them settle into silence, an act that seemed especially silly since the acclaim wasn't for him.

Nick was the oldest of the three Cantwell siblings who had inherited the house after their father, Norman, died in 1995, and he was the one who had proven most resistant to opening the place up to the public.

Having moved to St. John's to attend university, he then made his mark on the business community there the same way severe acne makes it mark on a freshman—unwanted, greasy, and leaving a wake of scars—Nick seemed happy enough to coast on the family's dwindling fortune and just stop trying, which he felt was the best way to stave off future embarrassment.

But Maggie, tired of turning down requests for weddings and other parties at the homestead, had, along with their somewhat apathetic younger brother Neil, convinced him to secure backing from the few relationships he hadn't squandered to get the place up to code, which they had been working on as they geared up to open to the public over the Victoria Day weekend of 2020.

Needless to say, Nick hadn't been happy with how his foray into the hospitality industry had started, and he was counting on this weekend to provide some review fodder from a group of patrons with a knack for writing and an eager audience.

"Folks, unfortunately we're having some issues with the back-up generator." As he began to address the crowd, several employees began moving through the room handing out candles. "Rather than forcing our poor guests to read in the dark and project their voices without our audio equipment, we're going to have to postpone the rest of the readings until tomorrow."

Groans filled the room.

"But fear not! Or fear some, hopefully. We had planned to give tours of the estate and share with you its macabre history, and now seems as good a time as any."

Jacob, who had been called away during the last reading

arrived back to Monica and Malcolm with two candles.

"Is this serious?" Malcolm asked him.

"I guess so," Jacob said apologetically as he passed out the candles and produced a disposable lighter from his back pocket.

"I didn't realize this was going to be that kind of weekend," Monica said but with a hint of excitement. Malcolm and Jacob looked to each other, both surprised by Monica's reaction.

"Are you able to come along, Jacob?" Malcolm asked.

"Uh, I think so?" Jacob checked his watch. It had crept past 9 pm, which was when he was due off, but he was thinking about his plan to try to finish his story. After a moment of fleeting consideration, he convinced himself his laptop would be dead with no ability to charge, meaning it was much better to get in this facetime with two writers than to sit alone in the dark.

"Before we get started," Nick Cantwell's voice boomed back over the crowd, "we did have another of our visiting wordsmiths here who says the circumstances won't prevent them from entertaining you with another tale."

The author climbed onto the dark stage, flicked on a tablet screen which threw off an intense blue beam and cast a gigantic shadow on the back wall as they began to read...

WHO AWAKENS YOU?
C.H. Newell

Amanita muscaria, Jared says. He holds up the bag of plump red toadstools, shaking them like it's meant to convince the others taking them is a good idea.

Winona scoffs. I'm all for Newfie shrooms, but nobody's going eating them Lewis-Carroll-looking things. Been reading bullshit on the internet, haven't you?

Jared snorts and shoves the Ziploc bag back into his duffel. He sits back, looking out the window as the Great Northern Peninsula landscape moves by the window next to the RV's dinner table. He's about to point out a flock of gulls moving in a ripple across the sun, but when he turns, he notices Marcel sound asleep, crammed into the corner of the futon in the back. Marcel had already been on a journey before getting on the road. He was back home visiting his parents in Liverpool after the Spring term ended—they threw a reunion with the Caribbean side of his family in attendance after many years apart—and just flew into St. John's the day before the others packed up the RV.

Jared flops his head back. He contemplates taking out his Canon to snap a few shots then decides against it. He knows there'll be plenty of time later. Plus, despite being a hand Winona hired on as a labourer, as well as a photographer, Jared's lazy, and he doesn't want to take out his camera and lens—he'd rather start in on the shrooms or at least have a beer.

Jared says: How much longer?

Brenda doesn't take her eyes off the road. She turns the rear-view mirror slightly so her eyes beam right at Jared. You seriously playing Are We There Yet? You're like a teenager.

Everyone goes quiet. Brenda clenches her jaw. The steering wheel's leather squeaks and crunches under the grip of her tensed fingers. Jared doesn't make a peep. Winona's trying hard not to bite through her lip to keep herself from laughing for fear of setting off the wrath of Brenda. The road trip from St. John's has been a long one, and everyone is getting on somebody else's nerves after nearly 1,000 kilometres. Winona spent most of the drive preparing an itinerary for their time in L'Anse aux Meadows. She wants to make sure they spend their time wisely. And it *is* her project. She intends to make use of every last minute. It was focusing on work that kept Winona out of the escalating vehicle drama. Now she knows they'll need a break once they get out of the car before anybody wants to spend another second longer together. She plans to get everybody drinking and spend their first night letting loose. That way they can wake up the following morning, shake off a hangover, and then get to work. She did pencil in Jared's suggested shroom trip. She doesn't have an aversion to hallucinogens, and she thought it was a fun idea to help them get closer to nature while out among the land.

Everyone is on the trip for a specific reason, all intending to work hard, though Winona more than any of them. She wanted to do something for her PhD dissertation that actually made an impact in the real world, outside the big white walls of academia. She wanted to put her own Indigenous heritage into her studies. It only made sense, given that she was studying archaeology, that she comb through some of the lesser considered history here in Newfoundland.

When Winona was little, her Mi'kmaw grandmother used to tell stories about the Beothuk meeting Norsemen, Vikings who came and settled here, who met the first people inhabiting this land. She always thought it was fascinating. She imagined a meeting upon the shores, two cultures converging at the ends of the earth. Winona knew the best and most obvious place to begin hands-on research was to head for L'Anse aux Meadows. She's never been there herself. They'll stay at the RV park, and they brought tents with them to find their own little place somewhere in the woods to set up camp for a night or two. She also thought going during *Lithasblot*—the pagan harvest festival— would be an appropriate time to connect with the Norse history embedded in the island and its history.

The aptly named Viking RV Park had few spaces left when Brenda called, but she managed to secure a lot to park her grand-parents' RV. Brenda hated coming from old money. Her white bourgeois grandparents certainly were never progressive; they can barely talk about her being a lesbian without mentioning Jesus. Still, she's thankful at times like these that she can get access to their toys, like the RV. She isn't too proud to ask, ei-ther. Might as well make use of the privilege, she figures. She's known Winona for what feels like forever, and so it's all the bet-ter to be able to help her out with the trip. Brenda is a PhD stu-dent herself. Her concentrations are folklore and language, hav-ing studied several different cultures. She's spent time studying Norse poetry, too. It felt like destiny when she first listened to Winona talk about the stories of Vikings meeting the Beothuk. Afterwards she actually spent months on end scouring her own resources to see if there was even a passing mention by Norse poets alluding to it. The least Brenda thought she could offer to

Winona, apart from little bits and pieces of Norse folklore, is use of the RV. Although at this point in the trip she'd rather drive the RV into the Atlantic and never see it again. Or at least she'd love to pitch Jared into the ocean.

Seriously, though, how much longer? Jared says, right on cue.

If there wasn't a wide green sign stating there's only twenty kilometres left to L'Anse aux Meadows, and only twenty-eight more to the RV park coming up over the horizon, then Brenda would have turned to see if she could reach Jared to smack him in the head. Instead, she lets the sign come into their vision and Jared takes note, not bothering to say another word.

After Brenda checks into the park, she finally brings the RV to rest and the whole crew all but falls out of the doors so they can put their feet on solid, stationary ground. Over ten hours cooped up did the trip no favours. Not to mention Jared's annoying way of doing absolutely everything, and the fact that neither of them know Jared well other than the fact he's a fairly well-known photographer around the Avalon. He was most of the trouble along the way. Marcel slept the majority of the time, and even if he'd been awake, he's easy to get along with, someone both Winona and Brenda had known for a few years already since starting their PhD programs at Memorial University.

Jared says, I'm going to go for a little walk. Have a look around for some trails, that kind of thing. Might find us a spot to pitch the tents.

Winona gathers everyone together in a circle first. She makes sure to lay down the ground rules: 1) get as drunk as you want as long as you get up on time in the morning; 2) no drinking or

smoking weed while working; and 3) do not leave garbage anywhere except a trash can—pack it in, pack it out. Once the rules
are explained Jared heads off into the distance, walking towards
a patch of forest with a wide trail cut into it. After a minute or so
he's gone. Brenda lets out a sigh of relief.

Oh, come on, Marcel says. He ain't that bad.

Brenda chuckles. You slept eight out of the ten hours I
drove.

Truth, Marcel says. He laughs, shaking his head at himself.

Winona takes out a piece of paper with her itinerary written
on it, looking over her plans. Guys, I don't want to waste any
time, even though I know we're all beat. So maybe if Jared finds
a good spot while he's off on his walk we can just go out there
with the tents and setup. And then we can just relax, have some
drinks. Sound good?

Marcel and Brenda give Winona a thumbs up. They all start
to unpack their bags and equipment from the RV, including their
tents, sleeping bags, and a slew of gear Winona brought from
digging tools to an axe for firewood. Despite the official status
of the land at L'Anse aux Meadows, Winona wants to have a
look in the surrounding areas—she isn't planning to start a major dig, but she keeps holding onto hope that maybe, if she's
lucky, they could stumble onto something worth dredging up.
She's been studying the few resources available to her about the
possibility of Vikings making contact with the Beothuk, and a
few places between L'Anse aux Meadows and the RV park feel
like they're worth exploring. She's under no delusions that she'll
go out there and, in only a few days, uncover hard evidence of
this potential, history-altering meeting, yet Winona has always
held onto a sense of faith as part of her studies. She knows that,
sometimes, luck and cosmic coincidence are just as much a part

of discovery as elbow grease and research.

When everything is unpacked, they stand around waiting for Jared to return. Marcel sees an elderly couple unpacking their own RV nearby, so he goes to help them, flashing his stunning smile and greeting them with his thick British-Jamaican accent. Winona and Brenda share a cigarette, sitting on a couple of fold-up lawn chairs. They smoke silently as the midday warmth washes over them and the sky slowly starts to deepen from its warm blue hue in the waning afternoon.

Beautiful out here, Brenda says.

Winona nods, puffing away. Can see all the stars at night when you're away from the city. My favourite part of camping.

I always wished I knew more about the constellations. All I know is the stuff I've come across studying folklore. Which is not that much.

The Norse name for the Big Dipper is *Karlavagnen*. The chariot of man.

Look at you, studying up. Making me look bad.

The two women laugh, finishing their cigarette. Winona puts out the butt and makes sure it's totally snuffed before she takes it into the RV and puts it in the garbage. She brings a couple beers with her on the way back out, handing one over to Brenda. They crack the bottles open, cheers, and chug.

Brenda says, Think Jared got lost?

Who knows, says Winona. Won't be gone long. He's not the rigorous type.

And you decided to spend grant money on him.

Winona sighs. Only because he's a photographer *and* a labourer. Not like the labour is that intensive, either. Setting up two tents. I got like, one bag of gear he'll be carrying for me.

So, what you're saying is, like always, it's the women doing all the hard work.

Winona winks. Well, Marcel's pretty handy. He's helping those old folk.

I didn't say men were completely useless.

They laugh just as Marcel makes his way back over to their RV.

Marcel says, Riot, is it?

Winona pats him on the back and throws an arm around his shoulders. Glad you were able to make it back in time for this trip with us, Marcy.

The three of them chat a few minutes. Then they hear Jared yelling indistinctly, halfway between the RV and the treeline. They see him waving, beckoning them to come his way.

He's seriously not going to come carry any of this, Brenda says.

Winona says, Not totally useless. Utterly, hopelessly useless.

Marcel picks up as many bags as his arms will allow. Brenda and Winona take what's left between them. They walk towards the treeline where Jared waits at the mouth of the trail, its opening a gaping maw lined with wooden teeth poised to swallow them whole. Before they go into the forest, Winona pulls out an old leather bracelet her grandmother gave her years ago, something she's kept ever since as a good luck charm; it broke a while back so she carries it on her now everywhere she goes. She kisses the bracelet and puts it back in her pocket, then heads into the trail.

After the tents are up the fire gets roaring. Winona makes sure everyone has a drink of some sort in their hand, hoping it'll cut away all that excess tension from the long drive. They all get half drunk. Marcel starts to sing sea shanties, belting his baritone voice into the trees. They managed to find a nice spot away from the park, tucked into a small clearing where they can sing and laugh as loud as they want without bothering anybody. Winona only meant for them to party the one night, so it was a good place for them to get rowdy and blow off steam for their first night out.

Brenda's still wide awake later when everybody else passes out. She lights a cigarette and walks out of the clearing towards the thick forest. She passes through a shadowy canopy where the moonlight disappears. A moment later she comes back into the soft, dim light near a cliff's edge. She hears the Atlantic Ocean, the waves crashing together almost invisible in the night, the water black as a starless sky. The rush of salt water hits her in the face and she breathes it in gladly. When she gets to the edge she stands there smoking, the cherry of her cigarette a hot red star in the pitch black. She listens to the waves closely. Something else emerges from the noise in the distance. She can't tell right away what it is exactly. She stops smoking, holding her breath to try homing in on the noise beneath the ocean's rhythm.

A creaking, croaking crack bellows, echoing around the inlet below the cliff's edge where Brenda stands. The sound carries a while. Another crack. Brenda can tell it's the sound of wood, but she can't imagine where it could be coming from, or even from what. She knows driftwood can't make that much noise. Before Brenda conjures another thought in her head, she sees a cloudy fog form out of nowhere, spiralling up out of the water and spreading into a wall. An ashy mast and sail come out of the fog, as if part of the fog itself. The rest of the ship floats out onto the water, its haggard frame not quite touching the water but barely hovering above the rippling waves.

Brenda watches on stunned. She rubs her face and stares, sure that the cloud-like ship and fog is only a dream. She wonders if she drank too much. But the ship remains. It keeps moving through the inlet. She keeps listening, hearing the groans of the vessel's wood. Its body lurches on over the water, but the decrepit thing looks close to death; one good smack against the shoreline's rocks and it could collapse into sawdust. Nevertheless, it keeps going. Brenda listens for any sounds indicating there were people aboard. How silly, she thinks, People aboard a ghost ship. She knows it's a ghost ship—she didn't get *that* drunk during the night. She's sure that legends of ghost ships came along with ghostly sailors. So, she listens intently atop the cliff.

That's when Brenda hears it: voices, lifting and lulling on the wind. She moves further down the cliffside on a patch of grass, trying to get closer. She watches the ghostly ship come to a stop in the bay past the inlet. The ship stays floating above the water. No more booming cracks from the vessel's weary body. Now only the waves and the wind make noise. Brenda hears the voices grow louder. More now, too. Many voices speak at once, their tongue not immediately recognisable to Brenda. She listens as hard as she can, not breathing, not swallowing.

Munu warned, a ghostly voice says. *Gereigir disturb okkarr dauðr.*

The words echo up from the bay, into the trees. They surround Brenda. She hears nothing but the words. Now she can tell the language is Old Norse, she just can't tell what the voice is saying. She feels the words crawling over her skin, wriggling into her ears. She tosses her cigarette out towards the ocean, turning to rush back through the trail towards their campsite. When she's back she slips into the tent she's sharing with Winona and tries to slide into her sleeping bag without much noise. She can't shake those ancient voices nor the sounds and the sight of that ship. She closes her eyes, but sleep doesn't come easy.

Brenda finally falls into a dream just as Marcel opens his eyes, hearing a noise outside his and Jared's tent. Marcel figures it's only Brenda or Winona going to pee. He settles back into a comfy spot in his sleeping bag and closes his eyes. The noise gets closer to the tent, so Marcel opens a single eye. Fingers press up against the tent's fabric. They wiggle around, feeling for something, anything. Marcel opens both his eyes in fright. He calms himself quickly, looking defiant.

Ladies, it's too late for this, says Marcel. He keeps his voice low, trying not to wake Jared.

No reply. More fingers press into the tent; two hands at once this time. Marcel's eyes go back to a state of uneasiness. He stares at the fingers and they look too fine at the tip. They don't look like full fingers, not even for Brenda, whose hands are fairly small. Marcel feels a shudder rush from his groin up through his stomach. He's cold all of a sudden in spite of being swaddled in his sleeping bag.

Seriously, girls, Marcel says. He's more stern this time.

The fingers stop pressing against the side of the tent. No noise anymore, either. Marcel relaxes, though he can't stop staring at the walls of the tent. Just as he starts to feel the goosebumps all over his arms settle back into the skin, he watches the side of the tent press inward. Marcel doesn't see any fingers. He sees the outline of a grisly, uneven human skull sink into the tent's wall, the jagged teeth grinning at him. He shrieks and turns away, unable to look at the haunting image any longer. He pulls his sleeping bag up around his head, burrowing into a blanketed cocoon.

You're dreaming, Marcel says. He repeats this to himself. He keeps repeating it until the moon recedes and the sun rises. He doesn't sleep a wink. All he sees when he tries to close his eyes for any longer than a blink is that ugly, smiling skull trying to sink through the tent right into his arms.

Neither Brenda nor Marcel speaks about their experiences when everybody wakes the next morning. Neither are totally sure they actually heard and saw what they believe they did, anyway. So, they keep to themselves, and go about the day with the other two. The group spends their morning at the L'Anse aux Meadows site, and in the afternoon, they walk some trails, looking for lesser travelled areas in the vicinity. Jared planned to bust out the mushrooms that coming evening, so Winona made sure they used their first full day wisely.

By suppertime the gang are beat and ready for grub. Jared starts in on the Coleman RoadTrip Grill that Brenda's grandparents keep in the RV. Apart from photography, Jared always had a love for cooking, so he's assigned as grill master for the trip. He tosses several moose burgers and sausages over the fire, the fat immediately sizzling atop the heat. Brenda, Marcel, and Winona sit around the campfire they started, opening a few beers.

Everyone into mushrooms and onions on their burgers? Jared says. The other three pipe in to indicate that's fine, then they get back to their conversation. Nobody will notice if Jared slips their stash of powdered shrooms onto the burgers. Especially not if they're on there with Montreal steak spice, onions, ketchup, mustard.

While Brenda, Marcel, and Winona laugh and chat by the fire, Jared goes about his business over the grill. A little later they're all chewing into the burgers and dogs. Everyone tells Jared what a great job he did with the food, and he smiles, chewing away knowingly. The food's gone in a matter of minutes. All the walking and hiking today worked up appetites. After the food there's cigarettes, a joint, and more drinks. Jared keeps his eye on everyone, awaiting the first signs of the mushroom trip spreading across his friends' faces. It's nearly an hour before Winona starts to feel strange, her face contorting as she feels a deep rot in her stomach. The others notice. At first, Jared pretends he doesn't notice a thing.

Honestly, Winona says, it feels like I just developed an ulcer, right here, right now.

Brenda rubs Winona on the back. You want to go back up to the RV tonight?

No need for that, Jared says. I put something special on the burgers.

Winona says, The hell was it?

Jared shrugs, grinning. Something magic.

Winona's eyes go wide, filling with rage. You didn't.

Jared swigs away the last of his beer and goes to the cooler for another one. He doesn't say a thing, just gets his beer and sits back down. He knows he's in trouble, but the look on his face shows to the others he really doesn't care.

You ever heard of consent? Winona says. I pity any women you've come across, Jared. Absolute fucking menace.

Oh, relax.

Winona starts to lunge at Jared, then Brenda holds her back.

Marcel says, Right, mate. Time for you to take a hike—literally. Get the fuck out of here for a while.

You're serious? Jared says, standing with his hands out and his jaw hanging in disbelief.

Marcel grabs a flashlight from his bag near the tents. He hands it over to Jared, pointing a finger towards the woods. Then he goes to Winona, trying to help Brenda calm her down. Jared grabs his backpack and storms off towards the trees, slipping away through the trail on into the night. Marcel goes to the cooler and takes out several bottles of water, handing one each to Brenda and Winona. They all hydrate, knowing they're in for a rough ride the rest of the evening.

I cannot believe this, Winona says. She puts her head in her hands. She already feels the world spinning away beneath her feet.

Brenda rolls her eyes. Well, Winny, if I'm honest it doesn't really surprise me. The guy is a total shithead.

Marcel nods. Can't really pick up for the guy anymore. Certainly not now. Guess all we can do is wait until we start tripping?

Even though he's an idiot, Brenda says, I hope Jared will be safe out there.

Winona spits, trying not to throw up as she feels the shrooms' poison gnawing at her gut. Fuck him.

The woods are lonelier, darker, and deeper the further Jared gets away from where they set up their campsite. They were already a ways off from the RV park. Now Jared's out where he hears nothing at all coming from the RVs at the park, not even a dull roar. The ocean isn't yet loud, either. He's still inland, deep in the trees. The only sounds are his feet crunching sticks and rocks under his boots, the occasional noise of a small animal flitting across the forest floor or through tree branches.

A strange sound of metal against metal stops Jared in his tracks. He hears it behind him, then suddenly it's gone. He stands still to listen for it again, but there's nothing. He moves on through trail after trail, one branching off the other, until he's not quite sure where he is anymore. The mushrooms are taking hold. Jared watches his vision ripple. The air seems to throb. He tries to reach out and touch the throbbing air, and everything ripples again. A second after that and Jared's vision returns to normal, except all sound for him has dropped away. He can't even hear his own breathing.

Jared hears the strange metal sound again, only louder this time. Through the bush on the opposite edge of the trail comes a tall figure cloaked in a flowing robe, its face not visible beneath a shadowy hood. It carries with it a rusty sword and shield. The figure steps towards Jared, who can only laugh.

These shrooms are good, Jared says. He reaches out to touch the figure, sure it's only one of the night's first hallucinations.

The tall, cloaked figure extends a bony claw from an arm of its robe. It clasps the bones around Jared's hand. Jared is struck still. He can't move. Somehow, he isn't scared. He feels like he's on the precipice of a great discovery, of experiencing the depths of the unknown. Suddenly, he hears the figure's voice in his own head. He doesn't recognise the language, not like Brenda. Yet he understands the words. He feels their meaning within himself. And he knows inherently what the figure asks of him.

The dark figure dissipates into fog. Jared immediately walks through a break in the trees, not a trail, just an opening through a patch of branches and shrubs. He scans with his flashlight along the ground as he goes, eyes wandering every which way in search of what the figure told him to find.

Who awakens you? Jared says. Who. Awakens. You.

Jared mumbles the words to himself and strolls through the trees, tangled in branches but never tripping, like he's dancing over the roots and rocks. A break in the trees lets a stream of moonlight trickle down onto the forest floor. There it is, the plant Jared seeks, illuminated like the woods and the moon came together to make a path just for him. Jared kneels down and picks one of the fat yellowish flowers, along with some of the stem and its leaves. He holds it up and looks over the henbane. The figure's voice returns, quietly telling Jared what to do.

Jared pulls out his bag of amanita muscaria and drops the henbane into it, mixing everything together. Then he chews and chews, swallowing the mixture dry. He smiles and wonders how long it'll be until the change comes. His eyes are wild in anticipation, his belly rumbling with untold hunger.

Hamask, Jared says. He doesn't understand the tongue in his own mouth. He only knows he is becoming something else.

Very little light makes its way to where Brenda finds herself. She can't remember how to get back to their campsite. She certainly can't remember how to make it back to the RV, either. Not out this far. She regrets running off from Winona and Marcel. But the mushrooms had taken hold and she freaked out, darting off into the forest before either of her friends could move an inch. She's never done mushrooms before, and she'd wanted to do them with her friends on this trip—on her terms. Goddamn, Jared, Brenda thinks. She wishes Winona didn't hire him. Maybe then she wouldn't be out in the wilderness, lost by herself. She realises it's not that far from the tents; it can't be, really. That doesn't help her now that the darkness is growing blacker, she has no flashlight, and the mushrooms have turned up all the sounds of the forest, a desolate symphony just for her.

Brenda saw no hallucinatory visions from the mushrooms, until now. At first, it's only the smell. Brenda's nose fills with the reek of decay. Her eyes catch the sight of treetops shaking in the distance. A patch of trees open, and through it steps a massive, bloated corpse—it appears ancient, yet full of life, dead but still vibrant. The corpse is black and blue all over with flecks of crimson spattered in patches. Its beard and hair, its finger and toenails, all overflowing as if the undead thing's body is hung with drapes. It moves towards Brenda, pointing directly at her. A screeching boom erupts from the corpse's mouth, the jaw hanging lower than ought to be normal. Brenda covers her ears. There's no language to the corpse's scream, only a wave of cacophony and a deathly stench of decomposing flesh and moist dirt.

Brenda turns away and runs blindly through the trees. She's smacked in the face with branches, her cheeks and neck clawed into thin red streaks. She doesn't stop, no matter how badly the forest tears her apart. Before she can think of anything else but running, she slams into Marcel as he runs right into her. The two of them tumble into a tangle of limbs, rolling over one another and eventually coming to rest against the stump of a fallen tree.

Jesus Christ, Winona says.

Brenda and Marcel are both winded. Neither of them can stand up; they try, but their legs are weak and wobbly from the collision. Winona tries to pull them both to their feet, though she's unable to help either of the two stand up just yet. Marcel rubs his head and neck while Brenda babbles.

Winona says, What is it? You okay, hon?

Draugr, says Brenda.

What'd you say?

A draugr. I saw one.

Winona isn't sure if Brenda's tripping out, or if she is, too. She knows they both probably are, but she also knows the look on her friend's face is more than a slight scare from a bad mushroom hallucination.

I swear, Brenda says. Couldn't be anything else. It was... black, blue... rotting. My god, the smell. And it was, walking, but it was dead. Had to be.

Winona says: We're all having a weird night. I get it.

I'm telling you, I saw it.

Brenda barely gets the words free of her lips without her jaw trembling. She grabs Winona by the arm, squeezing tight to the bone. There's no time left to talk once the draugr's bloated corpse comes shambling into the clearing where Brenda, Marcel, and Winona stand in a daze. The trio immediately snap out of it and run, hand in hand. They keep hold of one another as they pass through a maze of trees, the massive dead thing not far behind them with its hot, fetid breath so strong it turns the forest into a swamp. The stink crowds Marcel's lungs. He slows down his run, chest heaving, breath catching. He coughs and wheezes. He pulls his hand from the link with Brenda to grab his chest, stopping in the thick of the woods. In that one minuscule instant, that fraction of a second, Marcel separates far enough from his friends for the lumbering draugr to snatch him by the legs and haul him into a dark corner of the trees. After running a few feet Brenda stops Winona and they look for Marcel, calling out to him. All they hear is the crunching and munching of the draugr somewhere out there among the long shadows of the night.

We have to go, Winona says. She whispers, hoping the undead thing doesn't hear them; its disgusting sounds aren't far off. And she doesn't want to go, but she knows they have to, so she pulls Brenda off into another trail.

Back at their campsite, Winona and Brenda frantically grab a few things. Brenda chugs a bottle of water, trying to clear her brain from the mushroom haze. Winona does the same by stuffing her mouth full of marshmallows and graham crackers, chewing fast while grabbing her backpack. She looks around near the tents outside and finds the axe she brought for splitting firewood.

Let's go back to the RV, Winona says.

When Winona and Brenda start to leave the campsite, they look back to see the trees shaking. The draugr erupts onto their site and squashes the tents into the dirt beneath its swollen feet. It smacks Brenda with one of its fat, blackened arms—its skeletal fingers beating against her ribs, cracking one or two—and she goes flying into a tree several feet away from where the tents previously stood. Brenda lies on the ground where she falls, gasping for a full breath of air.

þú munu fill minn belly. The draugr's words come in a tunnel of rank air like a warm breeze carrying the horrifying scent of a corpse fire. It roars from an undead, decaying throat, pointing a bony finger dripping with dark green flesh.

Winona doesn't move, standing right in line with the corpse's finger. She holds up the axe as if to dare the draugr. Come hither, speaks the axe in its newly sharpened glory; Winona bought it specifically for the trip. It had only ever split a few pieces of wood hours prior. Now it's going to split into aged, brittle bone and soggy, rancid flesh. The draugr waits no longer and darts towards Winona, though its bloated body only moves so fast. Winona swings the axe up over her head from behind her, bringing it down in a crescent. The axe blade collides with the draugr's mossy skull as its turgid body barrels at her. It sinks into the draugr's head, splitting through wiry bone into the brain meat that pops out like old grey beef, spilling down the sides of the corpse's face. The draug falls over on its side, then all the way to the ground. It lets out a groan before going totally limp.

Cut its head off, Brenda says. She's getting up from where she fell, holding her snapped ribs with an arm against her body. You have to cut off its head, or else it could come back.

Winona wastes no time and swings her axe again, coming down onto the draugr's neck. She swings again, and again, and again. Finally, the draugr's head separates from the shoulders and rolls onto its side, the skeleton mouth half open in an eternal howl.

Anything else? Winona says. She wipes a slick of blood from her brow.

Burn it. We have to burn it and toss the ashes in the sea.

Death's a lot of goddamn work.

Winona still feels the ash on her hands, regardless of washing them. She's not sure if she'll ever get it off. All thought of the corpse's ashes leaves when she and Brenda find a monstrosity back at the Viking RV Park. A big fire burns in one of the lot's pits. It's the only light around; none of the RVs are running, and none of their lights are on at all. Not only that, the RVs are also smeared with streaks of blood. Next to the fire, Winona and Brenda catch a glimpse of glistening skin and blood and bone. Winona recognises a face in its mess: one of the old people Marcel helped unpack when they first arrived. She sees it's the old man. But he's no longer simply a man. Someone, or some thing, has gruesomely transfigured his corpse: the body lies prone on the ground and a large piece of his back is gone, revealing spine and ribs, through which his lungs have been pulled and now lie spread across his back on either side like eagle's wings.

Are you seeing what I'm seeing? Brenda says.

Winona silently nods. She wishes it were the mushrooms rather than the bleak picture of violent death before them.

Shrieking pierces the air, drawing the women's attention away from the bloody old man. Brenda looks around everywhere, eyes filled with madness. Winona grips tight to her axe. The shrieking continues, getting closer, closer. What comes through the fire's flames is beyond Winona and Brenda's comprehension initially. They watch a man draped in fur—a recently killed wolf, judging by the fresh blood, with its eyes and teeth intact—and dripping in blood pass over the fire pit, carrying with him a wooden spear whittled from a tree. His eyes are those of a rabid animal. His movements are odd, his entire body jerking and swaying with each motion. He breaks into a stride, running at Winona and Brenda with a terrifying energy. He screams, going berserk.

When the man comes closer his face is visible under the wolf hood rimmed with drying blood. Winona sees Jared clearly with his skin the pale shade of death, pupils dilated so wide there's no white left to his eyes, only abyssal holes sunken into his face. He charges, not slowing in the slightest. His eyes are fire and his yowling crackles on the air like electricity. Brenda feels the skin raise up all over her arms. She's shocked, frozen to the ground. Winona stands firmly wielding her axe, telling herself she has to use it, no matter if it's Jared coming at them. Because Jared is no longer Jared. Winona sees that already from where she's standing, and the closer he gets to her the more she can see his new ghastly form.

þú eru minn! Jared screams as he sprints, coming closer to the women with the spear raised above his head.

Winona swings her axe to clip Jared as he reaches them. But Jared dips to the side and the blade swings wide, sending Winona spilling into the dirt. He blows past in his berserk rage, again raising his spear. He stops a few feet from Brenda then releases the spear, taking her off her feet. The weapon splits through Brenda's midsection and the furious force propels her backwards, as the spear's tip digs into the ground and comes to an abrupt stop. Brenda's body wobbles on the spear, jutting from the soil like a macabre flag at half mast. Jared howls into the moon, his black eyes shining with primal pride.

All Winona can do is run for the treeline. She runs until her veins boil and her lungs feel dry, stretched tight across the inside of her chest. She hears Jared's grunting, frothing breath behind her. He sounds to her like a wild beast, some appalling creature that stepped out of the pages of a fantastical book. She pushes him out of her mind. She rushes as fast as possible through the woods without getting tangled up in her own feet. But the mushrooms haven't finished their tricks. And the forest becomes less familiar as Winona passes tree after tree, rock after rock, all of it blending into one dark, wild puzzle.

Quickly Winona descends into a state of utter panic. She doesn't recognise anything anymore. The second wave of the mushroom trip has washed over her, and she feels like she's just woken up into a strange new world. Jared's animalistic screeching still rises up over the trees, carrying on the wind to Winona who's not that far ahead. She runs a little more but the disorientation is soon too much. She sees only trees, a sea of dark green, no break in them for her to escape the grim forest. She thinks of her grandmother's strength as the darkness closes in around her. She refuses to stop, to let Jared—or whatever it is he's become—catch up and do who knows what to her. Winona runs through another thicket of trees and alder branches; she doesn't care where she's going, she only cares that she's moving.

And eventually Winona sees more of the moon's light through the woods ahead. She smells the salt water—it makes her think of her grandmother, that tiny little mahogany woman who loved nothing more than to jig cod. She runs faster and falls through the treeline out onto a cliff above the nearby bay. She scrambles to look for somewhere to hide, but she's at the very edge of the cliff. The only noticeable way out is either down the side into the ocean or back through the way she came.

No, no, Winona says.

From the woods comes Jared's chilling scream. Trees snap as he comes stalking through the forest. He breaks whatever is in front of him, raging his way towards Winona as he seems to follow her scent. He steps past the trees and sees Winona standing at the cliff's edge. His black eyes catch the glint of the moon, and for a brief moment he looks like he's smiling. His snarled, bloody mouth says different.

Please, Winona says, I don't know what's happened to you. But—

Who awakens you? Jared's voice still speaks the words in English, but it sounds like the voice of an ancient entity, something older than the dirt, the rocks, the ocean.

I don't know what that means, Jared.

Who. Awakens. You.

The thing that is now Jared lurches towards Winona at a frenzied pace. He no longer has the spear he left impaled through Brenda, only bare, bloodied hands stretched out in front of him like wretched claws. He's about to nab Winona when she drops to the ground, rolling to the side. Jared—that thing—topples over the side of the cliff and falls stone-like towards the choppy Atlantic water. He screams until the rocks and water devour him. Winona hangs from the cliff with roots, clumps of earth, and errant tree branches clenched in her fist. She lets her own scream out, using every last bit of strength left in her worn, tired body to pull herself up onto the cliff's edge again. She barely makes it up into the grass before collapsing in a heap of sweat and sobs.

Winona lies still, crying and breathing hard. She stretches her hands out into the grass, feeling every last blade between her fingers. She pushes her face down into the grass and smells the earth underneath.

Thank you, Winona says. She kisses the earth gently.

Winona gets up and walks back through the forest, just as the first sliver of dawn breaks through the dark blue sky. She walks until she reaches their campsite. She cries and covers up Brenda's corpse with a sleeping bag from one of the wrecked tents. After that she heads back in the direction of the RV park. Winona tries to ignore the old man and his crimson eagle wings, though the general stink of death on the air makes it impossible to ignore. She goes to Brenda's RV, washing blood and dirt from her face. Then she goes to get the spare keys from where Brenda stashed them before they left St. John's. Winona sits in the driver's seat, looking through the windshield at the corporeal chaos left behind in Jared's wake. She tries to remember the faces of her friends. All she recalls now is blood.

With tears in my eyes and an ancient song from my heart, I pray, Winona says.

She takes out her grandmother's bracelet, kissing the leather softly. She puts it away and starts up the RV, pulling out of the park. Winona doesn't care right now about whether Vikings made contact with the Beothuk, she only wishes they'd never come to this land in the first place. And she'll be ready for them next time they decide to return.

6

Jacob couldn't track Maggie down but did find Tracy Cantwell-Jackson while he was looking.

Tracy was Maggie's sister-in-law, having been married to her younger sister Niamh and them both taking on the same hyphenate. But Niamh had lost her battle to cancer during the first round of COVID lockdowns and Tracy, who found herself on the other side of the country from her native White Rock, B.C., decided that staying in Newfoundland with the support system of Niamh's family proved more appealing than trying to restart things somewhere else. Not that Nick and Maggie were particularly supportive, but at least they had the estate that gave Tracy something to work on and distract herself from the loss.

Jacob had been using his phone as a flashlight, making his way back to the lobby when he met Tracy doing the same.

"Aren't you supposed to be off?" she asked him, checking the time on her screen.

"Yeah, I was actually looking for Maggie to confirm that she doesn't need me anymore."

"I'd go on if I were you, with the blackout she might try to get you to stand in the corner with your flashlight on."

"Well, I want to stay, that's sort of the problem," he told her. "Nick is doing the tour now and a couple of the authors asked me if I wanted to go along with them."

"That sounds great! You should go for it." Tracy was aware of his ambitions and hopes for the weekend as much as anyone, only she was more supportive than her in-laws. "I'll cover you with Maggie if she comes looking."

"Really? Thanks, Tracy!" Jacob called over his shoulder as he turned and rushed back to the Matthias Room to meet with Malcolm and Monica.

She smiled as she watched him disappear in the darkness, but the smile contorted as she noticed a glow coming from around a corner at the far side of the lobby. Her brow furrowed in puzzlement.

She lowered her phone and followed the light, hearing the clacking of fingers on a keyboard crescendo as she approached.

"Hello?"

She spoke the words before she rounded the corner and the clacking silenced at once.

"Yes?" The voice that answered had a low rasp and the "s" slithered out.

Tracy came around the pillar and saw a face underlit by a laptop screen staring back at her. The direction of the light distorted the shadows into ghastly shapes, the twenty-first century version of a flashlight under the chin.

"Sorry, just with the blackout I wasn't expecting anyone down here."

"Luckily I was fully charged," the mysterious writer presented their laptop to Tracy, "and this seemed like a nice, quiet place to get some work done."

"Right! Well, please don't let me stop you."

"Actually, would you mind?" They waved a hand to the

empty chair across from them.

"Mind what?"

"I think I'm just about done. I'd love to hear some feedback."

"Oh, I don't think I'm the right person for that," Tracy replied in a mix of honesty and discomfort at the thought of sitting through a stranger's work-in-progress. "There are lots of people around who'd be a much better audience."

"Please!" they scoffed in retort. "Who should I ask? The literary blowhards or the pulp-pumping panderers?"

Tracy was dismayed by the contempt towards the other guests, and instantly asked herself why someone would choose to attend the event if they felt that way about the people here. But the aggression also scared her and made her instantly aware of being alone in the dark with this person, and a quick tally of the pros and cons of the situation in her head convinced her that accommodating the request might be the best way to deal with the situation.

"Fair enough," Tracy pseudo-conceded as she sat in the chair. "Let's hear what you've been working on..."

THE DEVIL IN I
Paul Carberry

The engine growls, emitting a low rumble I can feel through the cold metal against my thighs. With my arms pinned against my breasts, I lean into my restraints, and the chain links rattle off the bare floor. The straps tug the straight jacket into a tight embrace. No doubt a side effect of the tranquilizers, a trickle of drool runs down my chin. I'm helpless to wipe it away. It pools into a wet puddle between my neck and the collar of my vest. But the worst part of having your arms pinned against you is the itch. Under my knees and the back of neck is crawling. I can't wait to scratch myself. From the front of the cab, I listen to the windshield wipers racing across the window, the motor groaning to keep up with the torrential downpour.

Every turn causes the chains to yank tightly, tugging me in every direction. Defenceless in this straight jacket, I'm at the mercy of the reckless driver's will. Up front, they're listening to the radio. The smell of coffee wafts back to me, making my nostrils flare and my stomach growl. I haven't had a decent meal in days. After days of eating prison food, I have a wicked case of heartburn. And prison coffee has the consistency of sludge with the bitter aftertaste of diesel fuel.

An impenetrable fog settles over the city of St. John's. Another frigid November night where the weather is threatening to turn nasty. For the last twenty minutes, the police wagon winds its course through downtown St. John's. The vehicle shudders as the tires sink into potholes filled with rainwater, spraying slush over the pavement in giant waves. Outside, the wind wails, buckling the aluminum panels of the wagon in and out. It's as if the vehicle is a living creature, the iron bars and chains resembling the monster's ribcage. Red taillights flood the back of the wagon, casting everything in a malevolent shadow. Gleams of silver light catch on the cold, hard steel.

My brain is groggy from all the prescriptions they force feed me, my vision blurred, as are my memories of Lucas Green. And I have a splitting headache that won't go away. I've been in and out of consciousness over the last few days as I adjust to the medication. Oblivion is my only reprieve from the pain and torment. Haunted by disturbing visions of that harrowing night, I've suffered through restless sleeps ever since that tragic turn of events.

It had started out as fun date; it was our third. Lucas was handsome. Spiked, dirty blonde hair, chiseled jaw line, piercing blue eyes. And most importantly, that body. Infatuated, it was no wonder things progressed between us so instantly. Then things escalated, spiraling out of control as I observed from outside my body. Helpless to prevent the actions I had allowed to set in motion, Deborah appeared. Before I could react, Deborah took control, filled with rage, taking things too far.

I'm remorseful, even though I'm innocent of the crime that landed me in Her Majesty's Penitentiary; and he deserved almost every dreadful thing that happened to him. I can live with everything she did that night, except for his death. Somehow, my twin sister gets away with everything. No matter who I tell, no one believes Deborah killed Lucas. When they found me, his blood was all over me. But it was Deborah, I swear.

"No means no, right, Samantha?" Deborah says, her tone a harsh rasp. Since we were children, it was like she could read my mind.

Filled with rage and jealousy, I refuse to make eye contact with those reptilian green eyes. "You could confess," I hiss, speaking to her shadow.

"Why?" she snaps back. "It would only complicate things if I did. And you need to stop feeling bad about it. He didn't display any remorse for what he did to you."

"Just a misunderstanding," I lie. "Really."

"You're pathetic and weak," Deborah groans.

"I don't need you messing up my life," I spit back. "You spoil everything. Take things way too far. Every time."

"You need me."

"Not as much as you need me," I counter, sick of her attitude. "You'd only be a shadow without me. Without me, you'd be nobody."

"Without me you'd be just like our mother," Deborah snarls. "Knocked up and left alone to go mad. Now shut your fucking mouth."

"Don't hate me because mom never loved you." I spit out the words as if they were venom in my mouth. "You always reminded her of dad," I add.

"You and mom, two peas in a fucking pod," Deborah groans. "Golden hair, rosy cheeks, and intense blue eyes. Literally a princess from a fairy tale. And look at you now. You're like a skeleton with skin stretched over it. I guess Rapunzel isn't so beautiful without her beauty rest after all."

"Go to hell, Deb," I snap. I can't help but notice how her darkened features compliment her creamy complexion and exotic emerald eyes. No one would ever guess we were twins. Especially not now.

"Later," Deborah says, her tone resolute. Without another word, I hear her stand up.

Squealing brakes compound my headache as the paddy wagon lurches to a halt. Hinges groan as the orderlies toss open the doors. "I'll see you soon, little sister," Deborah whispers in my ear, her breath warm on my collar. Then her hideous laughter fades away. I can hear her climb over the console and plunk down in the passenger seat.

Heavy foot falls approach the doors, splashing water and crunching gravel. When they open the door, a blast of wintry wind assaults me, peppering me with droplets of icy rain drops with pellets of hail mixed in. Driven by the gusts of wind, the ice shards tear and rip at my skin. Forced to squint, the wagon dips as the orderlies climb up into the back. The springs of the ambulance groan in protest.

"It's time to go, Miss Beaton," a deep voice announces, void of emotion. "Don't give me any trouble; it's been a long night and I don't have any patience left." He thumbs the night stick dangling from his belt, strumming his knuckles off the vicious weapon.

I say nothing as they go about their business. With practiced ease, they unlock my chains in fluid progression. The orderly drapes a second jacket over my wrists, covering up my handcuffed wrists; a modest token of humanity I'm not accustomed to. They lead me outside, my feet dragging behind me.

Harsh autumn winds propel the rain against the orangish-brown brick of the Waterford Hospital, pattering against the barred windows with a relentless, methodical rhythm. The grumble of an approaching engine roars, rising above the raucous clamor of the storm. Beside me, the orderlies grunt and groan, complaining about their responsibilities. It makes me sick to my stomach to hear them. At least they aren't accused of a murder they didn't commit.

Standing in front of his squad car, Detective O'Reilly watches me from beneath the brim of his tilted fedora. To protect himself from the seething storm, he holds it against his forehead, pressed between his thumb and forefinger. Tucked between his armpit, a manilla fold stands out in stark contrast to his black rain slicker. With the rain lashing at my backside and the wind whipping the jacket from my hands, I'm exposed. I watch the detective pat his pocket, slide his hand inside, and produce a pack of cigarettes. He cups his hand over the coffin nail and flicks his lighter, igniting a brilliant red spark. I meet his glare with an idle stare. The orderlies drag me towards the stone steps leading to the front door.

A clap of thunder resounds in the distance and a flash of lightening illuminates the sky. In that instance, with the orderlies distracted by the luminous glow, I twist my head towards O'Reilly. The blustering wind sweeps my golden hair to the side, and I flash a thin white line of teeth. Behind the detective, highlighted by the incandescent light, a pair of green eyes glare at him from the bushes. Those horrible reptilian eyes go unnoticed by everyone except me. Her ebony hair stands out as a stark juxtaposition to her pale complexion.

I can see her snickering as she haunts the detective from the shadows.

Buried in the back of the Waterford, they keep the overflow section out of sight from the public eye. Desperately in need of modernization, these corridors echo an inhumanity from the past. Weathered, red-bricked walls border the cells, only broken by the rows of black iron bars. The slippers they gave me are worthless; heat leaks from my body. The floor is damp with condensation from the water trickling down the walls as the rain hammers the bricks outside. All along the seams and cracks, black mold ravages this ancient section of the institution. More insane asylum than medical facility, this is a depressing reflection of the Newfoundland government's views on mental health.

Thunder rumbles in the distance and the resounding noise echoes in the hollow space. I'm the only resident in this hellish section of the Waterford. The air is stale and it reeks of black mold and despair. There is no hope to be found within these walls.

"This is abominable," Deborah says, shattering the silence. She's just outside my cell, resting her forearms on the wrought iron bars. "I wouldn't allow my dog to stay in there. This place needs to be condemned."

Water drips excessively from the leaky window, falling to the cement below. A tributary forms, following a worn path towards the center of my cell towards a metal culvert. An appalling, rancid stench of raw sewage rises from the pipe. Thick strands of matted hair, covered in a moldy residue, have built up in the drainage, leading down into an abyss. Water bubbles up from the pipe as the flood waters gush into the sewers. I can't stand the smell. My stomach twists, knotting itself, forcing bile into the back of my throat.

A weighty silence remains between us. I refuse to acknowledge her. Every time I look at her, I want to scream. But I'm too fatigued from the pills the nurse gave me. My sister told me I could trust her, so I let her give me the shot without putting up a fuss. I didn't expect to get any sleep until this was all over. That was our plan, anyway.

"You know the detective is in Doctor Yarn's office now." Deborah breaks the silence. "I just wanted to let you know he'll be coming to speak with you soon." Not waiting for me to respond, she continues: "They're scouring our records, drudging up the past. They won't believe your story; the records are wrong. Just stick with my plan, and you'll be free."

I perk my head up. Strands of blonde hair tumble over my face, creating a shroud. Deborah leans into the cell, her jet-black hair blending into the iron bars. Long shadows cast her in darkness, splitting her into two separate halves. I can see tears welling in the corner of her emerald eyes. A single tear tracks over her prominent cheek bone. Her delicate features obscure the suffering within.

"What do you need me to do," I sigh.

"Stay in this cell tonight," Deborah answers, her tone demanding. "And you need to get another shot, just like we talked about."

"How do I do that?"

"Convince them you're crazy," Deborah cackles. "Shouldn't be too hard."

"But I'm not crazy." I hesitate. "You're real. They think I killed Lucas. I watched you do it. His blood is on your hands. This is your fault."

"But can you prove it?"

"Why are you being such a bitch," I cry, another side effect of my new prescriptions.

"Haven't I always kept you safe?" Deborah snaps. "Don't you trust me?"

I chortle. "You didn't need to keep me safe. If it wasn't for you, things wouldn't have gotten out of control."

"He was out of control," she spits, her voice a harsh croak. "I did what I had to do to keep you safe. Don't forget that, ever."

"How can I forget what you did," I murmur. My eyes burn and tears track down my cheek. Deep, hitching sobs catch in my chest. "What you always do." I bury my face into my hands, working my fingers through my matted hair, wondering when the next time I'd get a shower.

"Quit your belly aching. It makes me sick to my stomach hearing you cry like a baby. Listen, the doctor will be here soon. Despite his flaws, he means well. And Nurse Sally will keep you safe. You can trust her with your life. I'm going to go find out what the detective has in store for us." Deborah pauses. "That son of a bitch is up to something. Once you get your shot, you'll sleep. Everything is going to be okay."

When I glance up, Deborah's gone. I lay down on the cold, hard bench and continue to sob. With my back rounded to the iron bars, I tuck my knees into my chest and hug them close. Footsteps echo down the empty hallway. A man and woman are chatting, their words muffled by the storm. I can sense the rats scurrying through the walls. The grind of their claws over the cement is nauseating. Their squeaks and cries are worse. Dampness creeps into my bones, seeping in through the window. I get up and move into the corner of the cell. With my back pressed against the wall, I slide down onto my ass and tuck my knees into my chest. The floor saps the warmth from my body.

A clap of thunder rumbles overhead, sending tremors through the earth, rattling the foundation of the Waterford. Three seconds later I see a spark of white light catch in the cold black iron. The storm is alarmingly close now. I can feel the static electricity in the air; the hairs on my arm stand on edge. Deprived of sleep, food, and groggy from the drug cocktail, I fight off exhaustion. Another clap of thunder explodes like artillery fire, followed by a flash of lightening. Scared, I draw in quick breaths. I'm on the verge of hyperventilating. Each breath I take is a gargled hiss, the drugs numbing my tongue, unable to stop the saliva pouring down my throat.

I can hear footsteps approaching my cell. The faint echo of a man and woman's conversation accompanying the hollow echoes.

"No, I'll be making my own observations, Sally." Doctor Yarn says. "What I'd like for you to do is send one orderly in with a pitcher of water and some extra blankets."

I size him up through the veil of my hair that has fallen over my face. He still hasn't acknowledged that he's balding. Yarn combs his frail white hair over. Glimmers of light reflect off his scalp and the black rims of his glasses that are perched at the tip of his too-big nose. His thin lips are pressed into a weak smile. "And bring me a record of the prescriptions the penitentiary has been feeding her. She looks haggard and stoned."

Sally nods her head, holding a clipboard over her chest to cover up her cleavage; a move I've used occasionally when a boy's gaze lingers too long. Even in my semi-state of consciousness, it's easy to follow his gaze. Sally's uniform is bleach white, reminiscent of the traditional candy striper uniform—more driven to incite male fantasy than for the comfort. His eyes follow as she struts away. Her high-heeled shoes clack off the cement, the strident noise amplified in the hollow corridor.

Once Sally leaves, his gaze shifts to me. A somber expression crosses his face as he looks in on me with what I can only assume is empathy. He digs through his pocket, coming up empty handed. Then he touches his belt; the key fob jingles. It's almost embarrassing to watch him fumble with the keys. After what seems like an eternity, the latch to my cell opens with a solid thud. The hinges screech as the gate swings inward towards me, the shrill sound piercing my eardrum.

"You're here to ask me questions?" My voice comes out fragile, matching my emaciated appearance. "To evaluate me."

Yarn takes a step towards me; pieces of crumbled brick crunch beneath his feet. "I'm here to help you," he says, tapping his pen against the clipboard. "Nothing more. Whatever it takes to make sure you get better."

I suppress a fit of laughter rising in my stomach. How many times has he used that line? And how many times did anyone leave this hell hole cured? The government did not equip this facility to handle the health and well-being of the mentally ill. This disgrace of a mental institution conjures up images of antiquated sanitoriums, a monument to the misguided past.

"You can't help me..." My voice trails off. Why couldn't Deborah be here for this?

"I will do everything in my powers to make sure you get the help you need," he answers, sounding sincere. His eyes examine me. What could he be staring at? I look awful in this grey jump suit.

"I'm not the one who needs help. You're looking for my sister Deborah. But you can't help her either." I fix my gaze on Doctor Yarn. "Besides, she's not with us right now. I want her to come back."

"Well," Yarn paused, "shall we start by talking about her? Would that be okay?"

When I open my jaw, a low, groaning croak escapes my larynx. My tongue lolls around inside my mouth, as if something is pushing it aside to make room. "Why? You're just like the rest of them." My voice takes on a shrill rasp, making me sound like my sister.

"He won't believe you." Deborah's voice rises from behind me.

Yarn's eyes dart up, scanning the room, a perplexed expression on his face. "I won't judge," his voice cracks. He pauses, taking a moment to steady his voice before he continues. "I'm only here to listen…" another lengthy pause, "…to you."

"They all judge you, Samantha," Deborah spits.

I turn my head towards the barred window. "You're back. Thanks for coming."

Yarn scribbles his pen across the paper, the clipboard rattling nervously as he jots down a note. He shifts on his feet, fidgeting. Miraculously, he steps deeper into my cell. I can tell he's trying to get a good look out of my window. A booming clap of thunder sends him jumping backwards. When the flash of lightening strikes, his eyes grow wide with fear and his jaw hangs open; a silent scream catches in his throat. His Adam's apple bobs up and down as he swallows.

A whistling wind screams into the cell, knocking the window as another burst of lightening illuminates the room. Despite the bright light, mysterious shadows creep and crawl around the chamber. As the light diminishes, a glacial chill floods the room. A stiff breeze rushes past, tossing my hair around. Thunder grumbles overhead. The florescent light flickers and hums as the power surges. When the next flash of lightening strikes, I can see Deborah's elongated shadow fall across the cell and spill into the corridor. I wave my hand to the waning shadow, knowing my sister is still looking after me.

Yarn stammers, peering over his shoulder, his entire body

shuddering. He closes his eyes and takes a deep breath, exhaling slowly. "Why don't you tell me about what happened the night of Lucas Green's death?" he asks, tapping his pen against the clipboard, just one of his many nervous ticks. Something about the way he asks his question. He studies me with his eyes, taking in everything and processing it. But he wants out of my cell.

"He wanted to hurt her," Deborah's harsh voice hisses; my lips don't move.

Slack-jawed, Yarn glares over his shoulder. He can't see her, but I can.

"Did you mean Lucas tried to harm you?" he asks. He thumbs through the papers on his clipboard. The manilla folder that Detective O'Reilly brought is fixed beneath the medical records. He hadn't bothered to open it. With an insidious grin, he steps closer. "Or did he try to hurt your sister?"

Deborah laughs at his statement, but I ignore her. "Please just go away," I beg Deborah, pointing back towards the window. When I turn around, a flash of lightening tears the sky in half. I've pissed her off.

Not realizing who I was speaking to, Yarn answers: "I can't do that. If you want me to help you, we need to discuss all the things in your file." The electricity surges in the room, casting the room in wavering light. On the wall, Deborah's shadow dances around the brick, moving with an eerie grace, flittering in and out of existence. "Did Lucas try to…"

"Yes," I answer, cutting him off. I'm so sick of that question. It's the only thing that people believe. How many times have they asked that question over the last several days? More than I'm willing to count. Deborah laughs at me. She whispers something, her voice drowned out by the driving wind and precipitation.

"And how did that make you feel?"

"I was afraid." My voice quivers. With considerable effort, I push away the images that are seeking to rush back into my mind's eye.

"So, you fought back?" Yarn asks, tapping his pen against the clipboard.

"I fought back," Deborah answers for me in a snarling hiss.

"Deborah doesn't let anyone get away with anything. Even when I beg her to leave me alone, she just takes control of the situation."

"You mean," Yarn pauses, staring vacantly at his paperwork, "Deborah takes control of you?"

"No!" I roar. The electricity surges in sync with my pulse. "What I mean," I growl, "my sister attacked Lucas when she witnessed him trying to hurt me."

"Your sister is always around whenever you're in trouble?" Yarn questions, his tone incredulous.

He pulls the manilla folder out, laying it on top of his papers. He furrows his brow, pinching the bridge of his nose as if it hurts him to look at the content. "Let's start at the beginning, Samantha," he sighs. "Maybe it will help me understand you better."

I glance over at Deborah just in time to see her eyes roll, her long lashes batting. She shakes her head. A revolting smile creeps over her face. "Alright, let's get this over with." I'm speaking to both of them. But he doesn't appreciate it yet. Deborah stays quiet for a change.

"Did your mother ever talk to you about your biological father?"

"Rarely. It came up a few times when I was younger," I

recall.

"And you weren't curious about him?" Yarn asks, he taps his pen against the paper, waiting for a response.

"I am, but I gave up asking when I was five because I realized how much it saddened her." I feel a tear well in the corner of my eye.

"What did she tell you about him?"

"Not much really. Basically, they met at a party, spent enough time together to fall in love, then he disappeared, breaking her heart."

"Did your mother tell you she was pregnant with twins?"

"Yes." That was a lie. "And that the doctors told her she'd lost one. It was a miracle when Deborah came out alive."

Yarn stared at me, concentrating, wrinkles creasing his forehead. "Then," he stammers, "why aren't there records of Deborah? Not a single picture?"

"Because she detested me. I'm a reminder of the sorrow our father caused," Deborah explains, choking back tears. "I had my father's eyes, Samantha has hers."

Yarn nods his head, his pen scratching across the page. Before turning the page, he licks his fingers, his dry tongue scraping over his index and middle finger. "And your mother remarried after?"

"Right away," Deborah answers for me. Yarn still thinks that I'm the one talking to him. This time he doesn't search the cell.

"It wasn't proper for a young woman to raise a child alone. Embarrassing," I add.

"Then your brother was born a few months after they got married." Yarn's eyes search for the answer within the folder.

"Four months after," I recall. "She fit into her wedding dress without showing."

"Your brother died young." Yarn lifted a page up. "Sudden infant death syndrome is what the coroner wrote on the death certificate."

"Deborah smothered his face with a pillow." I watch the shame distort Deborah's pretty face, turning it sour.

"Why would she do that?" Yarn asks. "He was only a few months old when it happened."

"He was stealing all the attention," I retort, wiping a tear away from the corner of my eye. "Deborah couldn't stand it. She wanted to scare him, but it went too far."

Deborah refuses to establish eye contact with me, staring out into the storm. A gust of wind batters the Waterford with a barrage of hail. A crack of thunder booms, the lights flicker, and electricity surges through the lines. The weather always fluctuates with her moods, manifesting the dismal abyss that is her soul.

Yarn offers the typical explanation: "Are you certain it wasn't an accident? While your brother passed from asphyxiation, the medical examiner found the fibres from the bed sheet in his throat. They determined you couldn't have done it. Your mother swore you couldn't reach him from the floor and you were too small to crawl into the crib. I'm sure that you feel guilty about it because you couldn't help him, so you created a story to help you cope with this needless tragedy."

Not bothering to respond, I sit here, absorbing the information. I perceive what question is coming next, so I answer it for him: "Deborah shot him with a pistol."

"You mean your step-father?"

I nod.

"Now, why would she do that?"

"Because he thought if he killed me," I allow my eyes to wander over to Yarn, "he could stop her. He believed what you suspect. You both jumped to the same conclusion. The same one as everyone else." I peer at him through glazed eyes and continue, growing sick of the same old song and dance.

"And what conclusion would that be?" Yarn asks, his tone curious.

"That I have split personality disorder. My mom thought the devil possessed me. That's why she tried to save me by performing an exorcism on me."

Yarn flips through the manilla folder, dropping his pen to the cement floor; it rolls towards the drain. "The Vatican denied your mother's request. O'Reilly told me. I can't find it in here." His words blend together, agitated now.

A sadistic smile crosses Deborah's darkened face. "Oh, she tried anyway. Both of them paid for it. Hell, who knows, maybe it would have worked if there was a demon living within Samantha. But I'm not the devil. I'm real. Just like you."

"Wait a minute," Yarn stammers, his eyes darting back and forth. "Who tried to perform the exorcism. And what happened to them?"

"Two priests from the mainland showed up and performed a series of sadistic rituals to rid Samantha of the demon." Deborah bursts into a fit of cackling laughter. "When they left, I followed them out and made them pay for what they did to my sister. And my mother."

"Can you tell me their names?" Yarn asks. "And what did they do to you mother?"

"Easton and Sharp," Deborah spits out their names like they were poison in her mouth. Yarn's pen races across the page as he records their names. "They took advantage of my mother, knowing she was desperate. They took her money after performing a fake exorcism."

"Listen, Samantha." Yarn shivers, his voice faltering, eyes wide. "I don't understand what's happening to you. But you're very sick, and I suspect you need help. I'm going to make a phone call and make sure you stay here with us at the Waterford." He was already edging towards the hallway, his hands groping for the iron bars.

When he turns to leave, Deborah slithers past me, her shadowy form as swift as a summer's breeze and as frigid as an Arctic blast. She reaches out, curling her fingers around his wrist. Yarn stops dead in his tracks and draws a hitching breath. He spins around, his eyes bulging with fear. He stares at Deborah, then his gaze wanders over to me. Then he raises his arm, examining a blackened smear sullying the cuff of his dress shirt. He stares up at the ceiling, searching for something.

"How did you do that?" he stammers.

A boisterous grumble of thunder rocks the floor. The power dies, casting the room into complete blackness. The temperature plummets. A wintry chill settles over the cell. "Samantha…" Yarn's voice trails off. Flashes of lightening crack. A vivid cluster of lights snake through the horizon, casting the cell in silvery light. A scream escapes Yarn's throat, and he tumbles backwards, his backside slamming hard against the iron bars.

Deborah stands beside me, a shadowy replica of my gaunt frame. Blackness swirls and pulsates around her, illusions of movement dancing on the walls. A dark mist billows from my mouth, puddling into a sinister aberration. A stiff breeze sweeps it across the floor. The light vanishes as another clap of thunder roars outside. From the shadows, a pair of reptilian green eyes peer out from within the entombed darkness. The light filaments tinker and buzz as electricity labour to make its way back; water-stained bulbs emit a pale, yellow glow.

"Deborah!" I cry out. "He's trying to help. He just doesn't understand."

"No," Deborah's gargled voice speaks from within the shadows. "He's just like the rest of them." Her shadowed figure lurches forward. Before she can reach Doctor Yarn, I grab my sister by her ankle. "Let go, silly girl. I need to protect you," she snarls.

Yarn fumbles his way out of my cell. He trips over his own feet and falls hard on his backside. His head snaps and the back of his skull smacks the cement hard. I grip Deborah's foot, her legs pumping, working to throw my grasp. Yarn's survival instincts take over, and he drags himself away from the cell. Desperate, he starts kicking at the door. It slams shut with a raucous clatter. Deborah throws herself against the bars, and the gate jerks open. Yarn drives his foot into the door. Deborah screams out in a fit of madness as the gate crashes shut.

"Help me!" Yarn screams in terror. His shrill voice pierces through the darkness like a scalpel.

"What is the matter?" Sally demands, standing over Yarn and gawking down at him with a confused, frightened expression. "What are you doing lying on the floor?"

Yarn twists his neck, staring up at her, then back towards me. I observe his face twist and writhe as he tries to piece together the last thirty seconds.

"Where did Deborah go?" he challenges me.

Finally, he believes me now.

"You caught a break, doctor," Sally says, unimpressed. "The subject stayed put in her cell."

"How did you know to come down here?" Yarn stammers.

"I watched you exit the cell and lay down on the security

camera." Sally thrusts the key into the lock and turns the bolt. It falls into place with a heavy *thunk*.

"How? The power's gone out." The words tumble out of Yarn's mouth.

"What are you talking about? The power never went out," Sally says, bending down to pick up the clipboard. A frown wrinkles her face as she glares at the manilla folder. "You're not well, doctor. Maybe you should head back to your office for a break?"

"No, we have to observe Samantha…"

"I'm sorry," Sally cuts him off, lowering her head.

Yarn swings his head down the corridor, towards the approaching footsteps. Two orderlies stand beside Detective O'Reilly. "We need to have a chat, doctor. It's time for you to come with me in my car down to the station."

"What's all this about?" Yarn fumbles his way to his feet, clutching the bars to steady himself.

"Doctor Yarn," Detective O'Reilly waves a warrant at the doctor, "we have some questions concerning the relationship you have with your patients."

"That's a fake document," Deborah says.

"What?" Yarn barks. "This is preposterous."

"Why did you have the camera's disabled in this part of the building, doctor?" O'Reilly questions, an unlit cigarette dangling from the corner of his mouth.

"What in God's name are you talking about?" Yarn half screeches, half cries out. The orderlies step forward, but O'Reilly holds them back with the wave of a hand. Hidden behind them are two more police officers. A pair of stainless-steel handcuffs dangle from one officer's hands. They clatter as he strides forward. "What's going on here?"

"Doctor Yarn," O'Reilly sounds high and mighty, his chest

puffed out. "You are under arrest for suspicion of assault."

A police officer grabs Yarn by the shoulder, twisting him around, slapping the cuffs over his wrists. Once they lock his hands behind his back, the officer grabs a fistful of Yarn's shirt, guiding him down the hallway out of sight.

"You can't do this to me," Yarn screams as they drag him from view.

I remain in the corner, pretending to be oblivious to everything taking place just outside my cell. The only person who ever believed me is snatched away when I need him the most. No one notices as Deborah's shadow slithers up the wall and slips outside through a crack in the window.

"I'll be back," Deborah speaks to me from outside. "The detective switched out your dose of Amobarbital with a fatal dose of potassium chloride. You know what to do." The wind steals her voice, and she vanishes with it.

Once more, I find myself alone.

An orderly steps into the room, his nameplate reads BRAKE. This is the orderly Deborah warned me about. I can hear his heart flutter inside his chest, beating the rapid cadence of fear. Beads of perspiration drip down his face, his complexion pale and clammy. As he reaches out to take the syringe off the tray, his hand trembles, knocking the tray off the cart. His Adam's apple bounces up and down as he swallows anxiously. He bows down to pick up the scattered contents of the tray.

"Are you going to be alright, Aaron?" Sally asks as she rubs an alcohol swab over my shoulder, preparing to give me the fatal injection. Not willing to take any chances, Sally has two of the orderlies hold me in place. My heart thumps in my chest with anticipation. My mouth is dry, and I try to speak but my tongue cannot form the words. Instead, a trickle of saliva drips in thick ropes from the corner of my mouth.

"Yeah," Aaron stutters, "just rattled by everything that took place tonight."

Eying him suspiciously, Sally asks: "What took you so long to offer these accusations about Doctor Yarn, anyway. And why tonight?" She grabs a ball of cotton, pressing it against my shoulder, holding her hand out for the syringe.

"Thank you," I rasp.

"Of course, my dear," Sally answers with a motherly affection.

I roll my tongue around in my mouth, drawing in moisture. "Not you." I stare vacantly at Aaron, lifting my arm to point a finger. "Him." I allow the vague outline of a smile to surface despite the waves of panic crashing hard over me. "You released me from this torture." I revel watching him sweat, his mouth twisting in terror.

"Just doing my job," he mumbles, holding up the syringe as if it were a trophy.

"No, honey," Sally interrupts. "I'll be giving you the dose. He's only holding it for me." Sally holds out her hand, her fingers outstretched unknowingly for the mortal dose.

Aaron breaths a sigh of relief. He removes the plastic tip before handing the syringe to Sally. I roll my tongue around in my mouth, dispersing what moisture remains. With my head turned towards the window, I can see Deborah glaring at me, waiting impatiently. She doesn't expect me to follow through with her plan. Sally pinches the flesh of my shoulder. Her nails dig into my flesh, releasing an exquisite stream of endorphins.

"Don't be frightened," Deborah whispers into my ear. "We got them now."

My mouth shifts open into a gaping smile. "I'll miss you."

Sally jabs the needle into the muscle, depressing the plunger. The icy liquid drains into my veins. With each beat, the lethal dose creeps toward my heart. Outside, Deborah howls. The others stare out the window, thinking it's the wind. The orderlies ease me towards my bunk. Sally glances down at me for a moment, her tender smile reminiscent of my own mother's, and tears well in the corner of my eye. Before she leaves, she straightens out her skirt. "Aaron, can you get her settled into the bed please? I want her straps secured," she looks down at me for the last time, "so she doesn't fall."

The effects of the potassium chloride are already working; I'm lethargic, serene. My heartbeat slows to a methodical rhythm, my pulse all but non-existent. As Sally walks away, the rhythm her high heels make pounds into my skull like nails driven into a coffin. Aaron shuffles into view, working the straps as instructed. He yanks them too tight, cutting off the circulation in my wrists and ankles. But soon, that won't matter. When I try to speak, the fluids building on my chest muffle my words, the sound of my voice a distorted rasp.

"What are you trying to say?" Aaron asks, leaning forward, his breath hot against my neck. His nose scrunches, repulsed by my vile body odour.

"Thank you for setting me free," I croak. My insides are dying, my breath reeking of rot and decay.

"You're getting what you deserve," he whispers into my ear as he wrenches the wrist strip along the wall tight. The bones in my wrist snap.

A rattling laugh escapes my lungs. The fluids building in my chest gargle the supernatural echo. "I didn't kill your cousin."

His eyes grow wide with fear. "How did you know?" Aaron's face flushes with blood. "No one at the Waterford knew about that. How?"

"Deborah knew." My lips curl into a merciless smirk. "And now that I won't be here to hold her back, she's free to do what she wants."

"What are you doing in there, Aaron?" Sally calls out, poking her head into my cell. "We have lots of work to do tonight, and I'd like to get out of this section of the building now."

With the final strap secured, Aaron bolts up straight. Carried by a fear-induced sense of urgency, he turns to leave. Before he gets far, I reach out, snatching a handful of his pants. "You'll meet her tonight, after she's done with that detective." My words fade into oblivion with me.

When I awake, the world is pitch black. Wherever I am, it's freezing. Muffled voices speak nearby. My head is spinning, and my body aches all over. I want to sit up, but lactic acid flood my muscles, rendering them useless. The rhythm of my heart thumps inside my skull, pounding to get out. I realize my eyes are closed, but when I try to open them, I can't. They're stuck together. I push my tongue against my lips, but strands of thread prevent it from pushing my mouth open.

Foot steps approach and the conversation becomes clearer.

"It's a shame what happened to her," Yarn's familiar voice drones. "I don't get it, she was healthy."

"Well," a stranger's voice answers, "that's why we are here. An autopsy will determine what happened."

"Thanks for waiting for me," Yarn replies. "That corrupt detective had something to do with my incarceration, I know he did. There's no way Aaron Brake came up with those lies by himself."

"I'm still shocked no one knew he was Lucas's cousin. He

should have never been allowed near this woman."

A moment of silence passes between them.

"Let's just get this over with," Yarn shatters the silence.

The boisterous clamour of a zipper tearing open bores into my skull. An intense light shines against my eyelids. Metal instruments clang off a cold, stainless steel countertop. I feel the sharpened edge of scissor blades prod into my mouth, cutting the threads. My tongue slips into the back of my throat, gagging me until the doctor lifts my head up.

"What drugs were you feeding her?" the stranger asks. "Her breath is foul. They must have rotted her guts."

Next, the doctor removes the stitches from my eyes with surgical precision. "That's creepy," Yarn says. "It's like she's watching us with those reptilian eyes."

I can sense the fluids draining from my muscles.

"Is she breathing?" Yarn asks with a great deal of concern.

"Just a build up of gasses releasing," the coroner responds, his voice lacking any emotion. "I left my damn cart in room two, I'll be right back." His footsteps fade into the hallway.

I can hear Yarn pacing back and forth. Finding enough strength, I sit up. "Where is O'Reilly?" my voice a dry rasp.

Yarn stumbles backwards, tumbling over his feet and collapsing to the floor. "Sam—Samantha," he sputters.

I swing my legs over the edge of the autopsy table. My hands cradle my jaw, and I crack my neck, the vertebrate popping loudly. "Samantha is dead," I state. With my feet planted on the floor, I stand up. "Now tell me," I snarl, "where is the bastard who tried to kill me?"

"Deborah?" Yarn cries.

"Nice to finally meet you, Doctor," I grin at him, "and if you want to live, you're going to tell me where O'Reilly's family lives."

7

By the time Jacob had made it back to the Matthias Room Nick had already begun the tour, so he took a quick mental inventory of the ghost stories he had heard about the place and decided that the first stop on a tour built around the supposed true tales set in the building would be the sunroom.

Sure enough, he found Nick holding court, regaling the guests with a stilted take on the story of Victoria Power, the governess to the children of Aloysius Cantwell. Their story predated the house itself. Before the current home was built by Nathaniel, a smaller but still impressive building sat on the property. It was during that time that Victoria had lost Aloysius' youngest child, Elenore, during a game of hide and seek in the surrounding woods. It is believed that the girl, just six at the time, slipped on the sea-swept rocks and was stolen away by the undercurrent. While the family recognized the nature of the accident, the distraught Victoria never forgave herself and hanged herself from the birch tree they used as home base for their games on the first anniversary of the child's death. It was said that the spirits of the governess and the child could be heard playing and laughing in the woods around the tree.

Eventually, when Nathaniel, who happened to be Elenore's older brother, built Cantwell House he had the sunroom erected around the tree. No one was sure of his motivations, but it was assumed that since she seemed tied to the tree it was a way of protecting even her spirit from wandering too close to the shore. Others simply believed that since birch are so susceptible to infestation and blight that it was a means of protecting the tree that held such morbid sentiment to the family.

Nick patted a hand against the massive birch as he finished the story and the guests marvelled, only now taking stock of how large the tree, which according to the story was tall and sturdy enough for a grown woman to hang herself from over 200 years ago, truly was. Almost in unison, their eyes followed the bone white trunk up to the patch in the glass roof that had been amended as the tree grew through it.

"I didn't realize we were staying in Hill House," Malcolm whispered to Monica.

"More like Rose Red," she replied.

"Yeah, this place has got ridiculous stories." Jacob had tucked himself in behind them when he arrived, and they hadn't noticed him in the dark and his interjection brought a jump.

"Jesus, Jake, am I going to have to put a bell on you?" Malcolm was realizing how often the kid's entrances startled him. Jake chuckled.

"Just wait 'til we get to the dining room."

"What's in the dining room?" Monica asked, her interest and excitement reaching levels Malcolm wouldn't have expected.

"Well, no one really knows, that's the thing," Jacob told her. "There's a story that one of the Cantwells had built a sort of bomb shelter or something, basically a hidden room and the story goes that you enter it from the dining room. No one has found the entrance, but it's the climax of Nick's tour."

"When was it put in?" Malcolm asked.

"The story is that it was during the Second World War, so not that long really. Nick and Maggie's great uncle got spooked by the stories of German U-boats off Bell Island."

"And he didn't tell them where it was?" Monica prodded.

"Apparently the uncle and the rest of the family weren't on the best of terms. By the time he had the room built, Matthias was a bit of a hermit and wasn't talking to anyone. Nick and Maggie's father only inherited the place because he was named Matthew as a nod to Matthias."

"So, this family is very much weird old money."

"Oh, the weirdest of old money. Like, they trade on the whole merchant thing, but they had hands in a whole lot of other things before they started selling fish in Newfoundland."

"Y'know, I thought this place was a bit extravagant for a merchant family."

"Yeah, there's a lot of rumours about other stuff. People are aware that they were involved in some import/export stuff, but there's long been rumours of some shady stuff too."

The building rumbled as the power surged back on.

"Well," Nick looked at the brightened faces of the gathered crowd, "it seems the power wants to keep us on our toes tonight." He checked his watch. "There's some time left in the evening if you would like to return to the Matthias Room to continue our scheduled readings, or we can continue the tour."

The crowd murmured as they deliberated and decided that they would return for the readings.

"So, I guess I'm up soon. I should head back and get ready," Monica said cheerily as she walked away from Malcolm and Jacob.

After a moment of awkward silence Malcolm turned to Jacob.

"I read your story! Great work!"

"Huh?"

"Your story. Honestly, I was impressed you got it to me so quick."

"What do you mean? I haven't brought my story to you yet—I haven't even decided what story I'm going to give you."

"Oh. So, the manuscript waiting for me in my room wasn't from you?"

"No. But I wish it was. I promise I'll get it to you soon," Jacob assured him.

"It's ok. Take your time. It's just odd someone else had a story for me and left it unaccredited."

"Yeah, weird."

"Ok. I'm going to pop back up to my room. I'll see you back in the Matthias."

"Yeah, see you then," Jacob said, standing alone in front of the birch tree.

When Malcolm got back to his room, his foot once again hit a stack of paper instead of the plush carpet...

KEYS TO THE KINGDOM
Jon Dobbin

Snow careened against the four men, their snowmobiles trailing one after the other just close enough to keep in sight. The blizzard had come out of nowhere, the delicate calm of the forest broken by raking wind and striking precipitation.

None of them could talk, their helmets covering their faces, their machines growling too loudly, but they knew that they wouldn't make it home. They knew they'd have to hunker down and wait out the storm. They needed shelter.

It was only a few minutes later when one of them pulled his snowmobile to the side and stood from the seat. His faded snow-suit, patched with crosses of duct tape, barely visible through the wall of snow, drew the others to him. The first snowmobiler looked around, making sure the others could see him, and he pointed off in the distance.

A cabin peeked through a sparse group of trees, its sagging roof and porch frowning at them in the distance.

"Some snow," Aloysius Stamp said, a crooked half smile spoiling his ugly mug. Wish, the name most people called him, and the name he heard inside his head when he talked to himself, tossed a snow-covered duffle bag onto the cracked and curling linoleum floor.

"Poo, what a stink," he said as he trundled back out into the storm, tightening the hood of his snowmobile suit to leave only a portion of his face the size of a bologna slice to endure the elements. Wish slapped Moses White on the back as they passed one another on the remnants of what was once a patio.

"How did you find this place, Jer?" Mose asked, pushing his glasses up his nose and sliding a cooler across the same kitchen floor, wet with slush and snow. He eyed Jerome Chafe who'd managed to wrangle a chair from somewhere in the darkness of the cabin.

"Derrick told me about it," Jerome said after a long drag on his cigarette, "never thought I'd see it." He said the latter more to himself than anyone else. Mose, having given a subtle nod at the mention of Derrick, went back to work unloading their gear.

It was Wish who'd come up with the plan: three buddies out for a ride on the old snowmobiles, camping in the woods, maybe a bout of hunting (legal or not), and ice fishing. Old times. He had scouted the area out the previous year but didn't spend much time there—too busy, too drunk. Wish never knew anything about the cabin though, hadn't seen it in his lazy, meandering drives on his side-by-side or dirt bike. Then again, he wasn't a youngster. Kids always seemed to be able to find little pockets no one else could, find places they weren't supposed to be—places no one wanted them to be. Maybe it was their enduring connection to their imagination, or maybe Wish was just too drunk to remember any of it. Either way, none of them there were going to complain too much about shelter from a blizzard.

"Were you with Derrick when he found this place?" Jerome

stretched a hand across the table and patted Phillip LeGrow's arm. Phil was a tiny, young man, his thin, pale face almost hollow around his cheeks and temples. He was Derrick's friend. A good pal who had spent enough time with Jerome and his wife, Mona, that they were next to family. Derrick asked Phil to look in on the old man when he passed, wanted to make sure he didn't fall apart. Here Phil was, desperately gripping at the falling pieces.

"No, sir," Phil said and pulled his beer close to the table's edge. "I don't remember us ever coming this far into the woods. Though, you know Derrick, he pushed further and faster than any of us." Phil smiled at the thought. Derrick was his best friend; they'd known each other since kindergarten. He was a spark in the otherwise dim life of a teenager living in a small, isolated town. This place, this cabin... it was hard to believe it had anything to do with Derrick. It was dark and dank. It was cold and sad. It didn't feel right.

"Yes, he was like that, wasn't he?" Jerome said and crushed his cigarette on the old tabletop. He wheezed out a chuckle. "That was my Derrick."

"Started without me?" Wish said tossing two more duffles to the floor and making his way to the cooler.

"Only just. The boy here is nursing 'em, just for you." Jerome tilted his head and gave Phil a wink.

"Is that so." Wish pulled down his hood and eyed the table. "C'mon, Mose, b'y. Hurry up and sling those bags, we got some serious work to do."

Once Mose and Phil had crawled into their sleeping bags, Wish pulled out the liquor. Slapping away the beer cans and bottles, he slammed the twenty-sixer of rum on the table with a dull clunk. "Time to get down to business," he said and spun the cap off with one flick of his thick hand.

Jerome nodded and let his chin come to rest on his chest. Jerome was a bigger man, always a lover of food and drink. He'd really turned it up a notch lately, Wish thought as he poured up their drinks into red solo cups. Some people, when faced with a loss, will waste away to nothing. They forget to eat, move, live. They're the ones that are already dead, just going with the motion—a boat lost at sea. Jerome, well, he was of the other sort. The sort who buried their troubles in the pleasures around them. Course, it really wasn't pleasure anymore; it was a way to feel alive. A way to feel anything. Of the two, Wish reckoned that was the best way to be. Why not go out on a high note? Besides, he could always use a drinking buddy.

"Some snow," he said and handed Jerome the cup. Blizzard was probably the best word. Snow was sticking hard to the windows leaving little peep holes to watch it whip through the air. The snowmobiles were likely buried by now and Wish didn't relish the thought of digging them out.

"She's coming down." Jerome took a sip of his drink and sucked his teeth. "Was this in the forecast?"

"No, sir," Wish said after a swallow. Truth was, he had no idea what the weather was supposed to be like when he'd tried to set this all up. What he did know was that his E.I. check would be in, and he'd be able to buy some booze and gas. That's all he needed to know. The hunting, the fishing, that was just something to draw in Mose, have a DD present if they needed one. "Weather must've changed last minute. You know how it is."

"Probably the best thing to happen. Let me come out here,

see this place. This cabin was the last thing me and Derrick talked about. He got real excited about it, came home after his quad run just to tell me. His mouth moving a mile a minute, just like he used to do when he was a youngster, telling me about the latest thing on TV or the newest gossip around school. 'Dad, dad, there's this old cabin in the woods. Looks pretty solid too. I think I'm going to fix it up. Might be a good place to hunt.' He said that, but he meant a good place to drink."

"Hear, hear!"

"Well, we're certainly doing that now, aren't we, Derrick?" A quiver in his voice, Jerome raised his glass. Wish followed suit. After a moment of silence, they settled into their old routine, talking shit and drinking booze. A tradition nearly as old as they were. Wish figured it would be perfect if they had a pack of cards, something to keep their hands as busy as their tongues. A game of crazy eights or hundred and twenties would go a long way.

Leaving Jerome to stare into his cup, Wish stumbled out of his seat and began to poke around in some of the remaining cupboards. Most were torn open, tore down, or missing doors. Those that were left had some heavy water damage and might be moldy. "It'd explain the smell," Wish muttered as he struggled to open a drawer that refused to move. "Fuck ya then" he said and turned to the window. Something black passed in front of it. He jumped and turned around to see if anyone had snuck up behind him, but there was no one. Mose and Phil were still asleep, Jerome still at the table.

"You see that?"

"What?" Jerome said and dragged his face away from his drink.

"I think I saw..." But what did he see? A shadow? There was

a blizzard and they were in the woods. Any number of animals could have come around looking for shelter and run off when they realized humans had beat them to it. "Never mind, it must be the booze."

"I guess we should call it a night ourselves," Jerome said and drained the last of his rum.

"Just one more drink," Wish said and poured one up, his thoughts lingering on the black mass that passed before his eyes.

Phil woke with a scream trapped in his throat, the claws of his nightmare slowly fading from his memory. The cabin, he was still in the cabin. He pressed the heels of his hands into his eyes and blinked away the remnants of sleep. Pulling his phone from his pocket, he jabbed a finger at the home button—dead. He wasn't sure what he'd expected, maybe just force of habit. Derrick would have ribbed him for that, for keeping his face in his phone when the rest of the world passed around him. After Derrick died, Phil told himself that he'd change that. That he'd make Derrick proud. Maybe that's why he was out here, on a snowmobile trip with three men he barely knew—adventurous. Of course, he promised that he would look out for Jerome.

He sighed. The old fella wasn't taking Derrick's death too well. Drinking, missing work, crying. Maybe Phil wasn't doing the best job looking out for him.

A black mass loomed before him and Phil fell back, sliding over the silky nylon of his sleeping bag and slamming his back into the wall.

"Phil," Moses said turning towards him. "What time is it?"

Moses, Phil knew him better as Mr. White, was the principal of St. Mark's High School and not someone Phil thought he'd ever be on a snowmobile trip with. He never even had an inkling that Mr. White knew Jerome or Wish—especially not Wish. Mr. White was never the hard ass type, but he didn't let anything slide either: smoking on school grounds—detention; late to class—detention; fighting—suspension. That and a one-of-a-kind stern look of disappointment from behind Mr. White's perfectly round glasses. He'd been a good teacher.

Phil reached for his phone, felt its shape in his pocket. "Phone's dead" he shrugged.

The outline of Mose brought its arm up to its face. His old Timex Ironman watch illuminated the familiar glasses. "Give me your best guess, Mr. LeGrow."

Phil squinted out the windows—nothing but darkness, the night. "I guess, four…five?"

Moses smiled into the glowing watch. "Try ten."

Phil crossed to the window, careful not to trip in the tangle of sleeping bags. "Snow?"

"Looks like," Moses said stepping up alongside of him. "Seems as though we're buried."

"Jesus," Phil said and actively avoided the self-conscious sidelong glance he wanted to throw to his former teacher. "We're going to be clearing that out all day." Then, answering himself, "I s'pose that once we dig out the door, we just need to get the skidoos. Maybe not as much work…"

"If you think the cabin is buried, how do you think the skidoos will be?" Moses asked, shaking his head. "C'mon, let's get our sleeping beauties up and on their feet. We'll need everyone to be on this."

"Even Mr. Chafe…er…Jerome?" Phil said and thought of Derrick's father sitting and drinking as they all brought in supplies from the storm the day before.

"Yes, even Jer," Moses said but his face darkened some, his eyes softened, and he pinched the bridge of his nose between his fingers. "But we'll keep our kid gloves on for him."

"All right, b'ys," Wish said and coughed up a wad of phlegm. "Who's got a shovel?"

"I do." Phil always brought a shovel with him on snowmobile trips. It was a good habit to get into when you were riding around with maniacs like Derrick Chafe. There were more times than not that they had found themselves, and their rigs, nose first in a bank of snow and the powerful tread of the machine unable to get purchase. A shovel always came in handy.

The three men, each one old enough to be his father, stared at him expectantly.

"It's on my rig," Phil sighed, could feel his shoulders slump.

"Not much we can do with it there, Philly," Wish stretched his back and pushed out his bulbous stomach. "Jesus, what's that smell?" He waved a hand in front of his veiny, reddened nose and pulled open the old door.

The snow had crawled over the door and crept to the roofline, as far as anyone in the cabin could see, anyway. There was an exact replica of the door impressed into snow, it reminded Phil of his mother's dried flowers pressed between the pages of an old sketch book.

"What the hell is that?" Jerome asked from his place at the table.

Phil could see the sun at the edges of the snow, the melt running down in rivulets. There was something off with the imprint of the door, it looked like it was a handprint, like something had been trying to grab the doorknob.

"Don't get too excited there, Jer. Some snow fell away from it when Wish pulled it open," Moses said, wiping his glasses.

"Yeah, don't worry about it, Jer," Wish said. "I don't know my own strength."

"We better get started," Moses said and sunk a gloved hand deep into the snow. When he removed his arm a cascade of snow fell to the old linoleum. "This might take a while."

"All right," Wish stepped back and leaned against the wall. "Philly, you get started. Dig for as long as you can and come back—we'll switch out. Besides, us old fellas will have a chance to catch up some."

Phil nodded and dug his arm into the snow just as Moses had done a moment before. The snow was soft, wet. It would be heavy and thick, but it had to be done. Phil wondered how far he'd make it, thought that maybe if he could reach the snowmobiles and grab his shovel, it might be a big help for the others. He'd be able to sit back with a beer while they took their turns. With a nod to himself, he dug his other arm into the snowbank and pulled the snow into him in a bear hug.

The snow stuck together, molded, formed. As he pushed forward the snow did as well and began to spill around his shoulders and waist. For a moment it was like he was being embraced by the snow, that the snow was pulling him into it.

They spent their time reminiscing about the good old days when the three of them would run around King's Cove, rulers of their small domain. Wish brought out the booze before too long, and Mose was ashamed to say that he partook. Just a beer, mind. Just the light stuff.

"Glad to have you back, Mose," Wish said with a slap to the shoulder. "What with Jerome raising a family, and you off teaching the masses, I've had to hold the keys to the kingdom all on my own. At least Jer here came out on the weekends. What have you been up to?"

Mose knew this was going to come, knew that Wish would finally come around to it, the only thing that surprised him was that it didn't take nearly as much booze as he would have thought.

He straightened himself in his seat and mustered up one of his disappointed stares he used on his students. "Life isn't easy as an educator, Wish. Even before I was the principal, I had to put in a lot of hours to keep on top of things. And you know yourself that Jer wasn't the only one raising a family."

Wish nodded along, closed his eyes to emphasize his understanding, but Mose knew he didn't understand any of it. "I missed you boys though. The odd wedding and stag party every couple of years is hardly enough time to catch up with you."

"It's a hard ole life when tragedy is the only thing to bring us all together again," Wish said and made the effort to massage Jer's shoulder. "Hard to be happy to see someone when there is so much sadness around."

"How are you doing, Jer?" Mose leaned over the table and tried to draw the other man's view away from some spot on the wall. "How's Mona doing?"

Jerome stared off some more, his eyes flittering around the old wall just under the snow-encrusted window. Mose gave him time, was about to pat his hand, when the old fella blinked a few times and turned a sheepish smile to him.

"Mona is doing the best she can. We all are. Family, you know?"

Old fella? Jerome was the youngest of the three, had been a year under Wish and Mose in school, had a baby face into his thirties, forties. But he did look old. Drawn. He looked shallow, thin. Grief had taken a brutal toll on him, had sucked the life from him.

"Yes, Jer. That's clear as mud, me buddy," Wish said with a sidelong wink that made Mose feel sick.

"Where's young Phil gone to?" Mose stood and peered out the open door of the cabin, the pile of snow that stood in its entrance. "He must be gone for," he checked his watch, "Jesus, it's been three hours."

"Time flies when you're having fun," Wish said and poured Jer some whiskey. "Probably just trying to get to that shovel of his. Young fellas got all kinds of energy. Enough to spare."

They heard a thud above them. Mose flinched and fell to the floor.

"Mary, mother of Christ. Is he on the roof?" Wish stood and stared at the ceiling.

"I think I'll go check on him. Get him back in for a rest, take my turn. You're up after me." He pointed at Wish. "Don't go on a bender before I get back."

"Don't you worry, my son," Wish said to Mose's back. "I'll be right as rain by the time the likes of you gets back."

The hole in the snow was barely large enough for Mose to crawl into. Phil had made a tunnel, not unlike Mose's children made when they created a snow fort in his front yard. Mose never liked those snow forts. His father, a miner, had died in a cave-in when he was only three years old. Since then, imagining his father suffocating, covered in rock and dirt, always kept Mose away from enclosed spaces. Still, kids were kids. Their friends wanted to build snow forts, so they did too. Mose it might have been one of his friends, about to come in and give us their condolences, but he just stood there. Stood there and stared. I could tell by that stare it was Derrick. Every day he got closer, but Mona could never, would never see him. I didn't tell her I saw him, mind, I just had her look out the window every now and then judging to see if she saw what I saw. She didn't though." Jerome gripped his glass, his hand shaking.

"Then he started coming in the house. Not just some disappearing or reappearing bullshit either. He walked up to the door, opened it, and entered. Just like anyone else would, y'know?"

"Just like anyone else would," Wish repeated, but if Jerome noticed he didn't acknowledge it.

"We would talk then. For hours. It was like we used to do just a couple of years ago, before he got too cool for his old man." A smile peaked on the side of Jerome's mouth, but it quickly fled—scared. "Talk about his friends, family, sometimes even about you, Wish. And I asked him, y'know, what it's like. What it's like to be dead. And this, this is how I know it was him, how it was really him come back: he told me," Jerome was nodding his head now, "'Dad,' he said, 'it's the worst thing. I'm in pain, dad. Pain every single second. It feels like I'm being torn apart and put back together. It feels like I've been dead for hundreds of years, and then for just seconds. Dad,' he said, 'it feels like insanity. Like you're just about always cracked up—that you're at your limit and then they change the limit. They want to hurt you. They want you to hurt.' He said all that to me. He said it and then he screamed. He screamed like nothing I had ever heard before. Like a chorus of voices all moaned at the same time, but it was coming from him—from my Derrick." Jerome was crying, one meaty hand pawed at his eyes, trying to wipe away the tears.

"Jesus Christ, Jer. I'm... I'm sorry." Wish polished off the last of his drink, darting his eyes towards his bag, towards the next bottle, but was afraid to move. He didn't want to disturb Jerome.

"The worst of it, Wish, the worst of it is that I had to ask him to stop coming around. I had to ask my own son, my own dead son, to stop coming around. This child, my son, who was in so much pain, was in so much agony, and I had to ask him to leave me alone. Had to tell him to...had to tell him..."

"What happened?"

"He started to ask me to do things. They were simple at first, easy really. Tidy his room the way he liked, move his toothbrush to the sink instead of the holder, clean his old gun for him. Then they got harder, got worse. He...he wanted me to do things to Mona, to hurt her. To hurt others."

Wish sat forward; his cup crushed in his hand. "Did you, Jer? Did you hurt anyone?"

"Yes."

A crash sounded from above, as if a giant's hand scraped across the decaying roof. Wish jumped out of his seat, his head arching to the ceiling. A crunching, crushing, of snow echoed all around them; the cabin had come alive with sound. The snow at the windows shuddered and quaked, freed now from its mooring on the glass it fell freely. Still, light wouldn't, or couldn't, penetrate the windows—they were met with more darkness, with the night.

"No Jesus way," Wish said and rushed to the window closest to him. "No Jesus way it's night already." He clapped one hand to his forehead in a sloppy salute, cupping his eyes, and tried to see into the abyss.

"By's," He yelled, his voice directed back by the proximity

wouldn't have any part of it. Until now. He forced out a laugh as he crawled into the tunnel headfirst.

His shoulders scraped along the edges of the snow, and he found it hard to keep looking in front of him without his toque being dragged off by the narrow opening. Instead, he kept his head down, watched his own hands and knees as they pushed him onward. It was dark in the tunnel. The snow was thin around its opening, and it allowed some of the daylight to break through and color the harsh white a pale blue. That wasn't the case in the tunnel. Mose fought the urge to go back, to get the flashlight he had packed in his duffle. How far could Phil have gotten in a few hours?

His breathing came in heavy, gulping sighs. Mose felt the walls around him, felt them close in. He unzipped his jacket, freeing his neck and letting some cool air in. "Phil," he called, his eyes still focused on his hands. "Come on, time to switch out." Mose desperately hoped that Phil had already finished the work; he didn't know if he could spend much more time in the snow tunnel.

He chanced a look up, pushed his head into the snow some to accommodate more space, but stopped when it fell in clumps on his neck and shoulders. The tunnel went on, disappearing into the darkness, but it did angle upwards towards the roof. None of that made sense. The trail to the snowmobiles wasn't this far, and the snow itself was sure to spread out some as they got further away from the cabin. Going up was smart on Phil's part, the snow was thinner, and it would be quicker to break through, get a lay of the land. Still, wouldn't Phil have breached the surface before this? How deep was the snow?

To Mose's left he heard a series of crunches, dulled by the wall of snow to his side, but crunches all the same. Someone was running on top of the snow. "Phil!" he called out and pushed himself forward. He had to be close.

Mose made a good pace, his hands and knees moving in unison, the swishing sound of his snowmobile pants consuming him as he moved. Phil must have done it, must have freed himself, found the rigs, and was heading back to dig out. The opening, Mose had to find the opening.

He felt the foot before he saw it, his gloved hand clamping down on it as he rushed forward. Before he had a chance to look up, he was tangled in the legs and was falling into the body of Phillip LeGrow.

With a scream Mose pushed himself away, his breaths coming in shallow slurps, his lungs wheezing painfully. Phil was dead. Mose couldn't tell how it was done, but Phil's neck was turned at a strange angle.

"Wish! Jer!" Mose yelled over his shoulder. The tunnel was dark behind him, darker than he thought it could be. Then he heard the crunching above. If that wasn't Phil, who the hell was it?

Mose wanted to push backward, to go get help, but he didn't want to move. Not into the darkness anyway. It was oppressive, thick. He was afraid if he touched it, it would touch him back. He looked back to Phil but found no solace. Tears bulged in his eyes, falling in fat, warm droplets on his cheeks and snow. He turned back to the tunnel and the darkness was on him.

"Finally, a chance to get down to some real business." Wish made to refill Jerome's cup, but he hadn't touched the damn thing. "More for me," Wish grunted.

Mose hadn't been gone long, the lingering image of his two

boots flailing out of the hole in the snow still playing in Wish's mind. He found it so funny when he first saw it, but the humour faded with the heat. An urge to close the door came to him, but he resisted—the pile of snow detritus was in the way, regardless.

"C'mon, Jer, we're supposed to be having some fun out here. Sure, we hit a rough spot, but the boys will get us out. We might as well enjoy ourselves while they're doing it." Jerome had also faded; he had withdrawn, his eyes focused only on the wall in front of him, his breathing slow. It was almost like he was asleep.

Wish drained another glass and filled it again. He'd have to move on to another soon. Back home, this would have been a success. He would have counted off those dead soldiers on his hands the following Monday to anyone that would listen. A badge of honor? Sure. Why the hell not? Besides, it's the only thing he could brag about anymore. Money came in on the dole, Beth had moved in with her brother, and his house was falling in around him. All he had was the snowmobile and the booze. It was lonely though, real lonely. Not having a comrade in arms to joke about a hangover with, to tease into sickness, to share the burden. Lonely.

Then Derrick died, and Jer was looking to get soused. Jer came back to the battle, an ally, a friend, a brother. Sure, it wasn't nice what happened to bring him there. Jesus, poor Derrick. Wish would've never wanted something like that to happen (*right?*), would never want to see his friend in pain (*you sure?*). It didn't matter either way. Derrick had opened the door for Jer, and Wish was there to welcome him in. It was grief, and Wish had the solution.

He took a sip. The bite made him suck his teeth, pull a face.

He wasn't drunk enough yet. Sometimes, some nights when he wasn't drunk enough, he would wonder about Derrick and Jer. Should he feel guilty for what he did? For providing the means for Jerome's descent? Wish supposed that he should feel that way. That a decent human being might feel all sorts of guilt, but Wish hadn't considered himself a decent human being for a long time. And the loneliness, well it was gone. He had company, and if this weekend had gone better, he might have had the whole gang back together, still might. Though, he really didn't think that Mose would follow through. Maybe a Saturday night here and there. Maybe. That didn't really matter though. he had Jer and that was all the company he needed.

"Drink up, bud. I'm about to start a new bottle."

"I still see him, you know." Jerome didn't take his eyes off the wall, his voice a whisper. "Derrick."

Wish nodded along. Grief, that'll get him drinking again. "Of course, Jer, that's only natural. I'm sure Mona sees him everywhere too. Y'know, after my old man passed, I used to—"

"No, not like that." Jerry swung his head from the wall, his eyes bulging and wide, his neck tense. "Not like I imagine seeing him when I look in his room, when I see his toothbrush in the holder, not in the things I know he likes. I don't see him like that. I see him, Wish."

"Jesus, all right b'y," Wish said and hid behind a gulp of booze. Jerome turned back to the wall, his shoulders slumped, leaning heavily on the table.

"At first, well, I thought it may just be that. Y'know, wishful thinking, grief. But it wasn't. It wasn't. First, I'd see him out in front of the house, just standing there in the middle of the lawn, snow up to his knees. He was wearing the same thing he wore the day he died: green plaid shirt, faded jeans. At first, I thought

it might have been one of his friends, about to come in and give us their condolences, but he just stood there. Stood there and stared. I could tell by that stare it was Derrick. Every day he got closer, but Mona could never, would never see him. I didn't tell her I saw him, mind, I just had her look out the window every now and then judging to see if she saw what I saw. She didn't though." Jerome gripped his glass, his hand shaking.

"Then he started coming in the house. Not just some disappearing or reappearing bullshit either. He walked up to the door, opened it, and entered. Just like anyone else would, y'know?"

"Just like anyone else would," Wish repeated, but if Jerome noticed he didn't acknowledge it.

"We would talk then. For hours. It was like we used to do just a couple of years ago, before he got too cool for his old man." A smile peaked on the side of Jerome's mouth, but it quickly fled—scared. "Talk about his friends, family, sometimes even about you, Wish. And I asked him, y'know, what it's like. What it's like to be dead. And this, this is how I know it was him, how it was really him come back: he told me," Jerome was nodding his head now, "'Dad,' he said, 'it's the worst thing. I'm in pain, dad. Pain every single second. It feels like I'm being torn apart and put back together. It feels like I've been dead for hundreds of years, and then for just seconds. Dad,' he said, 'it feels like insanity. Like you're just about always cracked up—that you're at your limit and then they change the limit. They want to hurt you. They want you to hurt.' He said all that to me. He said it and then he screamed. He screamed like nothing I had ever heard before. Like a chorus of voices all moaned at the same time, but it was coming from him—from my Derrick." Jerome was crying, one meaty hand pawed at his eyes, trying to wipe away the tears.

"Jesus Christ, Jer. I'm... I'm sorry." Wish polished off the last of his drink, darting his eyes towards his bag, towards the next bottle, but was afraid to move. He didn't want to disturb Jerome.

"The worst of it, Wish, the worst of it is that I had to ask him to stop coming around. I had to ask my own son, my own dead son, to stop coming around. This child, my son, who was in so much pain, was in so much agony, and I had to ask him to leave me alone. Had to tell him to...had to tell him..."

"What happened?"

"He started to ask me to do things. They were simple at first, easy really. Tidy his room the way he liked, move his toothbrush to the sink instead of the holder, clean his old gun for him. Then they got harder, got worse. He...he wanted me to do things to Mona, to hurt her. To hurt others."

Wish sat forward; his cup crushed in his hand. "Did you, Jer? Did you hurt anyone?"

"Yes."

A crash sounded from above, as if a giant's hand scraped across the decaying roof. Wish jumped out of his seat, his head arching to the ceiling. A crunching, crushing, of snow echoed all around them; the cabin had come alive with sound. The snow at the windows shuddered and quaked, freed now from its mooring on the glass it fell freely. Still, light wouldn't, or couldn't, penetrate the windows—they were met with more darkness, with the night.

"No Jesus way," Wish said and rushed to the window closest to him. "No Jesus way it's night already." He clapped one hand to his forehead in a sloppy salute, cupping his eyes, and tried to see into the abyss.

"By's," He yelled, his voice directed back by the proximity

of the window. "B'ys, what's going on out there?" Wish tried again, this time facing the man-sized tunnel in the doorway.

"Wish, I need you to know," Jerome said, his voice carrying from somewhere behind. "I didn't *want* to do any of it."

Ignoring Jerome, who had clearly lost his marbles, Wish moved back to the window trying to get a glimpse of Phil or Mose, but only the dark greeted him.

"This was the only way," Jerome continued. He wasn't sitting at the table anymore. "You don't know what it's like to lose a child. You don't know the pain—as if God himself pointed his finger at you and said 'get fucked.' You can't know. A son shouldn't die before his father."

The night stared back at Wish, his eyes blinded by the little light that was being thrown out of the cabin. "Shut up, Jer. Just shut…" Wish felt like turning on the other man, turning on him and maybe decking him one. Sure, why not? The bastard wouldn't shut up, was acting crazy. Jerome deserved to be shut up, of course he did. But something drew Wish's eye. Was that movement?

"Mose," Wish turned back to the tunnel. "Phil."

"Derrick told me this was the only way," Jerome said, his voice lower than before.

"Moses, you out there?"

"He said that after you, after all of you, we'd be together again. He'd come back."

"Phil!" Wish said and plowed into the tunnel, into the darkness. He heard a slight cracking as he moved forward, he'd forgotten his plastic cup and crushed it in his palm, now his knee. He hadn't put on his hat or gloves. His fingers dug into the snow, the ache of the cold biting deep into his skin, his bones, but still he moved on.

"Derrick!" Jerome's voice rose up behind him, blubbering. "Derrick, come back to me."

Wish refused to turn around. He just needed to find Mose. He'd know what to do. He was a school principal, not some old drunk half in the bag. He'd take over; he was always the responsible one.

He crawled further and further into the darkness, further and further away from the cabin. His breath came in jilted wheezes, thick phlegm blocking his cough. Wish kept moving forward because the only other option was to go back to Jerome and deal with the crazy.

Wish stopped. It was a sudden stop, a stop that surprised even him. His body just stopped moving, ordered to a halt. It took him a moment to figure out what happened, but then he sensed it. Something was in front of him. Something stood in his way.

"Phil?" he said and forced one of his hands to reach out, hoping and not hoping to touch whatever it was that stopped him in his tracks. A shadow moved in front of him. It dislodged from the rest of the darkness and moved, slithering across the snow.

"Derrick?" The muffled voice of Jerome turned Wish back, an involuntary look over his shoulder.

"Mose?" Wish said and turned back to face the shadows, but instead they faced him with a crooked smile, sharp teeth, and long, terrible nails.

8

Just as the clock on the nightstand clicked to 12:14 am, Malcolm tossed the manuscript on the table and slumped into the wingback chair that faced the window. He had the curtains open so he could watch the storm that was still battering the windows. The darkness outside worked in tandem with the standing lamp illuminating his face to give the glass a murky funhouse mirror effect, the shadows pushing just past nature, forging an uncanny valley of gloom.

Who had put this manuscript in his room? Who had put the earlier manuscript there, for that matter?

He wanted to enjoy the spooky mystery of it all. Locked away in a seaside mansion over Halloween weekend while a storm raged, mysterious strangers kept leaving horror stories in his room, it was kind of perfect. But he found his focus constantly jumping to his own work, or lack thereof. He was too far behind with writing to enjoy that his weekend was turning into an episode of *Scooby-Doo* and that broke his heart a little.

He noticed the time and became aware that it was now, officially, Halloween and that he had been so caught up in reading the story left for him that he had likely missed Monica's reading downstairs.

He leapt up and ran out of the room, hoping the delay

caused by the blackout and subsequent tour had pushed the timing just long enough for him to get back down to the Matthias Room in time.

Sure enough, just as he pulled up in front of the large wooden door to catch his breath, he could hear Nick introducing Monica inside. He had made it just in time for her story...

THE ICE CASTLE
Erin Mick

"Want a beer?" The whole place smells warmly bitter—of exposed pine walls and half-burned logs left in the stove.

"Sure." Stock in the fridge is low, unreplenished in the waning days of cabin season, but the beer he hands me is still frosty-cold. "Generator was left on?" I twist the cap and it lets off a sharp hiss.

"I got Dad to run up and start it for us. Earlier today." He opens his own beer and takes a long, deep pull. I bristle and take a sip of mine to wash down the tension. It sparkles brightly across my tongue, carrying a sunny crispness discordant with the gathering autumn chill outside.

"That was nice of him. We should stop by when we head out. Say hi." I'm struck by a melancholic, snoozy kind of heartache. The same kind I used to feel as a kid around this time, that stubborn final week of summer when freedom and daily swims and too many ice cream cones gave way to new binders and the squeak of freshly-waxed gymnasium floors.

He chuckles. "Classic. Two minutes through the door and you're already planning our exit. Just relax, babe. Try to actually *enjoy* your last vacation weekend? Hm?" He grips my shoulders and rubs my arms like he's trying to warm me up. Like I'm frozen.

Placating me, I think. Outside the kitchen window, facing East, the mirror-side of dusk skims across the Atlantic, advancing for the shoreline faster with every second. I stare at the pink and orange waves as they foam and clamour up onto the rocks, willing them closer. *I dare you, come up here.* Up onto the grass, up onto the deck, in through the window. *I'll open it for you, I think to the waves. So you can come in and swallow us up.*

But I'm snapped back into the room when he lets go of my shoulders. Sighing at my lack of response, he moves over to the wood stove in far corner of the room and starts unceremoniously plunking in fresh logs from the small pile next to the sofa. He pauses, taking another long pull of his beer.

I yank the arm of my sweater down over my hand, putting the fabric between my palm and the sweating beer bottle, and I shove down thoughts about everything and more: thesis deadline, upcoming conference, the starting-back-up of teaching duties. All the things I signed up for, wished for, spent my youth daydreaming for, but now dread, and often despise.

"Babe, could you grab me another beer?" He downs the rest of the first one—*Must be a new record*—then fidgets with the BBQ lighter. Click. Click. Click. Nothing. Shakes it. Tries again. Click. A little blue flame spits out the end, like a smoldering snake-tongue hunting for prey. The paper in the belly of the stove flares and curls around itself, but the flame sputters and chokes when it reaches the logs.

I move to the fridge, talking over my shoulder. "I think you've got too many logs in there."

He leans back on his haunches. Examining his work. "I think you're right." He pulls some logs out, rearranges, and tries again. Click. Click. Click.

There are only six beers left. And one's a three-year-old

Black Horse everyone in his family has collectively agreed not to touch. *"Emergency beer!"* he told me once, with a wink. *"For safety."* I grab a non-emergency beer and take it over to him. Click. Click. The flame lights. This time some bark on one of the logs flares up hot and red, and the fire starts to climb the pile.

"There!" he says, satisfied. "Man make fire." He pounds his chest. I smile, charmed, despite myself. As usual. He wipes the soot off his hands and takes the fresh bottle, smiling at me, that first rapidly-downed beer already swimming behind his gaze. "Thanks!" He gives me a cool peck on the forehead, twisting the cap off the beer and tossing it into the fire, then closing the heavy iron door behind it.

There's a thought creeping into my throat, stubborn, sharp. It has been pooling at the back of my mind all day, scratching to get out. *Don't bring it up.* Don't bring it up. But it's already happening: "I miss her." I watch him closely as he struggles to control his reaction.

He tenses, taking a sip of his beer. A normal, human-sized sip, to delay responding. Then he nods. "I know you do."

"It is with immense sadness that we announce the sudden and tragic passing of one of our graduate students..." I try shake the memory away.

"Take your time," my supervisor had said. *"Take all the time you need."*

"How about forever?"

She had inhaled sharply, searching for the right thing to say. The thing a good mentor would say. *"Wouldn't...Kay have wanted you to finish your dissertation?"*

"I have no idea what Kay wanted. Clearly she didn't tell me everything."

Pause. *"She was your colleague."* Pause. *"And your best friend."*

Pause. "If you finish for any reason, finish for her."

Before I could stop it, the thought had come pouring out, landing on her desk with a dark thud: *"And I suppose all the funding attached to me and my project—all the funding you'd lose if I quit—that doesn't matter to you?"*

Her eyes, usually so gentle, had hardened. *"Because you're in pain, I'm going to pretend you didn't say that. Now, please, Cleo, take some time off. The whole summer, if you need it."*

"Babe?"

I snap back into the moment. "Hm?"

"Scrabble?" Miles is already holding the box. It's dusty, dragged out of some crevice for the first time in God knows how long.

"Sure."

He eyes me. "Where'd you go?" He visibly braces for my answer.

Truth? I look at him, considering. "I was just thinking…" *No, Cleo. Don't. You've already pushed it.* "I was thinking about how weird it'll be to go back. Without her." And just like that, with an eye roll he thinks I can't see, he lifts his second beer from the coffee table, where it has barely had time to form a new ring, and downs the rest of it. I feel my cheeks flare. "What, so, now you're mad?"

"I'm not mad, babe. I'm sad." He sets the empty bottle back down a little too hard, like a judge with a gavel, next to the first one. They clatter together. "And I'd love to go one single weekend—one minute!—" he wipes his mouth on the back of his hand, still holding the Scrabble box. And it's all so…*so Noah Baumbach*!…that I almost laugh, "—without thinking about how sad I am." He sighs again, more forcefully. "I lost a best friend too, you know."

It's not the same.

"I know. I know it's not the same."

"That's not what I was going to say."

"But I grew up with her. You know? And…" He's on a roll now, the beer swirling in his head, making it all spill out. "And… I know she was your best friend, I know that, and…and I'm so grateful because, well! Because she introduced me to you! And I'm so damn grateful for that. I am. But—but I…" He suddenly flares up, true anger, which is rare for him. "But! For God's sake, Cleo, I knew her for longer than you did!" He growls in frustration. "*You* moved here for university! *I've* known her since we were kids! Grew up together! In frigging East-Jesus, bay-town-nowhere, for fuck sake."

"It's not my fault I wasn't *born* here, Miles."

He ignores me. "And you're acting like you're the only one grieving!"

"That's not fair!" *Am I?*

"The point is: I miss her too." Looking away, he mutters, quietly: "And I found her too." He's begging me to engage further, to give him another reason to drown it all out. So, I say nothing. So, of course, he continues. "And on top of being sad about Kay, and on top of wishing I could have done something to…" He shakes his head, desperately, like he can jostle the last part of that thought right out of his skull. "On top of that, I also have to worry about you. I also have to see *you* going through those things over and over." He pauses. For effect, I'm sure. "And it's killing me."

That one blows me back a bit. I'm aghast, lost for words while the thoughts fly: *Killing you? Oh, it's killing you? I'm killing you? Great. One best friend down, one boyfriend to go.* I say none of it.

He huffs.

I throw my hands up, surrendering to the reality of a full-blown argument. "What? So, if I say something you're mad and if I say nothing, you huff at me. What do you want, Miles?" If Kay were here, she would chant in the background: *"Marital spat! Marital spat!"*

"We're not married!" Miles and I would shout in unison. The mood would lift. We'd all laugh. That's how it always went. She made everything around her better.

"I want you to enjoy this weekend that I set up for you. That my dad set up for you. He's letting us use his cabin, I took time off so I could be out here with you, and now you're just being miserable."

"I'm being *miserable*!?" My heart pounds furiously against my ribcage.

He tosses the Scrabble box to the ground, gesturing emphatically like "I give up."

I scoff. "Toddler."

"I'm getting another drink." He moves for the fridge.

"Oh! Great idea! Yeah, you know what? We've been here for almost half an hour, so a third beer is definitely reasonable." Up the road, the lighthouse foghorn lets off a long, low blare.

Miles pauses, leaning on the open fridge door. Then, slowly, he makes a great show of placing the beer he'd grabbed back onto the shelf. He says nothing—he doesn't have to. He has won: the drinking card has been played, so now it's a fight *I* started, instead of one he's been itching for all week.

The fridge door closes, the bottles clattering against each other inside, and he moves over to me, suddenly the very picture of calm and reason. "I don't want to fight." *Could have fooled me.* "Let's just..." he bends down, retrieving the Scrabble box.

"Let's just try to enjoy our time out here. As much as we can."

My heartrate is slowing. Annoyed as I am, I also know that the pressure valve has been released. The remainder of the trip will probably be smoother sailing. And he's right—I could *try* to enjoy my last weekend off.

"Fine." *No, still too angry sounding*. I try again. "But I'm allowed to use proper nouns."

He grins. "Deal. But no slang."

"Not even... 'cheugy?'"

"What is 'cheugy?' No, no way. No Gen Z slang."

"If it's good enough for TikTok, it's good enough for our Scrabble game."

He laughs, "We'll have to agree to disagree on that one."

"It's incredibly cheugy to use the phrase 'agree to disagree.'" He grins, and I can feel the mood lighten by the smallest fraction. The weekend can be salvaged. It can. I know it can. And yet, there's a weight pressing against the base of my skull, a heaviness. A tightening anxiety.

Outside, the final dregs of sunset-pink are sinking below the horizon of the Atlantic, plunging the shoreline into a hazy, purplish night. Miles moves to the chesterfield on the far wall by the stove and starts pouring the letter tiles out on to the coffee table. I join him, switching on the small table lamp.

Next to us, tucked into its corner, the fire in the stove burns molten hot, its flames hungrily licking the slats in the vent on the door. Like it wants to escape.

And we stay like that for hours. Sitting cross-legged on the floor, making words with the little wooden tiles by lamplight, chatting about the year to come, avoiding the things that are heaviest on both our minds. Then, when eventually neither of us can stand it any longer, when the fire in the stove has started to burn down to its embers, we curl up on the chesterfield, too tired to even make our way to the cabin's small master bedroom, and we both fall into the deepest, coziest of sleeps.

First, I'm dreaming of the day I met Kay. She was behind me in line at the Booster Juice in MUN Center in first year undergrad. She had tapped me on the shoulder. *"Excuse me, my treasure."* She reminded me of a Nan, instead of an eighteen-year-old girl. *"Your backpack is unzipped."* She had proceeded to zip it herself. We were friends immediately. Miles was with her that day, quietly reading the menu, paying me no mind. We wouldn't officially meet again after that for another six months—one of Kay's many schemes.

And then, I'm awake. And I'm coughing. Coughing like I've never coughed before. Like my lungs might crawl right out of my throat and flop onto the floor in front of me. My vision is bleary, obscured by a thousand floating spots of colour interrupting the darkness. *What the hell. What the hell.* I cough again and again and—

It suddenly stops. A new cough catches in my chest. My lungs seize and jerk and still I can't cough. Can't breathe. *Fuck. Fuck.* I jerk my torso out from under the blanket and roll off the couch, smacking my forehead on something and then landing on the floor with a dense *thud*. Fighting against my useless, empty, numb limbs, I reach up onto the coffee table, up, up, up to the lamp. I fumble for the switch, and with Herculean effort from my numb fingers I turn it.

The lamp helps—I can see now—but the light is all wrong. The room is hazy. Like we're in the clouds. *Kay?* I'm still half-dreaming. I'm on our trip to Ontario two summers ago. I'm thinking how the mist off Niagara Falls looks like how I always used to imagine Heaven must look when I was a kid. About the billows of smoke wafting off our campfire...

Smoke.

My lungs suddenly expand, unable to hold without a breath any longer, but the air I take in is liquid-dense and stings like acid.

I look over to the stove in the corner and black clouds are pouring out of it. I bring the neck of my sweater up to cover my nose and mouth, then, with a sudden burst of adrenaline, I'm up on my feet, stumbling to the corner. I lose my balance and catch myself on the stove's belly, and when I pull my palm away it's red-hot, already blistering, but I can't feel it. I throw open the stove's heavy door and crouch, looking up into the gut of the beast, up into its throat, at the simple exhaust flap in the base of the chimney.

Sure enough, the flap is closed—it must be stuck.

I reach for the poker next to the woodpile and jam it up into the throat of the stove once. Nothing. Twice more. Still nothing. My eyes are burning and watering, my lungs aching. *Come on, Cleo, come on.* With a final, impossible thrust, I jam the poker into the flap of the vent and with a sharp, shattering crack, like glass breaking, it opens. Like magic, smoke starts to rush into the chimney, up, out, dispersing into the night. *Window,* I think. *Go open a window.* But I fall back onto the floor. *No, Cleo, get up.* But I can't. I lie there, sweater still covering my mouth, and wait, trying not to pass out, while the smoke dissipates and my vision clears.

Seconds pass. Maybe minutes. Maybe longer. Eventually, there's a sharp pain seeping into my burned palm, and I'm relieved to feel it. I sit up, dizzy, delirious from the sensations rushing back into my limbs. Gingerly, I stand up and move for the window, turning the lever…

But it won't budge.

I try again, cursing my jelly-like muscles. Still, it won't budge.

I lean on the window itself, pushing with all my might. Nothing. *Locked?* I check. *Nope.* I move through the kitchen, to the door, turning the handle and pulling it—

But it, too, is stuck. Immovable. We never bother locking it, but I check the deadbolt anyway. As suspected, it's unlocked. *What the hell?* I try again, jostling the handle and pulling with both hands. My burned palm smarts, but I ignore it, willing the door to open.

It won't. Something's keeping it shut.

I move back to the window and cup my hands against the glass, looking out into the darkness. And it *is* dark. Oppressively so. I reach over to the switch for the porchlight and flick it on. Nothing. Flick-flick. Nothing. Flick-flick. Still darkness. I look out again, face pressed up to the pane.

And then I realize…the glass is foggy, coated in something.

"Ah, fuck." *How was this not in the forecast?* "Babe, there's been some kind of freak sleet storm, I think. We should leave as soon as it's light. Get back into town, if we can." Silence. "Babe?" He doesn't stir. I look over to his still form on the couch. "Miles?" Nothing. "God, you can sleep through anything! Miles!"

Then, like a droplet of cold water rushing down my spine, a realization overcomes me.

"…Miles?" He doesn't move. I rush to the couch and stand over him. His face is buried in the pillow, half-covered by the blanket. He's tucked himself way into the crease of the chesterfield, trying to be small so there'd be enough room for both of us. And he does look small. Smaller than he has ever looked. Childlike.

And horribly, nauseatingly still.

No. No, no, no, no, no.

I reach out and in the distance between me and him there's still room for doubt. But that distance closes entirely too fast, and in the split second it takes for me to touch is shoulder, to push him onto his back, for him to roll over, his arm falling out of the blanket and his knuckles hitting the floor with a sickening *thud,* my world, for the second time in less than a year, spins wildly off its axis.

"No." *Yes.* "No, Miles. No. No!" And then I'm shaking him, furiously, angrily, willing him: *be alive, be alive, be alive, you stupid idiot!* I shake even harder. "MILES!"

Somewhere deep in his body there's a wet *crack.* I freeze, pushing down the panic and the impending nausea, but when I let go of his shoulders he spills out of the couch and lands on the floor, brown eyes wide and pale. Empty. And a trickle of foam seeps quietly out of his mouth.

I scream. In fear, in frustration, in shock. I stumble back, out from between the coffee table and the sofa, and whirl around, away from the horrifying scene, trying to get my brain working.

The room swims.

Miles is dead. *Miles is dead. Kay is dead. "Call for help, Cleo. I'll cut her down. Cleo! Call 9-1-1!"* But now he's dead too. *Call for help, Cleo.*

Yes, call for help. I move to my jacket—hung on the back of a kitchen chair only hours earlier—and hunt in the pockets for my phone. I mentally prepare for saying it to the dispatcher, for saying the words out loud: *He's dead. My boyfriend, Miles Kelly, is dead.* But, of course, there's no service. It's all such a horrible, sickening cliché.

I try to focus on details in the room. The grain of the exposed pine on the walls. A single droplet of sap oozing from one of the slabs. *Breathe, Cleo, breathe.* The curtains around the window, white lace, dusty. The runner on the coffee table, blue, like my elementary school's front doors. Like the bracelet Miles gave me when I finished my undergrad. *No, don't go there.* The unfinished Scrabble game Miles was winning. *No, don't go there.* Blood. *Blood?* On the corner of the table. *Oh, God.* I reach up to my forehead, and my hand comes away wet and red. My whole skull aches, the entire side of my face sticky with blood. From when I fell off the couch. I probably have a concussion.

Okay. This I can work with. This problem I can solve. Dead-Miles is lying there, staring at me, willing me to make eye contact with him, but I refuse. Instead, I make my way through the kitchen, past the fridge, and into the cabin's small master bedroom. *If we'd just gone to sleep in here instead…* No. Can't go there. Not now. There's a window over the bed. I walk over, give the lever a try. It doesn't budge. *Focus. One thing at a time.*

In the ensuite bathroom, under the sink, there's a basic medical kit. I bring it up onto the counter, catching my reflection in the mirror. It's shocking—the open gash is still actively bleeding, trickling down and soaking my dusty-pink sweater in dark crimson. It's too big a gash for a standard band-aid, so I pull a roll of gauze out of the kit, tearing off a length and holding it to the bleeding cut in a bundle. I hold it there for a moment but almost immediately it's soaked with blood. I distantly remember something from a lifeguarding course I took as a teenager: *"Head injuries bleed a lot. Keep pressure on the wound."*

"There's no time for that," I say out loud. I try to wipe some of the blood off the side of my face, but it's no use. I take a fresh wad of gauze and press it onto the cut, holding it secure to my forehead, and use my teeth to tear off some medical tape from inside the kit and make a criss-cross over the fabric. "Good enough for now." *Why am I so calm?* I think back to the life-guarding course. *Shock, probably.*

There's a deep, creaking, otherworldly groan as the house shifts in a gust of wind coming off the bay. The storm is ramping up. I go back out into the main area of the cabin, keeping Dead-Miles in my periphery, refusing to look at him directly, and, once again, I press my face up to the kitchen window.

The sleet coating the window makes everything blurry, and it's dark, but if I squint, I can just make out the shoreline. Waves are crashing wildly up onto the rocks, glowing bluish-white from the moon now peeking out from a part in the clouds. There's another gust of wind and again, the whole cabin creaks and groans—but there's a strange quality to the sound. A high-pitched overtone, like metal on glass.

I back away from the window and try to think. The chimney vent—somehow, even with the heat from the stove—was stuck. *Frozen?* East-facing kitchen window, West-facing bedroom window, both also frozen shut. The door, jammed.

I turn around slowly on the spot, listening to every creak, every movement in the cabin's structure. I look over to the other main window, above the couch, South-facing, out into the woods that skirt the shore. I make my way over to it, still refusing to look at the body wedged between the sofa and the coffee table.

I stand on the couch and look out into the darkness of the trees. I can make out the peaks of spruce, touched by moonlight, stretching out into the night. But this window, too, is blurry, coated in sleet.

I once saw a giant ash tree after a storm like this one, bright red with early autumn foliage, every branch coated in an inch of perfectly-clear ice. It looked like a glass figurine. But I've never seen anything like this: the whole cabin sounds how that tree sounded as it swayed and creaked in the breeze. It sounded like it was crying out in pain, like it might shatter, leaves, branches, trunk and all.

There's another gust and the entire cabin groans in high-pitched agony.

And I realize: the whole place is frozen over. We're completely encased.

Then, behind me, I hear a movement. A quiet scuttle, a breath.

My heart leaps and I whirl around to look down at Miles. But he just lies there, staring out at nothing. Still dead. Still and dead.

It happens again—a scuffling sound, the kind you listen for when you're playing hide-and-seek and it's your turn to seek.

Slowly, I step off the sofa, over Miles' legs, and silently make my way into the kitchen. I look at the front door. Still closed. I tiptoe over to it, turn the handle, and pull. Still, the door doesn't budge.

The cabin groans again. My heart pounds. I put my back to the door and scan around, paying special attention to the shadows, but there are too many to watch at all at once, with only the light from the single lamp on the coffee table.

The base of my skull tingles. I am certain someone—something—is in the cabin with me.

No one is in here. No one is in here but you. You and Miles. And he's—

There. By the sofa, in the corner opposite the stove. At Miles' feet.

A movement. A shadow, just below the window. There's something there, I'm certain of it. Something quivering in a wedge of darkness the lamp can't quite reach. Watching me. I stare back, completely still, willing the thing to move again. But it, too, is unmoving. Patient.

I hold my gaze, trying not to blink, and my eyes start to water, but still, I cannot break my stare. Something deep in my stomach furls tighter and tighter, telling me not to look away, not even for an instant.

And then, Miles moves. I nearly scream but clamp a hand over my mouth, watching as with one swift slide—one swift *tug*—his feet disappear behind the coffee table. I gasp and direct my gaze to the other corner, by the stove, but I'm too slow. I look just in time to see his arm falling to the ground with a thick slap, dropped by the thing that had moved him.

I hold deathly still, staring at Miles' empty gaze, unable to look away. The shock of it all is wearing off, replaced more and more with every passing second by sticky, swirling fear. *I have to get out.* But first, I have to move. I have to move from this spot. *Cleo, you have to move from this spot.*

I eye the iron poker, still sticking out from behind the stove door from when I'd used it to force open the chimney vent. *Yes.* Keeping my eye trained on the shadows next to the stove, I take smooth, careful, very slow movements over to the poker.

I'm close, within reach, but Miles' body is in my way and I accidentally bump him with my foot. Horrified, I look down, just for the briefest moment, and it was a mistake. The thing dashes out from the shadow and into the kitchen, scrambling in my periphery, scuttling in the shadows until it rounds the corner, disappearing toward the bedroom. I snatch the poker and run for the kitchen window, where I plant my feet and swing the iron far behind me like a baseball bat, before hurling it forward, full force, into the window, which cracks and shatters with that single blow.

Relief floods my body. I drop the poker on the ground and pull a kitchen chair below the window, stepping up, ready to flee. I steady myself on the sill and swing a leg up through the window and—

I'm stopped. I lose my balance and stumble backwards, off the chair, crying out as I slice my hands on all the broken glass. The sound of my own shout snaps me back into focus, and I remember that I'm not alone in the cabin. I whip around, looking for any movement in the shadows of the kitchen. Nothing.

I clamour to my feet and reach out a bloodied hand into the empty window, hoping I'm delusional, hoping it'll reach right through, and I'll be able run out, out into the night, to the nearest road, to a passing car, to help.

But instead, my hand meets smooth, solid, glassy ice. Ignoring the pain from the burn, from all the fresh cuts, I ball my hands into fists and I slam them furiously against that stubborn, horrible ice, mind whirring. "What!" I hit the ice. "The!" Again. "Fuck!" Again, and again, I slam my fists into that ice, leaving bloody marks splattered across the smooth surface. But it remains unchanged. Solid, frozen, perfect, unbreakable.

I pick the poker up off the ground and slam it, tip first, hard into the center of the icy sheet. Nothing. Not so much as a fissure. *Again!* Nothing. *Cleo, you idiot, hit harder—again!* Nothing.

Determined, angry, painfully aware of the unknown presence keeping me company, I take the poker over to the front door and wedge the point of it deep into the space between door and frame. I pry with all my might, bracing with one foot against the wall, and, to my surprise, I'm suddenly thrown backwards by the door flying open. I rush forward, reaching out to see if I'm free.

But my hand meets cold, glasslike surface. "Fuck!" I wind up with the poker, ready to give that ice the swing of my life, but—

There's something on the other side of it.

A figure.

Dark, hulking and…human. *A person! Oh my god!* "Oh my god!" I laugh—I sound insane. I stand close to the ice and I shout at the person, hysterical: "This is a *crazy* I mean a really *crazy* situation, but I need your help! Could you—" Something about the figure's stillness stops me short. Something about the slope of its shoulders. The length of its limbs. Something about how it *feels*.

Wrong.

Bad.

That familiar, awful trickle of realization is crawling down my spine again. An all-too-familiar companion this year. But colder than ever before. More horrible. More horrible than the creak of that rope from that crossbeam five months ago. More horrible than the scene I know is still waiting for me if I turn around.

Wrong.

Bad.

Not human.

I back away from the door, holding the poker differently, like a weapon, gripping it tightly with both searing hands. I chance a quick glance over to the kitchen window, and to my horror, there's another figure there. I continue backing up, trying to watch both figures at once, mind blank with fear.

And there's a sound behind me.

I freeze, but I can't look away from the figures outside, so I stand there, in the middle of the cabin, paralyzed, breathing shallow, trying not to pass out from adrenaline and terror. Behind me, there's a shuffling sound. Something else too, like breathing, but laboured, grating. More shuffling, and then a steady *slide*. Another shuffle. Then, *slide*. I swallow against the bile rising in my throat. Shuffle, *slide*. Stuck in place, I glance between the window and the door. Neither figure has moved, which somehow makes them all the more threatening.

Then from behind me there's a new sound, a tugging, pulling sound, and then a series of wet snaps. *You have to look, Cleo.* The snapping sounds intensify, the breathing becomes more and more laboured.

I take one deep inhale. Two. Then, I turn, and I look...

At its gaping, empty face, at its elongated limbs. Like the ones outside, it's made of shadows.

It sees me and starts working faster. Pulling at him. Snapping. Breaking.

I...

I must have passed out. When I come to, I'm on the ground in the middle of the floor but I'm also, still, somehow, in that moment—the moment right before it all went black. I'm still turning around and taking in the horror in the corner of the room. I press my palms into my eyes, railing against the images now and forever burned there: Miles' body—mangled, twisted, folded—into the space beneath the woodstove, being dragged away, like an insect into a wolf spider's lair. Being pulled, by the shadow…below.

It makes no sense.

For a sliver of a moment, I'm convinced it has all been a nightmare, but my forehead is pounding from the open gash. I reach a hand up and find that my Macgyvered bandage has already fallen off, and my palms are coated in dried blood. I startle upright, frantically looking to the window, then to the door, the memory of those otherworldly figures still scratching at the base of my skull.

But they're gone, leaving just the milky darkness of the fog-laden Atlantic out the window, and the vast Newfoundland brush out the door. The ice, however, remains—the glow of the lamp gives it away, reflecting dimly in each glassy surface.

I'm still trapped.

Slowly, aware of the intense throbbing in my forehead, I turn around, back toward the site of that fresh horror, hoping that this, this one thing, wasn't real. Hoping that I'll see Miles there, just as he was before. Dead. Predictably, understandably dead. It's a horrible thing to hope for. But the alternative is worse.

I squeeze my eyes shut and finish turning around. *Open your eyes, Cleo. Look.*

My breath catches.

Worse. The only sign he was ever there at all is a streak of blood trailing into the darkness under the stove.

I grip the poker, next to me on the floor, and bring it along, crawling on hands and knees over to that dark space, my mangled palms crying out with every move. Halfway there, I suddenly feel the truth of my vulnerability. I look into the shadows under the belly of the stove, and they seem to look back.

I freeze, every evolutionary alarm bell sounding at five-alarm volume. Once again, I have the sense I'm in some kind of stand-off I cannot win. I stare unblinkingly into that darkness below the stove and then force myself forward.

One more inch.

Another foot.

Another yard.

And all the while, that coil of anxiety in my core tightens, and tightens, and tightens. *Don't blink,* I think. *Don't look away.* Another foot further and I'll be nose to nose with the stove…I hold my breath. *Steady, Cleo.*

And I arrive. The iron belly of the thing is still hot from the fire earlier. I lower my face toward the floor, slowly…slowly… to peer into the shadows.

But there's nothing there. Too much nothing. A gaping, velvety, impossible darkness that seems to go on forever. My mind locks onto a word for it: *tunnel.* Plunging back and down. Into the ground. But its edges are smooth, and they curve inward— not dug up and rocky like a burrow or a mine shaft. Instead, it's like the floor and the wall have simply melted into the hole. Melted, like the creature itself, into the shadows.

My vision swims, and I'm knocked back by a sudden draft of intense nausea, like when looking down from a great height. I pull away from the sickening darkness and force myself to take a few deep breaths in…

And out…In…And out…*"Just breathe, Cleo. I need you to stay on the line with me, okay? Can you tell me the address again? We're sending an ambulance…"* I shove the memory away and focus on breathing.

In…I try to focus on something in the room. Something solid. *No, not the blood.* Out… *No, don't look at the shadows. In…* I-N-S-I-G-H-T. One of Miles' lower-scoring words, and still, it had sealed my fate in our Scrabble game. It's still miraculously intact on the board atop the coffee table.

Out...I make a choice, snatch the *I* tile off the board, and scramble back over to the stove, aggressively burying the instant nausea as I look into the gaping mouth of that ominous blackness. I grip the poker next to me tightly, and then, with a single, determined motion, toss the wooden tile into the void.

It disappears instantly, sucked in by a silent force. I reach back to the board, grabbing the *N* tile and try again. Same thing: the tile leaves my fingertips in the smooth arc of a toss and then suddenly shoots straight back into the darkness, vanishing immediately.

Cursing myself for the fear gripping my stomach, willing it away, I reach out, just to the edge of the stove's door, feeling the air around the gap. My fingers, sticky and still damp with blood, detect a breeze. The void is drawing air from the room into its mysterious space.

I need to see how deep it goes. I need something heavier. Something you could hear, if it hit bottom. I glance around, zeroing in on the depleted woodpile tucked between the stove and the sofa. I select one of the logs, a sturdy one, unsplit and heavy, and set it right on the edge of the void, where the waxy hardwood floor of the cabin melts into nothing. With one forefinger, I gently push the log into the abyss.

It disappears.

I count.

One...Two...Three...Four... Outside, the wind starts up again and the whole cabin, uneasy in its icy prison, groans angrily. *Five... Six...* And then, somewhere deep in that otherworldly pit, there's the whisper of a splash.

A deranged laugh escapes my throat, followed dizzyingly

by another surge of nausea. "No, Cleo. No." I start the breathing again, in—

There's the creak of a footfall. Distinct from the increasing groans and creaks of the unhappy cabin walls. Then another sound—sharper, and quiet, but with intention. I stop mid-breath and listen.

It's quiet. Tap… tap… tap…Coming from the kitchen behind me. Coming from…

That now-familiar coil of anxiety in my gut gives a shocking jolt, like a snake tightening before a pounce, and my instincts tell me to keep as still as possible. To only make the slowest, most careful movements. Slowly, painfully, my blood rushing hot and fast, I crane my neck around until the shattered kitchen window is in my periphery.

There, beyond the smooth, glassy ice, the sun has decided to rise. Peach-coloured light is spilling in off the Atlantic, piercing through the cabin's frozen armour. And this might be a relief, this might be a welcome, lifesaving sight, if it weren't for *them*. All those figures standing backlit at the window, all those shadowy, almost-human things staring facelessly in at me, suffocating the very sunrise. The tallest of them stands closest to the icy pane, flanked by innumerable others.

Tap…tap…tap…

Losing grip on my remaining shreds of calm, I whirl around to face the window head-on, locking my gaze with the tallest figure. Despite an eerie lack of features, there's something in that dormant part of me, the part reserved for survival in some long-ago wilderness, that *recognizes* this one. From before. From the doorway.

My sudden movement was a mistake. A ripple of motion travels collectively through the figures, and I'm reminded of a kelp forest I saw once, waving with the tides. I hold my breath, listening to my deafening heart ka-thumping away in my eardrums.

Tap… tap…

The tallest figure has one elongated limb raised and it's… *pointing*? Yes, pointing. Pointing right at me. As I watch, the thing makes a subtle, almost graceful movement, pulling its pointed limb back, like an archer ready to let an arrow fly, and then bringing its sharp finger firmly down—*tap*—onto the surface of the ice. And again. *Tap*. And again. *Tap*.

And that's when I see it: the crack, forming in the spot where the creature is tapping, like the dent a rock leaves in a windshield.

Tap…tap…

The tendrils of the crack expand, slicing through the ice at an alarming rate. I had raged and pounded on that ice with an iron poker to no avail, but the shadow is breaking in with hardly any effort at all. Tap…And the others simply watch, calmly. Those foreboding kelp-like figures swaying behind their leader. I wonder why they don't just come in. Why they don't just get it over with.

Then I realize with a sick clarity: they're taunting me.

Tap.

The crack has spread across most of the window now.

Tap.

It expands again.

That coil in my stomach snaps and violently unfurls, jolting me into action. I look around, frantically, the likely uselessness of the poker in my hand suddenly weighing heavier than the iron itself. And then, as I look back at that space below the woodstove, at that ominous void, I have an idea. The stove's

iron belly sits almost a whole foot from the floor. I'm a lot smaller than Miles. I could fit, if I shimmied in, flat on my stomach.

I look back at the window, and it seems, somehow, that
even more shadow figures have gathered. The tallest creature
pulls its slender hand back one more time, pausing momentarily. And it knows—it knows that *I* know—that this will be the
final blow. It stares at me. I stare back, feeling something like
defiance. *Do it*, I think. And then I'm shouting, "Do it! Do it! DO
IT, WHAT ARE YOU WAITING FOR?" Even in the nothingness
of the thing's face I sense that it *grins*, and then...

Tap.

With a small, initial *clink*, there's a moment of intense, eerie
silence. Then the ice groans and lets off a high-pitched sound as
the entire shell around the cabin yawns and begins to succumb
to imminent collapse. There's a rush of frozen air that smells of
metal, and salt, and seaweed, and rocky shores, and then with
a great roar, the whole thing quakes, and rumbles, and then,
suddenly, shatters.

I hurl the poker at the shadows rushing in through the open
window, turn, and dive onto the floor toward the stove. I can
feel them all rushing in, filling every corner of the cabin with
their darkness, blotting out the accelerating daylight from outside. I do not look, I only crawl, desperately, toward that gaping
unknown that extends from below the stove. I grip the feet of
the stove with both hands, staring, determined, into the nauseating darkness. My whole body rejects the plan, begs me not to
go in there, not to follow where Miles had been dragged. But I
can hear them behind me—their laboured, inhuman breathing,
like wind through old shutters, overwhelming me as they spill
in and flood the room.

So, I take one deep gulp of the breezy air around the void,

and then, head-first, with the shadows beginning to nip at my legs, I pull myself in.

And I descend.

I'm in freefall, and then with a deafening splash, I'm not. I try to take a breath, but my mouth is flooded with a briny, metallic substance—seawater. I'm submerged and sinking. I flounder, flailing my arms around in the impossible darkness, railing against my muscles that are already cramping from the frigid cold. I give a hard kick downward, once, twice, once more with all my might, and when I finally heave through the surface with a huge, desperate inhale, I try to look around, to get my bearings, but there's nothing to see. All around me is the kind of darkness that feels physically heavy—not merely the absence of light, but the presence of a thick, inky, almost sentient Nothing.

The only grounding point I have is the freezing seawater keeping me afloat. I argue with my limbs, convincing them to move with more purpose—*Swim, Cleo. Come on!*—steering my mind from how deep the water beneath me might plunge, and what things might lie below. My eyes search the void for something. Anything. I look up, hunting for a square of light from where I fell, but there's nothing. I feel insane, like my eyes must actually be closed, and that if only I could open them, if only I could get my stupid eyes to work, I'd be able to see where I am.

Then, from somewhere in the infinite darkness, a sound comes dancing across the surface of the water and into my ear. A whisper.

I freeze, treading water, every nerve in my body on fire, listening. Again, somewhere in the nothingness, there's a whisper, a single word. I strain my ears, trying to be still, to stop the splashing of my shivering limbs in the water so that I can hear.

The whisper comes again, like the crackling of a dying fire: "*Cleo?*"

"Miles!?" *No, that can't be right.* But I heard it. I heard him. I'm sure of it. I flounder uselessly, trying to find the direction of the sound.

"*Cleo.*"

"MILES?" My voice echoes, like I'm in a cavern. *That's something. Cavern means walls*, I think. So, I pick a direction and I try to move in a straight line.

"*Cleeeeo.*" It's closer now; I'm getting closer.

"Miles? Keep talking to me." Even as I say it, I'm swatting away all the warnings in my chest, ignoring my own thoughts that keep up a steady rebuttal: *Miles is dead. Miles is dead. This can't be him. Swim away.*

"*Cleo!*"

Yes! I'm almost there! But…No, Cleo. Go back. You know this isn't Miles.

"I'm almost there! Keep talking!"

Then, like the wings of a moth against my cheek, the whisper is right next to my ear: "*Cleo.*" And it sounds nothing like Miles.

I swing out an arm next to my face and make contact, hard, with something solid, something that startles back with a splash. I panic and slip beneath the surface. I try to come back up, but I've lost any bearings I had. I'm being tossed around on sudden waves that grow stronger, and stronger. I break through the surface once, gasping, only to be plunged back down. There's a roaring sound all around me, a fierce rushing, as the waves gather and become angrier, and angrier. Each time I reach for air my lungs find only seawater.

This is it, Cleo. I've lost all feeling in my limbs. I've stopped kicking. Stopped flailing. I can't do it anymore, can't feel my body, can't feel my lungs. I'm overcome by a kind of extreme lightness, a calm, as I succumb to the waves and let myself float, tumbling around and around. *I'm an astronaut,* I think, *this is space.* I think of Kay. We got high and watched *E.T.* together one night when we finished our undergrad finals. *"E.T. phone home!"* she kept repeating, giggling uncontrollably. *"E.T. phone home..."* Space is so *nice,* I think, I *wonder what it tastes like...*I open my mouth, craving a breath of the universe, ready to know all its secrets—

And then, with a violent yank on my ankles, something pulls me down, out of space, back into my body, back into the moment, and my lungs are crying out not for space but for air. I'm being pulled down, down, down, faster and faster, the pressure in my ears threatening to explode. I clamp my mouth shut, *don't breathe, Cleo, don't breathe, don't breathe,* as still I am dragged down... down...My muscles find themselves again and I try to kick, but something is gripping my ankles with a tightness that threatens to snap my bones.

Just when I think I'm about to pass out from the pressure in my head and in my ears, just when I think I'll have no choice but to take the ocean into my chest, there's a surreal blue glow emanating from beneath me. I look down and, blearily, through the fog of rushing water, I see that I'm in a whirlpool, spiraling wildly around a circle of bluish-green light. But nothing is pulling me, no sinister presence is gripping my ankles, just the water itself. I brace my desperate lungs and will myself to hold on just a few seconds longer as the light below me grows bigger, and bigger, and I tumble and spiral down toward it...

But I can't wait any longer. I have to breathe. *Almost there, Cleo, hang on.* The light grows bigger, brighter, whiter. And my chest burns. *No, Cleo!* But it's too late. My mouth opens, ready to heave in a great breath, one that will kill me. My lungs shudder, and heave, and take in that final, fatal gasp—

And I breathe in air. Real, proper air. Crisp, cold, and tasting of brine. But it's *air.*

I hit the ground with a horrible smack, ejected from the whirlpool onto a slab of mossy rock. It's a miracle nothing in my body breaks, but I land hard on my side, and even as I cradle my skull from contact with the rock, my injured forehead lets off a yelp of pain. I curl in on myself, heaving in breath after stinging breath, and even in so much pain, after so much surreal terror, the green moss against my cheek is the most beautiful thing I've ever seen or felt.

I roll onto my back and look up at the whirlpool still swirling above me. It defies every law of physics, floating there. As a kid I'd go swimming in the summer months, and I'd hold my breath for as long as I could, looking up from the bottom of the pool, watching bubbles as they floated to the surface, getting caught on the undersides of all the floaties the other kids were on—dancing, silver orbs skittering across coloured foam, searching for the surface. The whirlpool looks like that from below: a dancing, silvery film, pirouetting around and around, stuck to the ceiling of this yawning cavern. I gingerly turn my head, trying to reckon with where I've landed. It *is* a cavern, the kind that speckle Atlantic cliffsides, carved by the ocean itself. A distance to my left, daylight—the mouth of the cave. From outside, I can hear the sounds of the tide sweeping steadily up onto the rocks.

"Cleo?"

I sit up, forgetting the pain in my forehead, and spin around. Against the far wall of the cave, huddled in one of its many crevices, there he is. Miles. Handsome as ever, crouching on one of the rocks. Unscathed. Smiling.

And I know it's all wrong. I know, just as I knew in the whirling darkness above, that this cannot be him.

But it *is*.

"Miles?"

"Cleo. I've been waiting." He rises to his feet and stands at his full height, one shoulder hanging just slightly lower than the other, as always. Graceful, like a dancer, as always. Strong, from a long line of dock workers and fishermen, *as always*. He's wearing the black flannel button-down he'd arrived at the cabin in the night before. The same jeans. He looks perfect.

Entirely too perfect.

"Am I dead?" *Dead hurts a lot more than I expected.*

He laughs. And it really is his laugh. Miles' laugh. "No, babe. You're not dead." He grins at me, opens his arms and gestures like, *come here*. And I do. I scramble unsteadily to my feet, dripping seawater, shivering. My toes, bare from when I'd fallen asleep on the couch, sink into the spongey moss that covers the rocky cavern floor.

He gestures again like: *come on, that's it.*

I move, one exhausted foot in front of the other, toward him. Toward *Miles*. Toward comfort. I get closer, and closer, and he keeps beckoning me, smiling, waiting with open arms.

Those arms should be cracked.

I shake away the memory of the horrible snapping, of the blood, of the limbs bending and cracking, of his body, too big for the space below the stove, being forced into it anyway.

That mouth should be gaping.

I push away the thought of that trickle of foam as it fell from his pale lips. It must not have been true. It must have been a lie. A dream. A nightmare. Because here he is, smiling. *This is the truth*. I tell myself. *I was wrong before.*

Those eyes should be empty.

I reject that false nightmare that had fooled me, the lie that told me his brown eyes had ever been anything but alive and sparkling and welcoming.

"I have to show you something," he says, still smiling. I focus on those eyes. Those brown eyes that are—

Not brown.

Not like the bark of a pine tree. Not like the rocks that line the coast.

"I found her, Cleo."

"What?" *You're wrong. They're brown. Brown like they've always been*. Brown like freshly-poured coffee.

"I found Kay." *What?* "She's here. I'll take you to her."

And just like that, the thought shakes loose.

Those eyes are wrong. *Not brown*. Black. Empty. I stop moving, planting my feet in the moss, letting the sensation of it keep me grounded.

His smile falters, just for a second. "Really, I know it sounds crazy, but she's here, babe. She really is." I say nothing, fixated on those empty eyes. "I'll take you to her." He beckons again.

"You're not Miles."

It laughs. "Who else would I be?"

"What are you?"

"Is that a trick question? I'm…your boyfriend? I'm…glad to see you?"

I ask again, more firmly. "What are you?"

And just like that, I'm right. The thing in front of me is no longer Miles at all. It looks like him, it moves like him, but once it drops the façade, it is suddenly empty. A shell. A disguise. Nothing more. The thing wearing Miles looks at me, appears to think, then leans back against the cavern wall, sinking deeper into the shadows. And I recognize it. Again. From before. From the cabin. From beyond the ice.

"We're your future." *We?* I look around, and the shadows in the cavern are all quivering. Alive.

"Just let me go." It doesn't come out like I'm scared—just tired. Just done.

"We really do have Kay, you know."

My breath catches. I'm shivering so violently I can barely speak, and the tips of my fingers are starting to feel hot, boiling. A word floats to the surface of my addled mind: *hypothermia*. Still, I get the thought out: "Liar."

"We do not lie. We have her. And we can take you to her."

"I don't believe you."

"Have it your way." The thing shrugs and starts to sink further back into the shadows, leaving.

"Wait!" It stops, looking at me. Smug. "Is she…okay?"

The thing laughs. It sounds nothing like how Miles laughed. It sounds like the gears of a machine catching and grinding to a halt. "She's dead. Remember?"

"But you said—"

"I said we have her. And we do. And you can see her. If you want. Miles too."

I'm shivering so violently I can no longer support my own weight. My knees buckle and I collapse, catching myself on the rocks, my mangled palms sinking into their mossy blanket. I have the insane urge to go to sleep. To just curl up and let it all go. But the shadows surrounding me are quaking with excitement, and it keeps me in the moment, keeps me from succumbing to the heaviness of my eyelids.

"She's dead, they both are," the thing continues, "but they're also part of something bigger. Something better. Something important."

What is this? An infomercial? "I've n-never…" I stutter on a violent shiver, but sheer stubbornness and exhaustion forces me to finish the sardonic thought: "I've never been much for pyramid schemes." A laugh spills out of me, turns to coughing, then turns into a final, aggressive shiver. And then, with a shocking abruptness, the shivering stops. My fingertips prickle and the rest of me is flooded with warmth. I'm suddenly so very, very warm. Too warm. Overheating.

Not good.

The thing ignores my joke, my pathetic display. "What is there for you, really? Out there?" The thing glances out to the open mouth of the cavern. "Stay with us. Be with your two favourite people. A version of them, anyway." The thing looks around him at the shadows surrounding me. "Feed the darkness. Help keep the balance."

"The balance of what?" Oh god, I'm so warm. I need to cool off. Even my damp clothes are suddenly oppressively hot. With great effort from my useless muscles, I pull off my sopping wool sweater and it slops onto the rocks.

"Of everything."

Outside, out there in the world, where everything used to make so much sense, the lighthouse foghorn blares, closer than it was from the cabin.

Then, there's a yell, a human yell.

The thing's gaze snaps back to the mouth of the cave; the other shadows twist and writhe. I can tell, even through the gathering fog of delirium, that it's *angry*. I wait, listening for more. Sure enough, there's a trill of loud, sharp sounds. They bounce off the outer cliffside and echo into the cave. A dog barking, I think. And more voices. More yelling.

The thing brings its attention back to me. "It will never be good for you out there again." It smiles a sickening smile, then crouches down from its shadowy spot, meeting me eye level. I suddenly realize it can't come into the light. Not completely. But of course it can't—it's a shadow, after all. "How are you going to explain all of this?" My stomach leaps into my chest. The thing is right: I went to the cabin with Miles, and I'm about to be found. Alone.

"Miles is gone. They'll just think he disappeared. Ran off."

"Will they?" It grins at me with Miles' face, and then stands up, pushing itself flat against the cavern wall. I watch as the thing pulls and yanks and tears itself backward into the shadows, peeling itself out of Miles' body as if it were a sticky rubber glove. With a final tug, the thing becomes one with the shadows, and Miles' body flops wetly onto the rocky cavern floor. Broken. Empty.

"Last chance, Cleo," whispers the shadow. "Come with us. Be part of something bigger." All the other shadows seem to beckon me in. The yelling from outside gets louder, gets closer. "They'll think you did it, Cleo."

"I didn't."

"You might as well have."

"What?"

Now, the shadows all speak in an otherworldly chorus, overwhelming me. "You can't invite the darkness in and expect it to leave with nothing, Cleo." I'm so, so hot. I can feel I'm about to pass out. Again. Any second now. "So, last chance.

Come with us. Be one with us. With Kay. With Miles. With everyone before who has ever called us in." I sway, my elbows about to buckle. "Or stay in the light and take the blame."

My arms give, and I collapse, rolling onto my back, looking up at the silvery dancing of the whirlpool above. Listening as the barking and the yells outside grow closer and closer. I open my mouth, trying to answer the shadows, trying to tell them what I want, trying to tell them that I've made my choice. But I'm so very, very tired.

I watch as the whirlpool above me begins to slow. It turns slower, and slower, and then stops entirely, freezing over, clear as glass. I watch as it fades to a dull reddish brown, disappearing completely in seconds—nothing more than a cavern ceiling. Nothing more than cliffside.

I look to the shadow, crouching behind Miles' discarded body. It's still waiting for my answer. I part my lips, ready to decide...But then, as if from a great distance, a woman's voice slices through the air, cutting me off: *"Show me. Show me!"* There's a snuffling sound. Hot breath on my cheek. Fur. *"Yes! Good dog! Good find! HERE! IN HERE!"* More voices. The piercing, shrill sound of a whistle.

Still, I lie there, fixated on the shadow, daring it to do something, to reveal itself completely. But it just stares calmly out from the darkness. They all do. Waiting. I think about the best advice Kay had ever given me when my relationship with Miles had gotten off to a rocky start: *"Ultimatums are always bullshit."*

So, I stare into that shadow, unafraid, thinking at it as loudly as I can: *ultimatums are always bullshit.* And through the pain, with great effort, I shake my head.

One last time, they speak, directly into my mind: *"Have it your way."* And they begin to leave, pushing themselves into the darkness, disappearing back into their own world. Leaving me.

The woman is beside me now, silver hair poking out from beneath a navy-blue hat with yellow letters I can't read. She's speaking to me but I can't understand her. She's wearing a yellow coat. It says SAR on it in big reflective letters. That one I can read, that one I know: *Search and Rescue*.

The dog is sniffing around Miles' body at the far side of the cave. I wish it would leave him alone. It lets off a single, sharp bark, so the woman stands, rushing over. Over to the dog. Over to Miles. I watch, as if in slow motion, as the woman crouches down, takes in the mangled, blood-covered state of Miles' corpse, and then turns back to look at me.

And she's horrified. Distanced from me, able to take in the whole gruesome scene, the woman's eyes travel down my side, to where my hand is resting in the moss. The horror on her face grows. Following her gaze, I feel around next to me on the rocks. And something is there. Something heavy and cold. I glance down, and there it is. The iron poker. From the cabin. Right next to my hand.

And it's covered in wet, dark crimson. As is most of my arm.

I look at the woman, desperate for her to understand: *No, no, that's my blood. It isn't how it looks. I didn't do this. It's a trick.* But she already has her radio to her mouth. The other searchers are already at the opening of the cave. Two men. One tall and thin, one shorter and stocky. They're seeing what the shadows did and I know I'll never be able to explain.

The woman is back at my side. She's talking, looking at me, waiting for an answer to a question I didn't hear. Unsure what's been asked, I just nod. Then she's unzipping her pack, all business, and draping something over me—something silver and flowing—like those bubbles in the pool when I was a kid, like the whirlpool that's no longer on the ceiling of the cave, like the strands of her hair escaping from her toque. She's asking me more questions, but she still looks horrified. Like I'm a monster. Like I might gobble her up. My ears suddenly clear, as if they'd been filled with water, and I can hear her.

"What's your name?"

"Cleo. Cleo Parker."

"Are you hurt anywhere?"

I don't understand the question. "What? I…Um, we came…we came to the cabin yesterday…"

"Yesterday?" She emphasizes the word heavily, shaking her head. "You're sure?"

I nod.

The other two searchers are standing over me now. One of them mutters under his breath, "Yes, b'y." The woman shoots him a look. I feel unmoored, like I'm missing a joke.

Am I speaking clearly? "Yes?"

"But sweetie, you've been missing for over a week. That's why we came to look for you."

I shake my head, "No, not that can't be right. The ice storm, it—"

"Ice storm?" She looks again, baffled, to the other searchers. They shake their heads solemnly. The taller man seems like he might vomit. He turns away when I look at him.

"Yes. And then…and then there was smoke. And…Miles… He…" I'm already losing the thread. The events as they happened are already fading. I battle to keep them in focus. "And we…I was trapped. I couldn't get through the ice. I tried. I tried to use the…" I look down at the poker, now a few feet from my side. Someone must have pushed it away. I look at the poker and try to get her to understand. I stare right into her eyes— they're blue, like the Atlantic on a clear day—desperately pleading for her to understand me: "I didn't do this."

"Okay. I believe you." But I can tell she's lying.

The taller man succumbs to his nausea and moves a few steps away, vomiting. The shorter man is turned away from me now, talking into his radio with urgency. "Uh...We need police in here. And..." he glances back at me, "and an ambulance." The taller man stands up, wiping his mouth, and the other man says to him, quietly: "Go out there and tell 'em to keep the father out of here. No matter what."

Miles' dad. My stomach plummets. *How am I going to explain this to him?*

The woman crouches next to me, pale, leaning on her dog—a shepherd-looking thing, all black, with pointy ears—who sits next to her, panting with excitement. Its eyes are darting around the room, and I wonder if it can sense that the shadows were here.

"I *didn't* do this," I say again, my voice shaking with desperation.

She nods, but she can't bring herself to look at me. "I believe you." Her eyes shoot to the bloody poker, nestled in the moss.

She doesn't believe me at all.

And lying there, half-dead, delirious, staring up at the stone ceiling of the cavern, listening to the waves crashing outside, and the crackling of the searchers' radios, desperately clinging to my memories of the events as they unfolded...I don't know if I believe me either.

I just don't know.

9

Monica's was the last reading of the night. His wouldn't be until tomorrow, so after congratulating her on her story Malcolm decided to call it a night and head back for some writing.

He was cautious opening the door and kept his eyes down, expecting another manuscript to be on the floor waiting for him, but there was nothing,

As he entered the room, he grabbed his satchel off the luggage rack, pulled out his laptop, and opened it on the table. After staring at the blinking cursor for a minute or so, he got back up and unwrapped the tissue paper from around one of the two coffee mugs and made himself a cup. If he was going to write all night, he'd need fuel. Once the coffee was ready, he sat back down and, again, stared down the blinking cursor. He got up, went to the mini fridge, and retrieved a beer.

Okay. Now he had everything he'd need. There was nothing that would stop his progress as he worked through the night and got, at the very least, a hefty chunk of his book done.

There was a knock at the door.

He looked to the clock, now reading 1:48am. Who the hell would be knocking on his door at this hour? Well, the gap was wide enough to fit manuscripts through so seeing that his lights were on wouldn't be a huge struggle. Still, though?

As he walked to the door another manuscript shot underneath and slid across the carpet. He ran to the door, unlatched the privacy lock, and flung it open to reveal...

An empty hallway?

Frustrated, confused, and feeling a sense of dread tickle the back of his brain, he closed the door, set the locks, and wedged a towel across the bottom to close the gaps. No more surprise stories.

But that didn't mean he wasn't going to read this one...

THERE'S NO SHIPWRECK 'ROUND HERE
Ali House

Wes found the wreck on one of his walks in the forest. Often, when he was bored or didn't want to do homework, he'd go wandering through the woods behind his house. In a small town that was far away from other towns, there wasn't much else to do, especially when his friends were busy. Toby had gone out fishing with his father, and as much as Wes would have liked to join them, they hadn't extended an invitation, and he didn't want to infringe on their father-son time together.

Usually, on his walks, he found nothing more than an oddly-shaped stone or some trinket that had been lost or thrown aside, but on this particular day he discovered a path he'd never noticed before. It was so overgrown and underused that he'd had to stare at it for a few minutes just to realize it *was* a path. Since it was something different and interesting, he immediately headed down it.

It was slow going, having to pick his way through the thick branches and tall grass, but when he finally broke free of the trees and emerged in a small cove, he knew the journey had been worth it. On either side of him the earth began to rise, climbing to at least twenty feet high. Pine and birch trees rose with the land, creating a strange kind of tunnel that seemed to exist outside of the rest of the world, secluding the cove. It was as if someone had created a mountain and then dug away a small path in the middle. The cliffs went out into the water for a bit before curving to the side, cutting off his view of the ocean proper, but he knew by the smell of salt on the air that this was connected to the ocean.

The ground in front of him sloped downward, turning from grass and dirt into sand and stones, eventually disappearing under the water. The tide was out, revealing a sight he'd never seen before. Amid the rocks were long strips of curved, red rusted metal poking out from the water, like the ribs of a long-dead whale. It surprised him to see the remnants of such a large vessel in the little cove, and he couldn't understand why someone would ever think to bring a boat of that size in here. No wonder it had crashed.

Making his way down to the rocky shore, he moved closer to the wreck, keeping clear of the pieces of rusted metal that littered the area. He'd never heard of a shipwreck around these parts, but here was one, just outside the town. And judging by the look of it, it had been here a while. How had nobody else discovered it? Was he the first person to find it?

As Wes continued to stare at the wreck, he tried to picture what the boat must have looked like before it was destroyed. It must have seemed massive in the tiny cove. Had there been people on the boat when it crashed? Did they make it to safety or had they gone down with the ship? Surely, with land so close, they had all survived.

Wes gazed at the cold water, which appeared gentle and inviting as it lapped against the rocks, but which he knew had drowned many people over the years. A shiver ran down his spine.

"Mom, did you know that there's a cove up north with a shipwreck in it?" Wes asked over breakfast the next morning. He'd considered keeping his discovery a secret, but last night he couldn't stop thinking about it, and his curiosity about the ship and what had happened won out. Besides, it was very unlikely that nobody else knew about this wreck, considered how long it'd been there.

She paused for a moment, her fork hovering over the scrambled eggs on her plate, before looking at him with a curious expression on her face. "No, Wes, I had no idea there was a shipwreck 'round here. It sounds awfully dangerous, though. I hope you didn't get too close."

"Of course not," he said as he looked down at his plate, trying to hide the hint of a lie in his voice. He'd gotten pretty close, but at least he'd been careful not to touch anything that looked sharp or go too far into the water. "I wonder what happened," he wondered aloud.

"Oh, the same thing that always happens," his mother smiled, waving her hand dismissively in the air. "I'm sure it's nothing to concern yourself with. Best to leave it be."

Wes had a feeling that his mother's words were less of a suggestion and more of a command. She was right that it was a dangerous area to hang around, but he didn't understand why she wasn't more curious about the ship. In his entire fourteen years of life, nothing interesting had ever happened in this town. Well, other than the time Old Bill nearly burned his home to the ground with a lit cigarette, but with Bill's drinking problem, he set something alight every five years or so. Meanwhile, a ship breaking up on the rocks of a hidden cove was exciting!

He couldn't get it out of his head. Why had they come here? What were they doing in such a small cove?

Throughout school that day, he tried to concentrate on his studies, but his thoughts kept drifting back to the wreck. After history class, he waited until most of the kids had left the room before going up to his teacher and asking her about it. Mrs. Ivany frowned and shook her head, saying that she'd never heard of a shipwreck happening around these parts, but the coastline was likely dotted with torn-up boats, so it probably wasn't anything special.

She was right; the island of Newfoundland was known for its treacherous coasts. But Wes wasn't interested in other shipwrecks—he wanted to know more about this particular one. Every time he thought about it, he could see the metal sticking up from the water like strange, rusted tombstones, marking the graves of people long forgotten to time. Every time he closed his eyes, he could see the water swirling and churning, and the boat breaking apart into pieces.

Once classes were over, he grabbed his backpack and headed home. If his history teacher didn't know anything about the shipwreck, then he doubted any other teachers would. Hopefully, the internet would have more details.

He spent hours searching but couldn't find anything helpful. There were a lot of stories about ships crashing off the coast of Newfoundland, but each story he read didn't sound like his wreck. By the time his mother called him for dinner, he still didn't think he'd found the right ship.

"Rough day at school?" his mother asked.

Wes realized that he'd spent the last few minutes staring at the wall while shoving carrots around his plate. Snapping to attention, he took a bite of potatoes. "No," he replied, "school was fine."

"Don't talk with your mouth full," his mother gently reminded him. "You seem like you have something on your mind."

He shrugged. "I'm just thinking about that shipwreck... wondering what happened and stuff," he said, taking another bite.

His mother shook her head. "I've already told you not to worry yourself about that nonsense. Whatever happened was years ago and it's none of your bother. And I don't want you going down there again. Shipwrecks usually have a lot of debris, and I don't want you getting tetanus or worse."

Sensing that the subject was finished, he tried to get his mind off the ship and concentrate on dinner, but as soon as he was finished eating, he said that he needed to do his homework and hurried off to his room. Was his mother right? Was he wasting his time chasing something that was none of his bother? The tone of her voice indicated that she was annoyed he was still thinking about it, which was strange. Normally she had no problem with him being curious about something. Maybe she was worried about tetanus. Or maybe she thought the whole thing was a bit morbid. Sure, a shipwreck seemed interesting, but there was likely a lot of tragedy surrounding it.

Unless, however, there wasn't. Maybe it was actually a heroic tale of people surviving the cold waters and safely making it to land. He glanced over at his homework, which was still inside his schoolbag. He should be working on that, but his mind kept drawing him back to the wreck.

After promising himself that he'd only look for another half-hour, he went back to his computer and resumed the search. He found a few reports of shipwrecks in vaguely northern areas, but nothing that sounded like *his* wreck. Sighing, he decided to switch tactics and search for ships that had gone missing and were never found. A half-hour passed, then an hour, then another. The night had grown dark before he finally found what he was looking for.

As he read about the private yacht which had gone out one night in the 1920s and never returned, he began to sit up straighter in his chair. He couldn't explain it, but there was a prickling along his spine, like the feeling of someone reading over his shoulder, and he instinctively knew that this was the story he'd been searching for.

The inhabitants of the yacht had set out on an evening pleasure cruise, although some now suspected that it was all a cover for smuggling. Nobody was sure what happened, but there were three popular assumptions: one, that the yacht had been sailing in unfamiliar waters and crashed against unseen rocks; two, that they had somehow angered the people they were smuggling with, who decided to sink the ship on purpose; and three, that the boat had been cursed. Since none of the ship-goers were ever heard from again, it was assumed that every person on board had died.

A chill went down Wes' back and he regretted how relentlessly he'd pursued this matter. The ship wasn't that far from the shore, so why hadn't anyone made it to safety? How could every person onboard die when land was so near? Another chill travelled down his spine and he felt thoroughly creeped out. Closing the browser, he finally took out his homework, hoping that it would help him forget what he'd discovered.

The next morning he was exhausted. Aside from staying up to finish his homework, his dreams had been filled with images of bodies floating in the water, lifelessly following the motion of the waves. At breakfast, his mother asked if he was feeling ill, but he said he was fine. Although he could have gotten the day off from school if he'd agreed, he'd rather have something to distract him from his thoughts.

"You comin' down with something?" Toby asked him in homeroom, staring at the exhausted look on his face.

Wes shook his head. "Just a terrible night's sleep. I was researching a shipwreck I found and stayed up too late."

"Is that for some kind of history assignment? Like, extra credit?"

Wes opened his mouth to answer, but then closed it. "Nah, it's not important."

"Well, I was gonna ask you if you wanted to hang out after school, but maybe you should go home and take a nap instead."

Throughout the day, Wes tried his best to stay awake, receiving a few helpful nudges from Toby when he started to drift off during class. When school ended, he trudged home, hoping to catch a quick nap before supper.

His dreams were filled with roaring waves, crashing boats, and screaming people. When his mother woke him up for supper, he didn't feel like he'd gotten any rest. She remarked at how tired he looked, and he mentioned that it was because he'd been up late, doing homework, being careful not to say anything about the shipwreck research. She said she was pleased he was studying hard, but that he'd have to start earlier so that he wouldn't be up so late. Then she playfully warned that if he were still up when she went to bed, he'd be in astoundingly big trouble. He rolled his eyes and promised her that he'd go to bed earlier tonight.

After supper he finished his homework, being thankful for the distractions that math equations and English assignments brought. He'd planned on reading a bit before bed, but only managed to read two pages before nodding off.

Wes awoke to darkness with the soft blue glow of the full moon filtering in through his window. The house was silent, and when he held his breath, it seemed that the rest of the world was silent, too.

Something felt off. There was a strange feeling inside of him that he couldn't explain and that he didn't particularly like. His hand reached for his phone to see what time it was, but it stopped before touching the device. No, that wasn't what he wanted. There was something else...

Suddenly he was on his feet, walking out of his room, his house, and into the woods. It almost felt as if someone else was in control of his body and he was simply along for the ride. It wasn't until he was nearly at his destination before he realized where his body was taking him. The cove.

Emerging from the woods, it felt like he was stepping into another world. Moonlight illuminated the scene, which was different than he'd been expecting. Instead of the rusted metal carnage from before, he noticed a shimmering boat softly bobbing on the water. He could hear a strange kind of music on the air, and then he noticed bodies moving on the front deck of the yacht, dancing and laughing. It looked like the best kind of party, and he suddenly wished that he was with them instead of so far away.

His feet began to move towards the scene and suddenly he found himself on the bow of the yacht. The people were dressed in strange, old-fashioned clothing and there was an odd shimmer about them. They smiled widely and invitingly, dancing around him as the music played on. He began to smile as he watched them, getting swept up in the joyful energy of the scene. One of them took his hands and he eagerly joined the dance.

Suddenly the yacht shuddered. The movement brought a moment of clarity to Wes and he stopped. The people around him continued to dance and laugh, but something in the air had changed, becoming more sinister. He wanted to enjoy the party, but the movement of the ship made him feel uncomfortable.

Another shudder almost knocked him to the side, but he managed to stay put. The occurrence didn't seem to bother the others, but he noticed that their movements had grown more frantic, more manic. The music had changed, taking on a strange, haunting, frenetic quality. Was it just his imagination, or did his feet feel wet?

Before he could look down, a third shudder sent him stumbling, knocking into one of the guests. The woman smiled at him, but then her mouth opened into a wide silent scream. Water suddenly coated her flesh, and her body began to swell, her skin taking on an eerie blueish colour that reminded him of moonlight reflecting off the water. Her eyes glazed over, turning completely white as they continued to stare at him, her mouth still screaming with no sound. Wes quickly turned away, but the other people on the boat had also transformed.

A loud screeching sound filled the air—the sound of metal twisting and breaking. His shoes and socks were soggy, and his feet felt like they weighed a hundred pounds. The ghastly people began to surround him, their waterlogged fingers reaching for him, pulling at his clothes, grabbing his arms. The action caused their skin to fall away from their hands, revealing stark-white bones that shone in the moonlight.

Panic overtook him and he shoved the hands back, trying to escape their reach. The water was suddenly up to his knees and chills ran throughout his body. Shoving through the ghastly crowd, he tried to make his way to shore, but the skeletal hands continued to reach for him, trying to drag him back. He kicked and punched, slowly making his way to freedom as the water continued to climb higher and higher. When he finally pushed the last person back, he began to swim like mad for the shore. Eventually he made it to land, breathing heavily as he collapsed near the trees.

Although he was free, he couldn't help looking back. The ship, which had once looked so beautiful, was breaking apart, decaying before his very eyes. The people were no longer on the bow of the ship. Their water-logged corpses floated in the turbulent ocean, their clothing agitated by the waves. More skin began to slough off each of them, disappearing under the water. The full moon reflected off the bones as their skeletons began to sink under the waves.

When Wes awoke the next morning, he wondered if it had all been a terrible, horrible dream. He couldn't remember going back to his house, so surely it couldn't have been real. But then he noticed the pile of wet clothing on his floor, and suddenly he could feel those skeletal hands grabbing at him again.

At school, he was putting his books in his locker when Toby caught up with him.

"Hey, didn't you say something yesterday about finding a shipwreck?" Toby asked, eyes wide with fascination. "You feeling any better today? Feel like showing me where it is?"

Wes paused, swallowing back the fear that threatened to overtake him. Putting a casual look on his face he shook his head. "No, I was mistaken. There's no shipwreck 'round here."

"Drat," Toby said, disappointment crossing his face. "Nothing interesting ever happens around here."

Shrugging his shoulders, Wes knew that nothing could be further from the truth.

10

SCRITCH. SCRITCH. SCRIIIITCH.

Malcolm woke in the wingback, now facing out to a stark grey wall of fog. His head spun to the clock telling him it was 8:53 am. He turned back to the computer, almost knocking the empty beer bottle into the full cup of coffee and spilling the latter over his laptop, which was also sleeping.

SCRITCH. SCRITCH. SCRIIIITCH.

As he caught the coffee and kept the laptop safe for him continue not getting any work done on it, the sound that woke him reprised itself. It was coming from the door.

Slowly and cautiously, Malcolm Hennessy pulled his tired body from the chair and lurched towards the door. He had glided past thirty-five a few years ago and found that he now understood what people meant by "sleeping wrong." Usually, it meant that the first twenty steps he took would be unpredictable at best but spending a few hours asleep in an armchair pretty much killed any plans he had to be mobile for the next hour or so.

SCRITCH. SCRITCH. SCRIIIITCH.

"I'm coming, dammit," he muttered to the noise he was making his way to investigate.

At the door, he discovered the towel he had wedged beneath it gone, but no new manuscripts were waiting. The door was still locked from the inside so after a moment's pause, he assumed that whoever has been messing with him and leaving behind stories had pulled it underneath from the outside. Unlike last night, he was more cautious opening the door, slowly peering through the widening seam between the supposed safety of his room and the unknown dangers of the hallway.

Once satisfied that nothing was waiting to pounce, he pulled the door fully open and saw Jacob run past his room at full speed.

"Jacob?" he called.

"Huh? Oh, Malcolm!" The bellhop turned, but the way he held his body told Malcolm that he wanted, no, needed to be moving.

"What's going on? The place isn't on fire, is it?"

"No, but Tracy is missing."

"Who?"

"Tracy Cantwell-Jackson, Nick and Maggie's sister-in-law," Jacob explained. "She hasn't been seen since last night."

Malcolm was still dressed from the night before and patted his pocket to insure he had his key.

"Okay, I'll come help."

He followed Jacob to the lobby where Maggie was standing around a small contingent of staff, working through the plan for the search. When she saw them enter, her worried expression hardened?

"Jacob, why is Mr. Hennessy here?"

"I saw him in the hall and told him what happened. He's come to help."

"I'm sorry, Mr. Hennessy—"

"Malcolm is fine."

"Malcolm, I'm sure you can understand that we're trying to keep the search tied to those we," she cleared her throat before finishing, "know."

"You think because I'm a stranger I might have something to do with this?"

The gathered employees shifted uncomfortably through the confrontation.

"No, it's just…Look, your new friend Jacob was the last person to see Tracy." Malcolm's head whipped to Jacob, who hadn't yet had the opportunity to share that information. "And just considering the delicacy of the situation, we're trying to keep the search limited to the staff as not to raise unwarranted concerns."

"What does Jacob being the last to see her have to do with that?"

She paused and collected herself.

"It doesn't. I was trying to say that we don't know much about the situation right now and we're gathering as much information as we can. Jacob said he spoke to her in the lobby last night during the blackout but—"

"Jacob, you saw her?" Malcolm cut Maggie off to get Jacob's side of things out for the whole group to know.

"Yeah, I was looking for Ms. Cantwell to confirm I could finish my shift and come on the tour with you guys. Tracy told me I was good to go so then I ran back to you."

"I can confirm as much of that as I was part of," Malcolm said, turning back to Maggie. "Jacob was gone, maybe, five minutes. He said he was going to check in with you about getting off work and he was gone just long enough for us to leave the function room and get to that sunroom with the birch tree."

Maggie sighed before prodding Jacob again.

"And you didn't see where she went?"

"No, I ran on."

"Ms. Cantwell—" Malcolm began to interrupt her inquisition.

"Maggie."

He smiled at the mirrored gesture and wondered if she was returning the same level of hostility under the platitude.

"Maggie, it's 9 o'clock in the morning. How can you even be sure she's missing?"

"Tracy heads up most of the grounds work here. She's up and often has half a day's work done by 8 but none of her usual morning tasks have been completed," Maggie said through an infuriating calm that made Malcolm question her preparedness.

"Even on a Sunday?" Malcolm asked.

"Especially on a Sunday with this many guests," Maggie quipped back. "But, if that isn't enough to pique your concern, please follow me."

The group began to follow Maggie and she quickly stopped them.

"Just Mr. Hennes—Malcolm."

He followed her though the lobby and into a section marked "Employees Only" as she explained Tracy's place in the family and how the loss of Niamh had devastated them all and how she and Nick would be beside themselves should any harm come to their widowed sister-in-law, who's already been through so much. She finished her exposition just as they reached a door marked with Tracy's name.

"If the idea that the lack of Tracy's presence this morning is raising premature concern for you, Malcolm," she almost spat his name, "then please let me know what you think of this."

Maggie opened the door to the office, which was in complete disarray with the chair tipped over, desk drawers emptied, and sheets of paper fastened all over the walls.

Malcolm stood in shock at the state of the place, then took a step forward to inspect the sheets when he realized that they were pages of a story, formatted just like the manuscripts that had been left in his room. That's when the door slammed shut behind him...

ENGOLIS
Brad Dunne

The *Rare Reef* was met with a salty welcome as it pulled into the isolated outport community. Its thirty-foot fibreglass hull certainly didn't fit in with the wooden punts and rodneys docked in the harbour. Hard-looking men working on their stages glared at this strange vessel. Darren O'Keefe and his young apprentice, Tim Bryant, took this all in as their barely sober captain docked. Darren and Tim wore black parkas with blue-and-yellow patches on the shoulders to identify them as federal inspectors from the Department of Fisheries and Oceans. They climbed up the wharf's wooden ladder and were soon greeted by a short man wearing a shirt several sizes too small without a tie. Darren guessed this must be the plant manager.

"Welcome," the plant manager said politely enough without offering his hand or name.

Darren observed as men, women, and children stared at them, looking out windows, performing chores as slowly as possible.

"Wanna drink before we head to the plant?" the man offered.

Before Tim could accept, Darren declined.

The plant manager nodded curtly. "Very well, maybe later. In that case, why don't I spare you some trouble and bring you a sample of our fish. Right to your boat. That way you can do your tests and have it over with."

Again, before Tim could respond, Darren stepped in and replied, "That's very thoughtful of you, but we must inspect the inside of the plant."

The plant manager abruptly turned and began walking. Darren and Tim followed. Now there were two lines of people flanking their path as they made their way to the plant. Children poured out of the school up the hill. Fishermen left their stages to join the procession.

"Rough crowd," Tim muttered.

Darren kept his focus straight ahead of him.

The austere steel and concrete rectangular structure stood out awkwardly amidst the outport's tiny wooden homes and stages. The hum of conveyor belts grew steadily as they approached. Just as they entered, the pissy stink of rotten cod washed over them. Tim immediately fumbled for his surgical mask. Darren dared not flinch. The plant manager looked at Tim then gave Darren an indulgent smile as if to say, *the young pup can't handle the smell of fish*. Darren pulled out his clipboard and went through the motions of inspection, maintaining a professional façade. Dressers ordered in assembly lines under the harsh glare of fluorescent lights beheaded, deboned, and filleted cod in less than thirty seconds apiece. They looked at Darren with equal parts hope and anxiety, trying to peak at his notes.

Darren picked up three packages of fish. "We'll take these down to the boat for some tests."

Darren and Tim left the plant and made their way back to the *Rare Reef* under the watchful eyes of the outport.

"I think I'm going to puke," Tim said. "I've never smelled anything like that. How can they stand it?"

Darren hushed him. "Wait until we're aboard the boat."

Once they were inside the cramped lab within the *Rare Reef*, which also functioned as their kitchenette, Tim said, "What's the point of even doing the tests? It's obviously rotten."

"We're going to need to cover our asses here," Darren answered as he observed scores of trimethylamine oxide under the microscope. The cod was rotten alright.

"Let's get out of here," Tim said. "They're going to gut us when we tell them they have to shut down."

"Absolutely not," Darren replied. "The Station would only order us back. And if we came back here with our tails between our legs, they'd have zero respect for us. Then it would get really ugly."

"How can they not know?" Tim asked. "That plant was the worst thing I've ever smelled my entire life."

Darren shrugged. "Denial is a helluva thing." He made some more notes then put everything away. The fish had failed every category. "Come on. Let's get this over with."

They emerged from the *Rare Reef* to find just about the entire community waiting for them on the wharf with hostile, hungry eyes. The plant manager stood with his arms akimbo.

"The plant is closed until it is brought up to standard," Darren announced. The people groaned dismissively. "All the fish in the plant as well as whatever was caught today will need to be dumped."

The last part drew curses and jeers.

"You're putting us outta work!" someone shouted.

"What do ye know about fish?" someone else shouted.

Tim looked nervously to Darren, who kept his attention fixed on the plant manager.

"And what if we refuse?" the plant manager asked, his face

turning a dark shade of scarlet.

The crowd cheered this.

"No fish will be accepted from this plant on my orders," Darren replied. "If you refuse to close, you'll have your license revoked, and you'll be arrested by the RCMP."

"The RCMP?" the plant manager asked with his arms held wide, looking around. "I don't see any RCMP."

This drew angry laughs.

Darren was about to respond when he felt something cold and slimy slap his face. There was a brief moment of shocked silence. He looked down and saw a cod starring up at him with a dead, glassy eye. Laughter and applause erupted around him. More flying fish descended upon them. Darren turned, grabbed Tim by the arm, and they walked back down to the *Rare Reef*, descending the ladder two rungs at a time.

"What do ye think of our fish now?" the plant manager shouted.

"Don't ever come back here again, ye buncha worthless townies!" a child yelled.

The skipper was still dozing in his cot. Darren shook him to semi-consciousness. The crowd was pelting the boat with fish now. He could hear the wet splatter as they struck the hull.

"Wake up," Darren ordered. "Get us the hell out of here!"

The skipper pulled himself out of the cot and stumbled up to his wheelhouse. The windows were smeared with the blood and guts of cod. The skipper laughed at this. As the *Rare Reef* pulled out of the harbour and away from the outport, Tim eventually started to laugh too. Darren removed his parka, which now stunk like rotten cod, and did his best to clean it. Tim handed him a bottle of rum. After some hesitation, Darren took a mouthful then passed it back. They did this a few more times.

"Three weeks into this trip and we only had to issue three warnings," Tim observed. "And then this."

"A full closure can get pretty nasty," Darren replied. "But that was definitely the worst I've experienced."

"As soon as we got there, they started getting worked up. I don't understand why they hate us so much. We're just doing our jobs. It's not like it's hard to meet the standards."

"We're outsiders to them. These outports on the south coast are isolated even by Newfoundland standards. Most of these people have only left their homes to go out to sea. They have no roads except maybe a bush path to the next outport over. They see people like us as meddlers coming in and telling them what to do."

"I hate the way they treat us like we're not real Newfoundlanders, that we don't know anything about fish because we're from St. John's. Sure, they're the ones who wanted Confederation!"

Darren took a mouthful of rum. "Don't take it personally. This is a good job."

"Yeah, they're just jealous," Tim added. "And you're not even from town, are you?"

"No, I'm from Petty Harbour."

"Wasn't your dad a fisherman?"

"He still is. Didn't want me going at it, though. Wanted me to get an education." Darren smiled at this thought. "Still couldn't get away from the cod, though, could I?"

They drank silently a little longer until they decided it was time to get whatever sleep they could. They got into the cots and strapped themselves down. Darren could still smell the rotten cod. That reek of ammonia. His mind kept replaying that moment when the fish struck the side of his face. His chest filled with fresh rage. He tightened his jaw and clenched his fists, imagining punching that plant manager right in his swollen stomach, followed by a knee to his double chin. The rum in his belly spread through his body and eased his nerves. He relaxed as the gentle sway of the ship lulled him to sleep like a giant cradle. After a brief, boozy nap, he awoke and looked to his left to see that Tim was at a near ninety-degree angle. They were both upright, bound to their cots like mummies in a tomb. The ship soon dove back down, and they were flat again. Darren heard waves smacking the hull. They were in a storm.

He released himself from the cot and went up to the wheelhouse. The sound of rain was like a mad marching band furiously drum rolling out of synch. The boat's lights illuminated the great waves rising and falling before them—thirty feet, easily. The skipper was so drunk he could barely stand.

"We have to run!" Daren shouted. "The hull can't hold up against this sea. Get between the crests!"

"Ah, shuddup," the skipper replied. "You worry about your chemistry set and leave the sailing to me."

In the distance Darren saw a lightning bolt vein its way through the sky followed by a boom of thunder that nearly loosened his bladder. The waves were now nearly fifty feet high. This was the worst storm he'd ever seen, and it was getting worse by the minute. He went back down to the galley and woke Tim.

"Holy shit," Tim said after feeling the swell of a great wave. "What are we going to do?"

"We're going to have to strap the skipper down to a cot and take over the boat."

"Isn't that mutiny?"

"It's that or drowning."

"Can you sail this boat?"

"I'm no skipper, but at least I'm sober."

"Well then you're no skipper."

Darren had to grin at this. They grabbed some sheets and headed up the wheelhouse. Tim looked out at the water and froze. Big black monoliths rose with angry froth and descended upon the boat's hull. The *Rare Reef* was a tiny capsule at the mercy of the sea. Darren elbowed him and nodded at the captain, who was oblivious to their presence, mumbling some incoherent shanty. They threw the blankets around him and used some rope to tie him down.

"What do ye sonsa bitches think yer doing?" the skipper protested.

Together they pulled him down to the galley and strapped him into a cot. The skipper fought them bitterly—his strength was more than a match for them both. But his drunkenness kept him uncoordinated. By the time they had him tied to the cot, he was out of breath.

"This is mutiny!" he bellowed between pants.

Darren ignored this and climbed back up to the wheelhouse. The waves continued to rise and fall with merciless intensity. He managed to get the *Rare Reef* between the swells and did his best to ride with the rhythm of the storm. But he knew he didn't have the skill to keep this going for long, especially with how quickly the storm was changing. A buzzsaw of dread began to churn in his gut when he saw a cone of light oscillating in the distance.

"Is that a lighthouse?" Tim remarked.

"That's impossible," Darren replied. "There isn't another operational lighthouse on the south coast until Rose Blanche. That's almost a hundred miles away."

"Well, then, this must be some kind of miracle."

"That's Engolis. But that was resettled years ago."

"I say go for it. It's the only chance we got."

Darren steered towards the light. The lighthouse was perched atop a promontory standing over the sea. At the bottom was a fjord carved into the island's impenetrable coast. Darren weaved the *Rare Reef* through the fjord's entrance, and the ship soon settled into its calmer waters. They waded deeper into the narrow inlet. Darren relaxed, feeling protected by the surrounding cliffs. Up ahead he could see the dark shadows of an abandoned outport with empty houses and collapsed stages. A bright flash exploded all around them with the sound of the hull splitting

"What the hell was that?" Tim exclaimed.

"I think we were just struck by lightning," Darren answered.

Smoke billowed up from the galley and they could smell something burning. Darren raced down the steps into water up to his knees. The lightning had blown a hole in the keel, and water was rushing in fast. The cots were on fire. He saw the skipper aflame, flailing his arms. Darren couldn't hear his cries over the sounds of the storm. He splashed water on top of the old drunkard until the flames were out. Swaths of flesh slid from his arms as Darren tried to pull him out of the charred cot.

"Help!" he cried out.

Tim crashed down and together they pulled the skipper out.

"We have to abandon ship!" Darren cried.

They each grabbed a lifejacket and got the skipper into one too. They tossed his unconscious body off the *Rare Reef* then plunged into the water with him. The cold took Darren's breath away. He fought to the surface taking deep mouthfuls of briny water as he struggled for breath. They weren't going to survive long out here. Their only chance was to get to shore.

"Swim!" he yelled.

Darren and Tim each pulled the skipper with one hand and doggy-paddled with the other, kicking furiously as they made their way towards shore. As they got close, Darren could see there were lights on in the houses. He wondered if this was delirium as his body went into shock.

"There's a boat coming!" Tim shouted.

Sure enough, a small dingy approached them. A figure stood at the bow with a lantern casting light over the dark water. There was another figure at the stern, manning an old make and break engine, directing the boat. Darren felt hands pull him from the water and into the wooden vessel. Once they were all aboard, they turned around and began approaching Engolis. Darren tried to speak, but he couldn't get any words through his chattering teeth.

"That's alright," a voice spoke. "You're alright now. Don't you worry."

Darren felt his grip on consciousness loosening. He leaned over the side and puked out a belly full of brine. The world faded away. The last thing he remembered was the sound of bells chiming as they pulled into the harbour.

Darren awoke in a small bed atop a stiff mattress. A shaft of light through the window cast a misshapen rectangle on the wooden floor. He could see dust mites floating in the sunlight. The old metal frame jingled as he sat up. He was wrapped in a multi-coloured quilt, which reminded him of something his grandmother would knit. At the far end of the small room was a wooden dresser with a large porcelain pot sitting on top of it. Darren considered it for awhile and realized it was a chamber pot. That's when he realized how badly his bladder needed to be relieved. He got out of bed and left his room. The wooden floor creaked beneath his footsteps, which startled him in the deep silence of the house.

"You're finally awake," an old woman's voice announced.

A squat, bulging woman with short grey hair greeted him. Her sleeves were rolled to reveal thick forearms roped with equal parts fat and muscle.

"I'm sorry," Darren responded, "but I really need to use the bathroom. Could you tell me where it is?"

"No plumbing I'm afraid. You can either use the chamber pot or the outhouse."

Darren didn't hesitate. He saw his rubber boots by the door and rushed outside. The surrounding neighbours spoke in hushed whispers as he walked towards the outhouse. Once inside, he went to unzip his fly and then realized for the first time he wasn't wearing his clothes. He was wearing some kind of old breeches with a trapdoor at the crotch. There was no time to ponder this as his bladder was moments from emptying itself. Darren fumbled with the buttons and managed to get the job done before worse came to worse. He closed the trapdoor and then took a moment to consider his clothes. In addition to his pants, he was wearing an old knitted guernsey, like something his grandfather wore.

That's when the memory of what had happened hit him. The *Rare Reef*, the skipper, Tim. He rushed back to the house.

"Everything alright, dear?" the old woman asked.

"My friends?" Darren asked. "Are they okay?"

"The older fellow was taken away in a helicopter this morning. Your younger friend is out in boat with Alton."

"Alton? Who's Alton?"

"Alton Best. He lives three houses over. His is the red one with white trim."

Darren stumbled. He was feeling lightheaded.

"Have a seat, ducky," the woman suggested.

She lay a hand on his back and guided him to a chair at the wooden table.

"You've had an awful go of it," she continued. "That was Alton who seen yous last night. Well, we all saw once the lightning struck. Oh my, what a sight to behold that was. The power of nature." She shook her head in admiration.

Darren looked around the kitchen but couldn't find a clock. He noticed candles on the shelves and windowsills.

"What time is it?" he asked.

"Around noon I'd say. No clocks around here, my ducky. Not much electricity neither. All's we got are a few generators in case of emergencies."

"I thought this place was re-settled?"

"It was about ten years ago. But a lot of us like to come back during the summer months to fish and live the old ways."

"Well, that's very fortunate for us because I'd say we'd have drowned out there if it someone didn't come rescue us."

The old woman waddled over to the stove and dropped a block of wood into it. When she opened the stove's door, he felt the heat of the fire. It made him think of the impossibly cold water when they abandoned the *Rare Reef*. He took a deep breath and luxuriated in the kitchen's warmth.

"I'm sorry," he said. "I didn't even introduce myself. My name is Darren O'Keefe."

"Barb Hussey," the woman replied. She glanced out the window. "That looks like Alt's boat coming into the harbour. Your young friend will be with him."

"Excuse me," Darren said and left the house.

Engolis was a wedge of saltbox houses nestled into the cliffs of the fjord. The community was shaped like a witch's hat with its stages and wharves spreading at the base, and the homes funneling quickly to the tip. At the top was a church presiding over the community, and behind it was a small trail leading into the sparse hills. Women were out hanging clothes to dry on their lines. There were even little children running around between vibrantly painted houses and fences. The only mechanical sounds in the outport were the *putputput* of the make and break engines.

Darren walked down the gravel, car-less road to the landwash as Alton was bringing his boat, heavy with cod-filled nets, up to his fishing stage.

"Looking good!" Tim said, who was dressed similarly.

Darren grinned then extended his hand to Alton, which was met with a hearty shake. "I guess I owe you my life. Two of us both."

"T'was the Christian thing to do," Alton replied with a mischievous grin Darren couldn't comprehend.

"So, a helicopter came for the skipper?" Darren asked Tim.

"That's right," Tim answered after some hesitation.

"What about us?"

"What do you mean?"

"How are we getting out of here?"

"Oh, right. Another chopper will be back to get us."

"Were you talking to anyone from the Station?"

"Yeah, they told us to sit tight."

"Don't you worry," Alton chimed in. "We'll take good care of yous while you're here. Now, why don't you lend us a hand."

They retrieved some long gaffs from Alton's shed and began unloading the cod from the boat. Darren and Tim worked slowly and deliberately to get the gaffs' hooks into each cod's gills so as not to damage them. Once the day's catch was all aboard the stage, they began gutting and fileting the fish. Hungry seagulls squawked above them, descending into the water, greedy for cod guts and heads. It felt good to work up a sweat under the sun, smelling the salt from the lapping waves. They salted the triangular filets then spread them on wooden flakes to dry.

"I'll have to keep ye fellows on," Alton said. "Are ye sure yer from town?"

It was evening now, and the sun was setting. Darren returned to Barb's house. She had a supper laid out with cod, mashed potatoes, and swiss chard, which he ate with some of Barb's homemade mustard pickles. He couldn't remember feeling so satiated. As he finished his mug of tea, a thick tiredness seeped into his bones.

"You've had a long day, my ducky," Barb said. "You go on up to bed and let me take of all this."

"Are you sure?"

"Yes, my love. It feels good to take care of a man so long after my husband died."

"Well, if you insist, I won't argue."

As he stood up, he felt an urge to embrace Barb with a kiss. She stared at him with expectation in her eyes. He smiled at her and walked away, trying to understand what had come over him. Before entering his room, he noticed on the wall beside the doorframe a small key hanging from a tiny nail.

"Barb?" he called out. "What's the story with this key?"

"Oh," she said, a little embarrassed. "That's a bit of old superstition. If I told you what it was for, you'd think I was foolish."

"Try me."

"They're for the spirits. Lost spirits. They use the key to unlock the door to the other side."

Darren nodded his head and examined it.

"See," Barb said. "You think I'm foolish."

"No, not at all," Darren insisted. "I think stuff like this is fascinating. I actually did a few folklore courses at university as electives for my science degree."

They smiled at each other. Again, Darren felt the urge to embrace her. Instead, he said goodnight and went to bed.

He lay down on his small, stiff mattress. But after spending weeks aboard the *Rare Reef*, strapped to a cot, this felt like the peak of luxury. He fell into a deep sleep the likes of which he hadn't felt since leaving St. John's, which was—how long ago? He couldn't remember. After the last couple days, it felt like years.

In his dream, he was back in the plant. The fetid stench filled his mouth and nose until he couldn't breathe. He ran looking for a way out, but there were no doors—only brick wall. The sound of scraping metal surrounded him. The plant workers were sharpening their knives, coming to fillet him.

Darren woke and took a great gulp of air. He had a pain in the guts. After weeks of eating processed food on the *Rare Reef*, all the fibre from the swiss chard had his stomach doing cartwheels. The stomach ache must have given him bad dreams, he figured. He looked out the window and saw the outhouse standing in the tall grass. Moonlight gleamed on the chamber pot. He couldn't do it. The thought of popping a squat on the floor was too demeaning. And surely Barb would hear him in this quiet house. Hell, she'd probably hear him from the outhouse given how quiet this entire outport was. What if the pot was just for display? How the hell was he supposed to clean it without running water? He couldn't allow Barb to do that. His stomach lurched. Time was up. Darren swung out of bed and went out into the chilly night to do his business.

There was no toilet paper in the outhouse. Not even old newspaper. He sighed and pulled off a sock. The job now over, he dropped it into the abyss. Something in the darkness seemed to slither. He froze. A rat squeaked and Darren bolted from the outhouse. Once outside, unable to control it, he started to giggle. Amidst the deathly quiet, it sounded a little insane. After he finally managed to get it stifled, he instinctively looked around to make sure no one had seen him. The community looked different. It was in tatters. The houses were gutted and falling apart. The stages were all decrepit and spilling into the water. The entire outport was a giant rotting corpse. Behind him something scurried in the bushes, shaking the branches. He turned around and approached them. There was what sounded like childlike whispers. Then he heard a bell chime and the air surrounding him seem to pop. He looked around and this time the community looked normal again. All the houses were neat and tidy. He realized then how cold he felt and went back inside. Once in bed, he dismissed the whole thing as some kind of residual dream logic.

The next day, Darren woke up a little after dawn. The rich

scent of fried bacon filled the house. He came to the kitchen as Barb was finishing getting breakfast ready. She laid a plate with fried eggs on the table as Darren sat down. He dipped a strip of bacon into the creamy orange yolk.

"This is probably the best egg I've ever had in my life," Darren beamed.

"Collected them fresh this morning," Barb said.

Darren looked out the window and saw a proud rooster standing sentry outside a coop. He hadn't noticed it before.

"Will you be setting out with Tim and Alton soon?" she asked.

"What do you mean?"

"For the salmon."

"First I've heard of it."

There was a knock at the door. Alton let himself in with Tim in tow.

"Not ready yet?" Alton exclaimed then addressed Barb. "You let him sleep in."

Barb gave Darren an indulgent smile.

"What's this about salmon?" Darren asked Tim.

"Alt says there's a great river for salmon not far from here. Just a short hike."

"Are you kidding me? What about the chopper coming to get us?"

"Oh, don't worry about that," Tim insisted. "Let's enjoy the time we have here."

"We have to get back to the Station," Darren pleaded. "Christ, the *Rare Reef* sunk. There's going to be so much paper work to do."

"You've already been here a week," Alt said. "What's another day?"

"A week?" Darren exclaimed. "What are you talking about? We've only been here two days."

"Right," Alton replied with that mischievous grin. "I gets fooled up sometimes. Happens when you're old, see." He and Barb exchanged glances like they were co-conspirators.

"C'mon," Tim kneaded Darren. "When was the last time you took a vacation?"

Darren thought it over. He couldn't remember the last time he'd gone salmon fishing.

"Fine," he concluded. "But I'm telling you right now, I'm useless with a fly rod."

Alton clapped him on the shoulder. "No better time to learn than now."

After breakfast they set out. They followed the steep, narrow trail from behind the church. Darren soon felt beads of sweat on his forehead as he struggled up the boney hill. His breath settled into a heavy rhythm, and he could feel his heart pumping. When they crested the hill, the blood in his temples was throbbing. He took a deep breath and looked around. Bare, rocky hills rose and fell for as far as he could see, lightly accented with stunted trees, shrubs, bog patches, and little muddy ponds. By his feet was a patch of violet blueberries. They looked ripe enough to eat, which was strange for this early in the year. When had they set out from St. John's? June, wasn't it? He couldn't remember. He reached down and plucked a handful. They had a delicately sweet and fruity flavour.

"Nice, aren't they?" Alton asked, knocking back a handful himself. The few teeth in his mouth were stained purple.

They continued hiking. Now warmed up, Darren felt the stiffness in his body loosen. He'd spent too long cooped up in his labs hunched over a microscope and neglected fresh air and exercise. The muscles in his hips, back, and neck sang. And the air was so fresh. Each deep breath untied some knotted muscle in his body. After about an hour of hiking, they took a water break. Darren sat on a large boulder, thoughtfully deposited by some glacier a million years ago. As he sat and drank from his jug, Darren watched a fly buzz towards a pitcher plant, lured by its nectar bribe. He observed the fly try to pitch on the carnivorous plant's gourd, only to slip into its deadly lagoon. Soon it would be broken down by the plant's enzymes and the tiny midges living inside into bug soup.

"Our provincial flower," Tim said, watching the same natural phenomenon as Darren.

"Alright," Alton announced. "Just over the hill yonder now, and we'll be at the salmon river."

They crested another hill, and as they descended into the valley the trees grew in density and stature, stretching towards the sun. Darren heard the steady drum of the flowing water. The trail broke onto the river. Sunlight dappled the gentle, steady stream. It was the sort of setting millionaire amateur fly fisherman from the mainland paid fortunes to get chartered in for. Alton smiled while Darren and Tim took in the scenery. They set their packs down and got their rods set up. They spread apart, and each chose a rock to stand on and cast their lines. Darren relaxed his mind and eased into the meditative calm of delivering the line, bringing it back, and casting it again. After a couple casts, he moved downriver, searching for the fish. He lost track of time, deeply focused on his work. Then he felt a tug. A thick, nearly three-foot salmon leapt from the water, holding Darren's line in its mouth.

"He got one!" Tim cheered. Alton came running with a net.

Darren could feel the fish's strength in his hands as he wrestled to reel it in. Alton splashed into the water up to his hips, net at the ready. Just as he felt the strength in his wrists and forearms wane, Darren managed to pull it in towards Alton who netted it.

"Looks like a male," Alton said. "Must be seventy pounds, at least."

They brought it over to the riverside. Darren broke off a heavy branch. Alton lay the salmon on the rocks, then Darren gave it a few good whacks with the stick right where its brain would be. Alton pulled the hook out from its mouth. A tiny splash of bright blood speckled its jaw. Alton handed Darren a knife.

"Would you like to do the honour?" he asked.

Darren took the knife and sliced the gills. Tiny spurts of blood pumped from the salmon's neck. He brought it over to the river and drained its blood, squeezing it out with his thumb and forefinger like a tube of toothpaste. Red rivulets plumed around his feet. Once bled, Darren tore into the salmon's belly with his knife and gutted it. Once he was done, Alton clapped him on the shoulder.

"I don't think anyone is going to top that one," Alton said.

And it was true. Between the three of them, they managed to catch a few more salmon and a couple trout, but nothing compared to Darren's catch. As the sun began to slide into the late afternoon, they packed up and headed home. As they were hiking, Darren kept imagining Barb's reaction when he showed her the salmon. Once they descended the trail behind the church into Engolis, Alton gave Darren a wink and a nudge with his elbow. Tim followed Alton back to his house. Barb was waiting for Darren at the door, an apron tied around her slender waist. Her long black hair was tied into a wavy bun. She smiled at Darren and followed him into the kitchen.

"What a beauty," she said after he took out the salmon. He delighted in the admiration in her eyes. "You go get cleaned up, and I'll get supper ready."

After supper, Darren felt like he was glowing with the rich, oily flavour of the salmon. After tea, he helped Barb clean up. He grabbed her lithe wrist and pulled her towards him for a long, deep kiss. They headed to bed. She wrapped her limber body around his and they made love. Soon afterwards, Darren fell asleep with his arms wrapped around her.

When he awoke the next morning, his arthritis was acting up. He leaned over, pushed Barb's grey hair aside and kissed her wrinkled forehead. They got up and made breakfast. He looked out the window and saw Tim and Alton shuffling towards the harbour. In the window, he could see his reflection. He was briefly confused to see an old man staring back at him then he smiled. Age certainly had a way of catching up. The sky was grey and hard. It was going to be a cold one. He went back to his room to retrieve his guernsey. Beside the doorframe was a tiny nail surrounded by the faint outline of where a small key once hung.

11

Not long after Maggie had left with Malcolm, Nick Cantwell had arrived and dispersed the employees, guaranteeing them that there was nothing to be concerned about and that Tracy would surely turn up, likely having just gone to the nearest town for supplies.

He encouraged them to go about their day and get the Matthias Room ready for the next round of author readings, slated to start in less than an hour.

Jacob wasn't as easily subdued as his coworkers and tried to approach Nick to ask about Maggie and Malcolm, but Nick had already moved on to prepping the rest of the day's events.

Instead, Jacob found Monica on her way down for breakfast and pulled her aside to update her on what was happening, directly disregarding the orders laid out by Nick.

"Malcolm is missing?" Her tone carried more confusion than concern.

"Well, I don't really know," Jacob confessed. "Tracy is missing, I think, and Malcolm went with Maggie to look for her and now they're not back and Nick is just telling everyone to ignore it all."

"How long have they been missing?"

Jacob's shoulders dropped. He knew how the next bit

would sound.

"Like twenty minutes."

Monica didn't say anything to Jacob at this. She could see in his look that as he said it out loud, he realized he might be overreacting and there was no need for her to confirm it for him. Still, he was concerned, and she would help how she could.

They sat and she coaxed a more in-depth breakdown of events from the bellhop and while she didn't land at his level of panic, she did feel like something was off.

"I'll tell you what," she felt she had an acceptable offer. "There's another set of readings beginning in a few minutes. If Malcolm isn't back by the time it's over, then we sound the alarms. Okay?"

"Yeah, that sounds alright," he relented, and she decided to change the subject.

"Malcolm mentioned last night that you're a writer too?"

"Kind of, I mean, not like you guys. I'm trying."

"And you're giving Malcolm one of your stories to read?"

"That's the plan. I stayed up last night trying to finish it up."

"Well, when you're ready I'd like to take a look too!"

"Okay, sure!" Jacob suspected that Monica might be just making the offer to appease him and calm him down a bit, but he really didn't care.

"Great! The next panel is about to start, I should pop in there. Are you coming?"

"I'll be by in a bit!" He was back on the clock today.

Monica left him and got back to the Matthias Room just in time for the first reading of the day…

MERMAID COVE
Tanith Frost

Every town has its secrets.

The young man paused, pen poised over his paper. The ideas were there; the question was how to relate them in writing. In one sense, it didn't matter—no one would see what he wrote. But it felt good to mark it down, even if he had to work by lamplight in his parents' draughty attic so no one would know what he was thinking. He wore an old quilt like a shawl and pulled it tighter around his shoulders before he set the pen down again.

Most towns have skeletons in their closets. Mermaid Cove has... something else. Something hungry. The Cove hasn't taken a victim in almost a decade. Is that why we had such a slow summer? Why the older folks are putting up storm windows when I don't remember them doing it any autumn before?

The wind whipped around the eaves, whispering a promise of the hard winter to come. The young man shivered then reached for his battered old notebook. Its silver coils strained with his notes, photocopies he'd taken from old school projects, and photos of photos he'd found all over town.

The archives had burned down before he was born, but everyone owned a piece of history here.

He swallowed hard and wrote the words that had kept him

awake since he'd begun taking his questions seriously just a few months before.

Ten years. No one talks about it, but they know it's past time. What happens if the sea grows too hungry?

And what becomes of our souls if we feed it?

Spindly pine trees whipped past the side windows as Alex pressed her foot harder on the gas pedal of the rental she'd picked up at the airport almost an hour before—hours later than her flight was supposed to land. She'd meant to arrive in Mermaid Cove around lunchtime, but bad weather in Toronto had held her back. Now she'd be lucky to make it before supper.

Her foot descended again, and the speedometer crept toward 120 km/h. She hadn't seen a cop since she'd left the divided highway behind well outside St. John's, but she kept an eye out.

Alex's teeth clicked painfully together as the car jolted over a pothole. She muttered a curse, then glanced at the stack of papers on the passenger seat.

"Sorry, Gran," she muttered to the photo paper-clipped to the top of the stack. The silver-haired woman in the picture smiled back, beaming like she hadn't a care in the world—not her granddaughter's filthy tongue, and certainly not any knowledge that at that very moment her own clock had been running out.

Alex passed a sign indicating that she should take the next exit for Mermaid Cove and slowed the vehicle. As the road curved around a wall of rock, the view opened up. Afternoon sunlight sparkled off the waters surrounding a small island, and for a moment it was all too easy to imagine real mermaids frolicking in the water. Alex's breath caught in her throat.

This was what Gran came here for.

Gran had vanished ten years ago. The trip to Newfoundland had been her return to adventure, her first solo voyage since Gramps' death the year before. She'd sent Alex letters gushing about the scenery, the kindness of the people, the pubs she'd visited along the way. And then... nothing. Her last letter had mentioned a planned stop in Mermaid Cove to try to catch a glimpse of the legendary creatures.

According to police reports she'd made it. She'd gone on the boat tour.

And then she was gone.

Alex tightened her grip on the steering wheel. Everything was in her notes under Gran's picture, but *everything* didn't amount to much. In the end, Gran had been written off as a tourist who was swept away by a rogue wave. Tragic, but no one's fault.

But for Alex, the wound had never closed. There had been no body to bury, and something was still begging to be laid to rest. She'd always intended to come out to follow Gran's steps. There was no chance that what she did over the next few days would bring Gran back to her, but maybe visiting this place would finally let her heart settle.

Alex dropped to the speed limit as she drove onto the causeway.

She'd meant for her first stop the be the bed and breakfast, but there was no time for that when businesses would soon be closing for the day. Instead, she'd head straight for Beaumont's Boat Tours and hope she wasn't too late to speak to Mariel and Benjamin—the last people to see Gran alive.

Mermaid Cove was, as Gran's last letter had gleefully hoped, a charming village perched high on the rocky shore at the edge of the ocean. It didn't quite give the impression of being trapped in time, but it came close enough. If the siding on the buildings was plastic it at least looked like wood, and the electric streetlights were shaped like old gas lamps. Alex leaned over the wheel and craned her neck to take it all in.

An older woman, her silver hair pulled back into a bun, stood from where she'd been pruning her roses. She frowned against the sun then offered a wave as Alex passed.

But when Alex looked back at her in the mirror the woman stood with one hand pressed to her chest, eyes closed, lips moving as though in prayer.

Alex's GPS told her to make a left onto Old Cove Road, which followed the edge of the water at the T-intersection just ahead. She waited for a few slow-moving cars and an ATV to pass before she took her turn.

The road sloped down toward a dense cluster of shops and restaurants. Alex drove slowly, noting the signs in front of the businesses. All of them had a nautical theme, from Wavy Day Gift Emporium to a waterfront coffee shop that had taken the daring risk of placing a white mermaid on a green background in their logo. There were mermaids everywhere, painted on signs, sculpted from stone, and wrought in iron on a pair of lampposts outside of a small, white building marked TOWN HALL.

All along the street, folks stopped what they were doing to watch Alex's car roll past. Some raised a hand to greet the stranger. Most smiled or nodded.

Gran had said Newfoundland was a friendly place, but something about this place seemed strange, too eager to Alex's city brain.

The road curved and descended again toward a marina cradled at the end of the cove. And there, in front of a squat red building, stood a sign with another mermaid painted on it—this one a buxom brunette wearing nothing but strategically placed starfish, her hands held out to offer a bounty of gold coins.

BEAUMONT'S BOAT TOURS
Whales, Mermaids, Birds
Benjamin and Mariel Beaumont, proprietors

Gravel crunched under the tires as Alex pulled into the parking lot out front. She left the car and climbed wide steps to the porch, pausing to examine the CLOSED sign hanging from the railing. Layers of webbing covered it, and a clump of spiderlings clustered near one corner. Alex blew gently on the dark mass, scattering them.

Only September, but the place had been closed for some time.

Alex knocked at the door and waited. When no one answered she walked back down the steps and followed a well-worn path around the side of the building. An enclosed porch with a white door and a narrow staircase leading up to it jutted out from the side of the building.

Two signs had been taped to the inside of the window.

PRIVATE RESIDENCE.
NO SOLICITORS.

Alex took a deep breath and knocked, and a minute later a face, its surface a map of fine lines, appeared in the window. The woman frowned at Alex but opened the door a crack.

"Yes?"

"Mariel Beaumont?" Alex stuck out her right hand. "Alex Anderson. My grandmother was the woman who was taken by a rogue wave here ten years ago." She'd practiced this speech in her mind a hundred times. "I'm retracing her steps, and according to the police your boat tour was her last stop before the beach."

Mariel was what Gran would have called "a handsome woman," but her guarded expression gave her the kind of hardness Alex associated with depression era portraits. Still, she held the door open wider, standing in the doorway to the rest of the house and giving Alex room to step into the porch and out of the sun.

"Do you have a minute to answer a few questions?" Alex asked.

"I've had plenty of them for some time now." Mariel leaned against the doorframe. "It's been a hard year. Benjamin's been too sick to go out and I can't manage tours by myself. I've never told the stories like he does." She gazed past Alex out a little window that gave a view of the boats and the water. "S'pose I should be glad for a bit of company. Gets lonely, doesn't it?"

Alex wasn't sure whether she was meant to answer, so she offered a sympathetic smile instead.

"Not sure what I can tell you that I didn't tell the police," Mariel said. "What is it you're looking to know?"

Alex hesitated. She'd planned this part out, too, but it sounded silly now.

"I'm just following her steps, making sense of it," she said.

"They claim Gran went down to the beach alone, that no one actually saw her swept away. Was she warned of the danger?"

"Yuh." Mariel sucked the word in on her breath. "We always warned them not to go alone. Town's got signs up now."

Alex frowned. "That's the part that troubles me, I think. Gran was... she loved the idea of adventure, but she wasn't one to take stupid risks."

Mariel smiled sadly. "You'd understand if you could hear how Benjamin told his stories. About the beginnings of this town, how the sisters—the mermaids, that is—saved a handful of sailors from drowning when every other soul on their ship was lost to a wreck, how they offer their blessings to the town to this very day..." She paused. "That is, they always have."

"But this year was hard," Alex prompted when she said nothing more.

Mariel nodded. "The tides will change, though. They always do. The sisters have never abandoned us before."

Alex frowned. She'd come expecting a kitschy gift shop, and the mermaid theme of the town had seemed appropriate enough, something to give the town a distinct flavour and draw the tourists in, but Mariel spoke like a true believer.

"I hope things turn around for you soon," Alex said.

"Oh, I think they will." Mariel smiled again, and for a moment her dark eyes were flat, shark-like. Alex blinked, and the effect was gone. "Would you like a cookie before you go, dear? I just baked them this morning. Molasses."

"Thanks."

Mariel turned and went deeper into the house. She walked with a hitch in her step—not quite a limp, but a favouring of her left leg.

The inside of the house beyond the doorway was dim, and

cool air drifted out.

"I don't suppose I could speak to your husband?" Alex called.

Mariel didn't answer, and Alex stepped into the house to ask again.

She stopped, struck still and speechless as her eyes adjusted to the darkness of the living room.

The walls were painted a deep grey-blue, the curtains at the big side window drawn tight. On the opposite side of the room a handsome stone fireplace stood cold and dead, the emptiness of its black maw in stark contrast to the mantel above, where a profusion of *things* lay in bountiful disarray.

In fact, every surface in the room, from the antique sofa to the wooden chest being used as a coffee table—both of which looked old and water-damaged, like they'd been hauled up from a shipwreck—was covered in baubles.

Flotsam and jetsam, Alex thought. It looked like an underwater treasure trove filled with glass bottles, cutlery, chipped bowls and vases. A pile of fishnet was piled in one corner, and a rusted anchor leaned against the wall. And above the fireplace, a framed oil portrait depicted a mermaid with dark eyes and shining brunette hair—the same one as on the sign outside, maybe, but in gorgeous, lifelike detail.

A chill crept up Alex's spine like cold seaweed brushing over her skin, and she took a deep breath to calm her racing pulse. The air was heavy, damp, and smelled of sickness.

Or worse.

Calm down, she ordered herself. But her heart still pounded.

This wasn't a show put on for the tourists. It wasn't even true belief. It was obsession.

"What did you say, dear?"

Alex spun around to face Mariel, who stood in the doorway to a brightly lit kitchen, a cookie in a plastic baggie in one hand.

"I, uh—I was wondering whether your husband was available to talk."

Mariel swallowed hard. "He hasn't been capable of conversation for some time, love. If it's any consolation, I doubt he'd remember more than I do." She held out the cookie, and Alex accepted it. "Be careful if you go down to the beach."

"I will. Thank you."

The mermaid in the picture seemed to be laughing at her.

She backed into the entryway. It felt like surfacing, like she'd left behind an underwater mausoleum. It was all too easy to imagine a drowned sailor shambling out after her. She'd intended to ask more questions, to ask to see the guest book, to get help retracing Gran's exact steps. Now all she wanted to do was leave.

"I wish you luck in finding what you're looking for," Mariel said behind her. "May the blessings of the mermaids be with you."

"And also with you," Alex said, feeling like she was in church. The sunlight on her face as she stepped outside did feel like a blessing, and her heartbeat slowed.

She reached the bottom of the steps before one last question occurred to her. "Which way is the—" she began, turning.

But Mariel had already retreated into her home and closed the door behind her.

By the time Alex was in her car, driving back up the hill toward the parking area over the beach, she had nearly convinced herself she'd overreacted.

Sure, Mariel was odd. Some people just really got into their work, that was all.

But it was hard to shake the ocean-deep chill or the creeping unease that had touched her in the house.

She parked in the lot at the top of the cliff above the beach and walked to the low fence at the edge, marvelling at sunlight that lit up the waves and warmed her skin. She slipped her jacket off and laid it over the railing then leaned over for a glimpse of the beach below.

It wasn't, as she'd expected, a sandy beach but a stretch of round rocks with low waves lapping against them. To her right, closer to the open ocean, the beach turned to flat, rocky land that jutted up from the water.

The fence was lined with red and white signs reading DANGER - UNSUPERVISED BEACH, ACCESS PROHIBITED.

Alex was glaring at one of the signs as though she could spite it into submission when someone cleared their throat behind her.

"No lifeguards on duty after August 31."

Alex turned to find a young man of maybe eighteen standing several metres back. Thick hair flopped forward over his eyes, and dark-rimmed glasses had slid down his nose as he looked toward his feet. He pushed them back up and smiled awkwardly.

"It's nice down there but dangerous." The young man came closer to stand beside her. "You don't want to go down there. Trust me."

"Not unsupervised, anyway." Alex held out her right hand. "Alex Anderson."

"Roy Mercer." His handshake was as uncertain as his eye contact. "Not a qualified lifeguard."

"I suspected not." Alex sighed. "My grandmother was a victim of a rogue wave ten years ago. I'd like to go down, just for a minute."

"You can't."

She smiled. "How often do those waves come along?"

"Three in my lifetime, maybe."

"Then I like my odds." She turned and headed toward the wooden steps that led down to the beach, stepping over the rope that had been tied between the posts at the top.

Roy grabbed her arm, and she turned back.

"Miss, you really shouldn't." His cheeks had darkened. "It's..."

"It's what?"

He pulled both hands through his hair, making it stand up in wild clumps. "There's something down there that takes people. But it's not waves."

Alex frowned, then chuckled. "I get it. How much for *your* mermaid tour?"

Roy's brow furrowed. "What? No. I just—look." He dug through his bag and pulled out a battered coil-bound notebook that fell open to a taped-in page covered in faded notes and drawings.

The drawings were nothing like the depictions of mermaids she'd seen around town. These had the same basic shape—fishy tails, human heads, torsos, and arms, but that was where the similarity ended. These ladies of the sea had hair that hung in clumps, claw-like nails, and gaping mouths packed with fangs. Their eyes, wide and white, stared off the page like those of deep-sea anglerfish. She shivered.

"Has anyone told you how the Cove got its name?" Roy asked.

"Mariel said mermaids saved some sailors."

"Not exactly." Roy flipped to another photocopied page, this one covered in tiny handwriting. "This is a letter from one of the sailors, describing the horror of it. The original burned with the old museum fifty years ago, but there are still copies."

Alex eased herself down a step, away from Roy. He spoke like Mariel. Like he really believed.

Roy looked out over the water. "They used to call it Hag Cove. Not like the ghostly hags that are said to haunt some parts of the island. *Sea* hags. And they didn't save anyone. The sailors who survived were the ones who escaped having those teeth rip the flesh from their living bones." He gestured toward the village. "They changed the town's name so long ago that no one remembers exactly when. All these images of beautiful mermaids sunning themselves on the rocks, as though these creatures would ever expose themselves to warmth and light..."

"Then I guess I'm safe." Alex looked toward the sunny sky and forced a smile. "I'm just going to take a peek. Stay here if you want."

She turned and hurried down the steps, her white sneakers flashing over weathered wooden beams. No other footsteps followed, and she was glad of it.

Her chest tightened as she pieced together what the kid was implying. Sailors drowned, flesh stripped from bones... Alex had never felt entirely comfortable with the rogue wave story to explain Gran's disappearance, but the alternative Roy was offering was impossible, and too horrible to think of.

The air was cooler on the beach, shadowed as it was by the cliff above. Alex wished she hadn't left her jacket behind.

She walked over the stones, letting them roll under her feet. Salt on the air stung her nose, along with the dank smell of rotting seaweed above the tide line. Finally, she stepped up onto the flat rocks. She'd seen pictures of them—this was where they said Gran was swept away.

She looked up, expecting a view of sparkling water and the boats sheltering in the cove.

Instead, she found the air filled with fog so thick she couldn't see the cliff behind her. It moved in thick swirls, pressing closer. She couldn't hear even a hint of the cars passing on the street above.

Then a new sound reached her. Singing, many voices in chaotic harmony, coming from the water.

She stepped closer, though her heart raced, and her mind screamed at her to run. Her body seemed to be under someone else's control, and as the voices grew louder a strange calm came over her mind. She found that she cared less, even though her body still said she was afraid.

She peered into the water. It was deep here, and dark. Pale shapes moved in the depths, writhing and twisting together before coming apart. Indistinct—the water had grown murky, and now a smell of rotten flesh rose to meet her. She tried to pull back and found she couldn't. One of the shapes brushed against the surface, almost—but not quite—breaking its tension, bowing the water upward.

Sea hags.

She tried to scream but couldn't find her voice.

Closer, the song urged—not in English, but Alex understood. *Such wonders we will show you when you visit our home in the dark and the deep.*

She felt her balance shifting, threatening to pitch her into the water.

Then she was hauled backwards, a hand on each of her arms. She lashed out, and her fists connected with bony flesh.

"Hey!" Roy cried. He fell backward, pulling Alex down with him onto the rocks and away from the water. He was on his feet again seconds later, still pulling her by the arm. "Come on!"

Alex didn't argue. The voices were no longer singing, but screaming, and she found that their control over her muscles was gone.

Something breached the surface. Alex didn't stop long enough to let her brain process what it was seeing. She grabbed onto Roy's clammy hand and let him pull her with him through the fog.

Gravel slid under Alex's feet as she raced for the car and skidded around its back end. She'd left Roy far behind by the time she jammed her foot down on the brake and pressed the button next to the steering wheel.

Nothing. She held the fob close to the starter and tried again.

A knock on the window made her jump as her brain filled with visions of sleek monsters with clotted hair and lantern eyes.

"It's me!" Roy yelled. "Miss Anderson, please, it's fine! They can't get up here."

Alex took a shaky breath and leaned her head back. Slowly the white spots that had crowded her vision began to fade. The window wouldn't open, so she cracked the door instead.

"Car's dead." Her voice shook in a way that frightened her.

"I know." Roy's skin had turned ashen. "The sisters don't want you to leave."

Alex stared blankly at him for a few moments before she realized he was talking about the things in the water. She gripped the wheel tight.

"The sisters? Or you people?" She shoved the car door open, sending Roy stumbling back, and looked around. She expected to see the rest of the townsfolk circled around the car and closing in, a terrible cult of the mermaid come to claim their next sacrifice, but they were still alone. "What is it with this place? Do you feed those things? Worship them?"

Roy adjusted his glasses and raised his hands in surrender. "Nobody here wants to hurt you."

Alex glared at him, arms crossed, the car door still open in case she needed to lock herself inside.

"Fine. You deserve the truth." Roy lowered his hands. A cutting wind whipped up from the water. "You want to get a coffee and talk?"

"I'd rather call someone about this." Alex gestured at the car and resisted the urge to kick it.

Roy reached into his pocket and held out an old flip phone. "Use mine. I imagine yours is dead."

Alex checked. Sure enough, the trusty smartphone she'd charged overnight was now flashing 1%. As she watched, it shut down completely.

She grabbed Roy's and stalked away, peering down over the fence to the beach below as she held the phone to her ear. No fog. No monsters. No singing.

Like she'd imagined all of it.

A few minutes later she walked back to Roy and handed him his phone.

"Pileup on the highway," she said dully. "Tow-trucks are

tied up." Alex slumped back against the car. "I could call the police."

"I imagine they're busy with that wreck." Roy's brow furrowed. "'*Mermaids are trying to eat me*' probably doesn't rank quite as high on their list of priorities."

A harsh laugh caught in Alex's throat as she looked deep into Roy's eyes. "Is that what's happening here? Really?"

He shifted uncomfortably. "I mean, there's more to it."

She'd scoffed at his claims, but that... whatever it was on the beach had proved he wasn't delusional or a liar. And he did seem like he wanted to help.

"Coffee, then," she said. The wind was digging its icy fingers under her sweater, and her need to get away from the water hadn't lessened at all.

A few minutes later they sat in the cozy little coffee shop with its view of the water, steaming mugs in their hands. Alex sat with her back to it, and noticed that Roy kept looking over her shoulder, watching.

"So what do I do?" she asked, keeping her voice low. There were only a few other people in the shop, but the bearded man who stood behind the counter had been drying the same cup since they'd entered, acting like he wasn't keeping an eye on them.

Roy chewed his lower lip. "I don't know. Honestly, Miss—"

"Alex, please. You saved my life; I think we can skip the formalities."

"Sure. Alex. Anyway, I've only really been studying this since graduation. I don't remember when your grandmother was... lost..." He trailed off and looked at his hands.

Lost. Alex thought back to what he'd said about the sailors, about the sea hags' sharp teeth and claws that tore flesh from bone. She thought of her grandmother and how there were worse fates than being dragged to sea by a rogue wave. Bitter coffee rose in her throat.

"But?" she asked.

"There are people who know more. But they're not going to tell you."

"So, tell me what *you* know." Alex strained to keep her voice even. She wanted to yell at him, shake him, anything to get him to spit it out.

Roy reached for his notebook, glanced at the fellow behind the counter, and seemed to decide against it. "I told you about the sailors who survived, about them calling it Hag Cove. Somewhere along the line, though, people settled here. Not in spite of the hags, I think, but because of them."

"Mermaid blessings," Alex whispered, remembering what Mariel had said. *The tides will turn. They always do.*

"Precisely. This town does well most of the time. Weirdly prosperous even during downturns, except when it's been too long since the mermaids took a human to feed on."

Alex shivered. "A sacrifice?"

He met her gaze without hesitation. "Exactly. They say the town will be destroyed if the sisters don't get what's due to them. The sisters are generous when the town pleases them, but they have a temper that no one wants to test."

Alex leaned closer. "Say this is true. Say someone in the past made a deal with the sisters—flesh in exchange for blessings and protection, and it's still going on today." She tried not to think of Gran as she said it. "Deals are broken all the time. We just need to find out how to do it."

Roy's fingers drummed against the tabletop. "Everyone here in town knows a little about what happens, but I'd be willing to place a bet on who would know the most."

"Mariel."

Roy nodded. "She's... she knows a lot about them. More than the tourists ever hear, I'd bet."

Alex felt the blood drain from her face as she imagined every treasure in that house being given as blessings from sea hags. In exchange for what? Delivering outsiders to them?

It sounded insane—or would have before her visit to the beach. Now all she could think was how much sense it made for the people here to offer tourists instead of their own citizens.

She studied the young man who sat across from her. He was obviously scared out of his mind.

"Why are you helping me, Roy?"

"Because this sucks." He spoke bravely, but Alex caught a slight tremble in his voice. "Because I've never been okay with this, but people like me, if they try to leave and tell anyone... bad things happen. I guess helping you end this is my only way out, too."

"Good enough." It wasn't, not really, but it was all Alex had to work with. "So, if we go talk to her now—"

She stopped. The barista was stalking toward them, brow furrowed.

"Roy, your mother just called," he said. "Benjamin Beaumont has died. Mum needs you home to start cooking."

Roy exchanged a quick glance with Alex.

"I'm kind of in the middle of something."

The man, whose nametag read CARL, frowned. "She was distraught. Better get going, finish this up later."

He left them but didn't go far enough to be out of earshot.

Roy's smile looked forced, and Alex wished he hadn't made the effort. "Okay, see you later, then," he said, a little too loudly. "Give me time to deal with mom, we'll meet at eight." He leaned in to whisper. "That'll give Mariel a while to get deep into her cups, too, loosen her tongue. I hate to do this while she's in mourning, but maybe, now that it's too late for Benjamin, she'll think about helping you."

Roy gathered his things then headed out after flashing her a concerned look.

No one harassed Alex in the street as she walked back to sit in her car. It seemed like the safest place for now—a small pocket of space that was hers and not the village's.

Of course they didn't bother me, she thought as she tried to relax into the driver's seat, her eyes firmly fixed on the top of the stairs in case something decided to try to climb up to claim her. She tried to start the car again. Nothing happened.

They know damned well I'm not going anywhere.

Eight o'clock. The front room of Beaumont's Boat Tours was dark, but a light blazed in a window in the part Mariel now lived in alone.

The temperature had dropped as the sun went down. Alex hugged her arms tight around herself and paced the parking lot, waiting for Roy.

The air was still now, but wind chimes clanged gently on the porch. She stopped to listen, caught by the familiarity of it— almost a tune, disorganized harmonies...

She forgot the cold as a warm fog settled over her mind. A part of her was aware it was happening, and of how similar the chimes sounded to the singing she'd heard on the beach, but her ability to care faded.

Silly, she thought. *What singing? I imagined it.* Of course, something had moved under the surface of the water. Probably seaweed. Of course—

She bit down hard on her tongue, sinking into the pain, letting it bring her back to herself.

No. I remember what I saw.

But something wanted her to forget.

She peered behind her into the darkness. No sign of Roy. She'd promised to wait, but what if he wasn't coming?

What if he *couldn't* come?

Still feeling calmer than she knew she should, she climbed the steps at the side of the building.

She knocked. And waited.

It was several minutes before Mariel opened the door. She looked older than she had just a few hours ago, her face blotchy and tear-streaked.

"Well, look who's here," she said, her words slurred. "Come to pay your respects?"

"I have." Alex followed her in and closed the door, leaving it unlocked. "And to ask you a few more questions."

"Ah." Mariel collapsed into an old armchair and poured a fresh glass of rum from the half-empty bottle on the table beside her. "You want one?"

"I think not."

Mariel shrugged. "Suit yoursel'." She squinted at Alex. "Someone's been telling you stories, I suppose."

Alex crossed her arms. "Truer than you told me."

"I'd say. But not the *truest* stories." Mariel blinked, and a tear spilled from one eye. "Benjamin told visitors what he knew, see? Told them about beautiful mermaids, kind and protective..." Her chest hitched. "Bless his heart."

"What kind of deal with the sea hags brought their blessings and kept the town safe?" Alex asked. "And how do you end it? Because it *is* ending, Mariel. Tonight. No one else is going to suffer what Gran did. Especially not me."

Mariel pushed herself to her feet, stumbling slightly.

"You came here to follow yer gran'mudder's tracks. Let's do it. I'll take you on the boat, tell you whatever stories you want."

Alex laughed. "So you can toss me in as payment for whatever deal you people made with those devils?"

The door swung open and Roy stumbled in, his arms held behind him by Carl the coffee jockey. The older, larger man had no trouble steering the boy into the living room with his free arm while his other hand held a large hunting knife ready for action.

Alex's stomach sank.

"Found this one skulking around outside." Carl gave Roy a shake. "Told you to go home to your mother."

"There are always those who won't listen," Mariel said, her voice suddenly clear. Alex looked back and found her standing up straight, though she still limped as she walked toward Roy. "Our success depends on such a delicate balance," she said speaking softly to the wide-eyed young man. "Those who don't support it are a danger to our way of life and must be dealt with. You were warned."

Roy struggled, but Carl held him tight.

"Well?" Mariel looked back to Alex. "Shall we go for that boat ride? I'd say your friend's life depends on it."

Alex looked to Roy, searching eyes that were too bright against his sweaty skin.

"They'll kill me anyway," he said, the words coming out in a rush. "Run, before they—"

The handle of Carl's knife came down against Roy's temple and he slumped to the floor.

Alex turned and ran—not for the door Carl had entered by, but for one that looked like it led to the shop at the front of the house. She burst through it, boots pounding against the weathered wood floor, and crashed into a rack covered in keychains and necklaces. She shoved it aside, raced for the door, and turned each of the three locks before she tugged at the handle.

It wouldn't move.

Slow, heavy footsteps caught up with her. She bolted toward an ice cream bar that sat empty and silent at the far end of the room, but Carl caught the back of her jacket and hauled her close, his arm an iron bar pressing her to his chest.

Mariel smiled as she entered the room.

"Blessings of the mermaids on you, Carl," she said, and Alex felt him bow slightly. Mariel smiled, and her eyes were as deep and dark as the ocean itself. "Tie them up, please. We're going for a little ride."

The boat thumped over the waves, jostling the pair of captives and pressing them against the back of the boat. Mariel stood just ahead in an open-backed cabin, steering and humming a shanty. Alex supposed Benjamin and the tourists would have stood out front during tours, him spinning his tales while Mariel piloted the boat.

Roy hadn't awakened since he'd taken his hit to the head. Alex had been conscious for all of it, though, struggling against Carl's iron grip as he hauled her to the boat, trying to get to her feet to jump out like a landed fish onto the dock. But it had been over the moment Mariel had ordered Carl to leave them and pulled away from the dock.

Alex might have got herself overboard, but there was no way to swim with her hands tied. She focused instead on the rough rope that bound her hands—slowly rotating her wrists, widening the openings.

Icy water from the boat's deck soaked into her jeans.

"Story time," Mariel called back over her shoulder. The boat slowed suddenly, though the engine still rumbled. Roy moaned and opened his eyes.

She grabbed Roy by the back of his coat and dragged him across the deck, toward the front of the boat, then left him to return for Alex.

"I'll walk," Alex said. The boat still pitched on the slow waves, but she got to her knees, then got her feet under her. When she stumbled, Mariel made no move to catch her. Mariel bowed slightly at the waist and motioned for her to go ahead, and Alex walked, feeling like she was drunk, toward the bow.

Roy sat slumped on one of the benches that ran around the edge of the deck. Alex sat beside him and returned to work on the ropes.

"Once upon a time," Mariel said, and smiled. "Benjamin always liked to start that way. Once upon a time there were ladies of the sea who possessed great magic. Twelve sisters, each of them strong, and unstoppable when they combined their power. It was the kind of magic that could change the world if only someone offered them enough in return for their favours."

The boat rocked suddenly to one side. Alex's hands slipped, and the knots tightened again. Her heartbeat echoed in her ears.

"The sisters ate well in their undersea home but loved nothing more than the taste of human flesh. There's just something about the meat of a creature that's been raised in the light of the sun—something tender and warm. So, they sang to lure ships onto the rocks, or called storms to sink them on the high seas. Then they'd drag their prey down below."

She spoke as though she were spinning a tale of princesses and knights, true love and heroism, all soft and musical. Alex's stomach pitched like the boat.

"But one of the sisters, the youngest, had a weak heart. She found a sailor knocked out cold in a wreck and was so taken by his innocent beauty that she couldn't bear the thought of seeing him torn apart by her sisters. She returned him to land. Her sisters were enraged. They had brought the ship down fairly, and every soul aboard belonged to them."

"Was he a prince?" Alex asked, a hard edge in her voice.

Mariel gave her a sharp look, but she smiled. "Only in the youngest sister's mind. Good enough?"

Alex turned her left wrist again. *So close...*

"Good enough."

The water outside the boat churned like it was boiling. Alex dared a glance overboard and wished she hadn't. The roiling waves were filled with pale shapes moving through the moonlit water. Her breath caught in her throat.

"The sisters threatened to kill the youngest if she didn't return their prize to them," Mariel continued. "So, she made a deal with them—they would use their magic to make her human, and she would lure him back to the sea. She went to him. Spoke to him. He offered her food and conversation, and she warmed herself by his fire and in his bed. And in the end, she found that she couldn't give him to her sisters."

"Touching," Alex muttered. Beside her, Roy raised his head. His glasses had disappeared somewhere along the way and he squinted at Mariel, then at the water.

A hand appeared at the edge of the boat, pale-skinned, with fingernails that were more like talons. It gripped the wood tight, carving deep claw-marks into it before falling back into the water.

"God," Roy whispered.

"She knew they would never be safe if she didn't repay her sisters," Mariel continued. "So, when a stranger came to town, she lured him to the water instead. The sisters dragged him away and asked the youngest to return to them. She refused. Instead, she made another deal. The sisters would continue to sustain her with their collective magic. They would protect her town and her prince, offering gifts and blessings to those in the town who made these small sacrifices.

"But it's harder now." Mariel spat on the deck. "The world watches, and it's harder to make people disappear. We became afraid to act, we left it for too long, and look what's happened to poor Benjamin."

Roy took a deep breath.

"Don't," Alex said, but she was too late. He launched himself off the bench, head low, running straight for Mariel. She stepped to the side, but his shoulder caught her, spinning her around. Mariel crouched, grabbed Roy around the waist, and threw him over the side.

"Roy!" Alex heard her own scream as though it came from a distance, drowned as it was beneath the delighted shrieks that rose from the water. She tugged again at her bonds. Once, twice... the ropes held. She forced herself to relax, twisted, and her left hand came free, then her right.

It was too late to save Roy. But that didn't make it too late for her.

She ran at Mariel, hoping to catch her while she was distracted. But Mariel turned back, grinning. Her eyes were bright, and she looked twenty years younger than she had moments ago. When she darted to the side there was no limp, no sign of stiffness or pain.

All thought except survival disappeared. The shrieks and wails from the water continued, but Alex barely heard them. She and Mariel circled each other on the deck of the little boat.

"There's nowhere to run," Mariel said, smiling, her eyes

black and cold. "They've marked you, and they will have you."

"We'll see."

Alex faked a lunge to the left, then darted into the cabin. The little room was filled with useful things—more rope, a first aid kit, a fire extinguisher, life jackets.

An axe.

She tugged the weapon free of its moorings and scrambled back toward Mariel.

She was right. There was nowhere to run. Nowhere to hide... unless Alex could get control of the boat and make it back to land.

Alex ran at Mariel, axe held high, and swung it downward. Mariel dodged, but the axe caught her arm and she screamed. Alex's blood turned cold. It wasn't the scream of a woman, but of the hags.

Mariel bared her teeth and ran at Alex, all composure and cold humour gone. Alex backed toward the side of the boat and dodged at the last second, copying Mariel's own move, ducking and grabbing to send her over the edge.

But Roy had been tied up, easy pickings. Mariel twisted as she fell, grabbing onto the side of the boat.

"Here's your sacrifice!" Alex shouted, bringing the axe down, aiming for Mariel's hand. She let go and splashed into the water, disappearing into the foam and the darkness.

Alex pulled in deep breaths of the frigid air and waited for a wave of dizziness to pass. A hard stitch had formed in her side—one she hadn't noticed in the moment, but that now felt like someone was cutting into her with a scalpel.

The hags swarmed, coiling around each other like snakes.

"Take her," Alex gasped. "And leave me alone."

She hurried back to the cabin. The boat was still running,

and every control clearly marked. The engine roared and moved forward—more slowly than Alex liked, but she made herself hold back. She'd only run smaller vessels before, and on calmer waters, and couldn't afford to capsize now. She turned and headed back toward the lights on shore.

Something hit the boat hard, rocking it. Alex gritted her teeth and looked over the side.

One of the hags breached the surface, graceful as a dolphin but monstrous in form, seaweed-like hair flying out behind her. Alex screamed.

The eyes were now white and wide, the skin deathly pale, but the face was Mariel's. The youngest sister, returned to her true form.

Against her better judgement, Alex urged the old boat to go faster.

The engine stalled and died. The sea, too, fell quiet, the water smooth as glass.

One twisted hand appeared over the side of the boat, followed by another. Mariel hauled herself up and dropped to the deck, a puddle of sea water spreading around her as her tail twisted, pushing her forward as her arms dragged her toward the cabin.

Alex took up the axe again and ran at her, screaming. Mariel's jaw swung downward, opening her mouth impossibly wide, revealing a mouth filled with teeth ready to tear and maim.

Alex aimed for her face and swung the axe.

She didn't see the long, muscular tail whipping toward her until it was too late. The impact knocked the air from her lungs and lifted her, sending her flying off the boat. Alex hit the water with a painful slap and felt herself dragged beneath the surface.

She gasped, taking in water that burned. She screamed, and

no sound came out.

When she opened her eyes, everything was blurry.

The burning, crushing sensation in her chest went on, but her mind remained clear.

Why am I not—

A searing pain tore into her left calf, and she tried to scream again. She pulled away, and someone laughed.

Mariel appeared in front of her, close enough to see, to touch. Alex tried to reach out to claw at her eyes but found she couldn't move.

"Don't worry," Mariel said, her voice clear even beneath the water. "You won't die. Not right away. My sisters have learned that when you start with the extremities and use a little magic, you can make a human last a long time."

More pain, bright and searing, from her left wrist. Alex sucked in another salt water breath and tried to scream, and Mariel laughed. She grabbed Alex's arm and held it in front of her, showing off the ragged stump where her hand had been.

"Maybe not so long this time," she mused, and licked the stump with a long, writhing tongue. "It has been so long since they fed."

She released her, and Alex sank into the depths, surrounded by a mass of tails and claws and biting teeth.

She wished she could drown, but the mermaids withheld their blessing.

Salt water splatted against the floor, dripping from Mariel's clothes as she entered the home she'd shared with her prince for over two hundred years—one she'd filled with treasures from the sea, with memories.

With love she'd do anything to protect.

She carried a moon snail shell, large enough that she needed both hands to support its weight and that of the water her sisters had filled it with. She walked with strong, certain steps.

The first sacrifice had been enough to restore her youth and her health, and for that she was grateful. But this time she'd asked for more and could only hope the second sacrifice had been enough.

She entered the bedroom and sat on the edge of the bed. Benjamin lay as she'd left him, his head on the pillow, his lips dry and pulled tight against his teeth, the eyes beneath his closed eyelids sunken deep in his skull.

"I'm sorry, my love," she whispered, and held the lip of the shell to his mouth to pour the water in a little at a time. "I took too long. I swear it won't happen again, no matter what the cost."

She tipped the shell, pouring the last of the blessed water into her beloved's lips, then smoothed back the hair from his death-pale brow.

Her sisters had made no promises, only bade her take the water and use the magic as she wished. There had been no question in her heart of what she'd wanted.

She drew a deep breath and leaned in to place a kiss on his cold lips.

"Come back to me," she whispered. "To warmth, to sunlight, to life."

Those were her gifts to him. He never had to know what the mermaids' blessings truly cost.

"Sisters, please," she whispered, and held the shell to Benjamin's lips again. One last drop of sea water slid out, and she set the shell aside.

Benjamin's chest hitched, and his eyes opened.

12

Malcolm hadn't shown up during the reading. Neither had Maggie or Tracy. Monica had been watching the doors hoping they would appear, and she wouldn't have to fulfill her promise to Jacob. Instead, he burst in almost as quickly as the applause died down to hold her to it.

"Did they show?" he asked, craning his neck to scan the room for any of the missing.

"No, but I still think it's too soon to be sounding the alarm bells." Before she could finish Jacob had already started making his way toward the stage.

"C'mon," he called over his shoulder.

She followed him as he stormed toward Nick, who was standing to the side of the stage, behind the wall of speakers and out of view of the crowd.

"Mr. Cantwell!" he called before Monica could catch and subsequently stop him.

"Yes, Jacob? How can I help you?"

"Malcolm Hennessey is missing," the bellhop blurted as Monica arrived at his side. "So are your sister and sister-in-law."

"Are they?" Nick's tone carried the same passive aggressive self-righteousness as his sister.

"Yes!"

"How long have they been 'missing?'" Cantwell was measured and reasoned and infuriating.

"Tracy since last night, Malcolm and Maggie since this morning."

"No, I'm afraid you're mistaken," Nick stated as he gestured behind them. They turned to see Maggie Cantwell approaching.

"Were you looking for me?" she asked.

Jacob's mouth fell open.

"Yes, our young friend's imagination had cooked up a story that you had gone missing." The siblings spoke as if Jacob wasn't standing there.

"Oh, that's right. You're a writer, aren't you, Jacob?" Maggie inquired.

He stammered for a moment before Monica stepped in to confirm.

"Yes, he was actually working on a story for Malcolm."

"That's perfect! Mr. Hennessey, Malcolm, had to leave urgently and his reading is coming up next," Maggie stated. "Do you think you could fill in for him and read from your story?"

The succession of shocks had just left Jacob speechless, so Monica once again stepped in for him.

"I'm sure he could." She turned to him. "Jacob, do you think you're ready?"

"I, uh, I mean, uh…" He leaned back and looked out at the awaiting crowd gathered for Malcolm's reading. The concern he'd had for the missing author now morphed into stage fright. "Why did Malcolm have to leave?"

"I'm not entirely sure," Maggie replied. "I had to step away and take a call from Tracy, who had to head into Corner Brook for supplies. By the time I was off the phone and informed him she'd be back this evening, he excused himself, apologized for having to miss his reading, and left to retrieve his things and leave."

"Oh." Jacob now found himself offended that Malcolm left without saying anything too him. Partially because of the unresolved mystery, but mostly because it left him unable to pass along his story.

That settled it for him. If Malcolm was going to leave without giving him the opportunity to share his work with him, he'd share it with everyone else.

"Okay, I'll do it. Can I print my story in the office?"

"Sure, hurry back though," Maggie said. "You don't want to keep your audience waiting.

Jacob bolted as Monica stood with the Cantwells.

"Ms. Weller, I'd imagine you'd want to return to your seat to take in Jacob's story?" Nick asked.

She eyed the siblings suspiciously as she slowly turned and walked away. They returned her glare, albeit with grins that enraged her.

As she got back to her seat, Nick climbed the stairs to the stage and began vamping an introduction about how, unfortunately, Malcolm Hennessey had been called away and was unable to read from his work for them, but not to worry because their event was going to be able to exclusively premiere the work of a fresh and emerging voice in genre fiction.

Monica thought of the oddities in the transpiring events. That Malcolm, who only yesterday had driven across the island specifically to read at this event had left without completing the task. She was worried for him. Maggie was so prepared to debunk it all, quickly offering Jacob's story as a solution. It was almost too convenient.

As Nick stirred up fanfare, all heads swung to the door where Jacob timidly re-entered the room, a freshly printed manuscript trembling in his hands.

He crossed the room, stepped up on the stage to the mic, and took a deep breath…

NO CANDY
Mike Hickey

She wanted to do it alone.

"It would be scarier that way," she told her mom.

With the world in turmoil, six months into a pandemic that people were sick of referring to as "unprecedented," Zena's parents had opted out of taking her trick-or-treating. Her asthma had improved over the last couple of years, and she was relying on her puffers less and less, but it was decided that she was still too compromised to go door-to-door soliciting candy from strangers.

She was heartbroken until her dad came up with a compromise.

He had waded through the pandemic conspiracy theories and racism that seemed to populate his Facebook feed and discovered a post about an alternative idea, which he pitched to Zena. She responded with apprehensive acceptance that grew into excitement as the day drew closer.

It was basically a spooky version of an Easter Egg hunt. Zena and her mom would go out for the afternoon, finding some safe ways to keep her spirits high before stopping into McDonald's for their traditional Halloween dinner of Chicken McNuggets and that sickly sweet orange drink. While they were gone, her dad would decorate the house and hide candy throughout.

When she came home, he'd turn out the lights, pipe in some creepy sound effects, and she'd go through with a flashlight trying to find the treats.

But when they popped out of the car, she announced her intentions to go through the makeshift haunted house alone. That hadn't been part of the plan and her parents were weary to let her wander through the dark home by herself, but they relented, and the small girl ambled up the stairs in her Frankenstein's Monster costume. She turned back and waved to her parents, who were snapping photos on their phones, before opening the door with a creak and disappearing into the darkness.

Ruby Jenkins was leaning against the door of the car in a daze, her cardigan pulled tight around her to stave off the October chill as she absently watched leaves fall from the large sycamore at the edge of the parking lot across the street. She could have pulled into the lot but didn't want to step foot on any property belonging to the police department.

A whoosh startled her back to reality: the sound of a small girl, about Zena's age, kicking her foot through the pile of leaves that had accrued against the sidewalk along the edge of the street. There were two children, their mouths and noses hidden behind orange face masks with black jack-o'-lantern patterns on them. The boy was on the sidewalk carrying the large pumpkin they were undoubtedly on their way to carve, probably after arguing over whose mask they'd base the design on. It reminded Ruby of the afternoon she had spent with Zena in a pumpkin patch last year, trying to keep her busy while Jasper decorated the house, doing all the Halloween things she could think of to occupy their time and satiate her daughter's obsession with the holiday.

Her lips involuntarily curled into a smile thinking about the time they spent together, before remembering that it was the last time they'd spent together. Tears welled in her eyes, and the corners of her mouth trembled as they retreated as low as possible, but at that moment Jasper emerged from the door of the station. He waved to the cop who had led him out the door without turning back and began to scan the parking lot for Ruby. Seeing her parked on the street he started moving toward her, removing his disposable mask to reveal a tentative grin. She matched it, diverting her eyes as she walked around to the driver's side, wordlessly.

He sighed and shook his head. The tension wasn't necessary. He had been with Ruby when Zena seemingly evaporated inside their home, and he was the one who had spent the last year being dragged back and forth to the station for questioning. He was at the point where he almost wanted them to just charge him with his daughter's disappearance so he could prove his innocence in court and hopefully end the harassment he had been facing.

That didn't seem likely, though.

He was the one who had carefully turned their home into a haunt attraction complete with animatronics, strobing lightning, thick fog, and all the other spooky accoutrements required for a quality dark house, and he was the last one to enter the place before Zena went in alone and hadn't been seen since. But the thing that had constantly held up progress with the investigation was the supreme strangeness of it all.

The Jenkins were the ones who had called the police and helped lead them through the home. The property had been scoured and nothing was found to be suspicious, other than the lack of Zena.

The couple even had a solid alibi; just as Zena had entered the house, their neighbours, the Callahans, had come out to join them and had been standing on the sidewalk chatting with them until they had all considered how long she had been inside. In fact, it was Dale Callahan who'd gone into the house with Jasper to see what was taking her so long.

They had entered the house with Jasper calling out for her in the darkness but only hearing the cackling of witches playing through their audio system answer him. Before long, he and Dale were charging through the house turning on lights and searching rooms. It was seeing all the lights that brought Ruby and Marcia Callahan in, and when they met a panicked Jasper coming out of the basement the call to 911 was placed.

It had been isolated. No other children had gone missing that Halloween night. In fact, considering the collective cabin fever of everyone who had spent the bulk of the year locked down, it was a relatively uneventful October 31 for the constabulary. Three teenagers tried to slip out of a mini-mart with an eight-pack of beer under each of their costumes and the over-zealous shop clerk called it in. And when Arthur O'Grady's dog, Milo, had gotten out Arthur had tracked him to his neighbour, Mary Ellis', yard. She saw him snooping around and thought it was a prowler trying to sneak a peek and alerted the authorities. Otherwise, the local police only had the disappearance of Zena Jenkins to focus on.

The year that followed without any answers had been a trying one. The girl had simply evaporated into thin air.

The words seemed to absorb all the moisture in Jacob's mouth as he read them. He took a deep breath and tried to compose himself, but he started to cough, losing control. It took a sheer force of will to keep himself from hyperventilating, thinking of the connection between the story he'd crafted and the one he was now at the heart of.

Nick didn't want to watch one of his employees stand on a stage in front of an assembled crowd and cough uncontrollably at the first event being held since the onslaught of the global pandemic, so he uncharacteristically came to the rescue, rushing to Jacob with a glass and pitcher of water. Jacob brushed the outstretched glass aside and grabbed the pitched with two hands, quickly gulping down half the contents.

From the back of the room, while Jacob's tale was unfurling, Monica found herself caught in his narrative. She had mostly been humouring him through the weekend, but she was impressed with the young scribe's story so far. At the same time, when Jacob had come to a temporary halt, she thought the parallels between the narrative of someone disappearing without a trace on Halloween and the ongoing mysteries that had overtaken their weekend were a bit concerning.

Satiated, Jacob continued his story.

While her parents were grappling with grief and allegations, Zena Jenkins was wading through a world she had come to refer to as The Darker.

In it, she was in an approximation of their home, the same as she had known it, but in a constant haze of gloom. She took some solace in the familiarity. After the year stuck in the house through lockdowns, she had joked with her dad that she would have been able to navigate the house in the dark and now that had been proven true.

Less comforting was the state of limbo she was existing in, just hanging on to our world enough to remind her what she was missing. She could see the shadows of her parents and hear them calling for her, but their voices were distant echoes that came from no source but every direction, filling her head.

Malcolm Hennessey stood in the back of the room listening to Jacob's story. At least he thought it was Jacob's story. He couldn't see who was telling it, just a shadowy form that resembled Jacob and he was so focused on deciphering the words, he couldn't deduce whose voice it was that echoed around him. He just knew that whoever they were, they were describing the strange state he had been in since the door to Tracy's office slammed behind him, and that chilled him to the bone.

The Matthias Room was plunged into darkness for the second time in as many days for him, only this had more permanence. It wasn't the darkness of the blackout; it was more akin to when your eyes adjust to the night. The room was there, and it was the same, and he could see it while he shouldn't have been able to. But the people were globs of shadow, undistinguishable aside from their basic forms, and he was trying to rely on his memory of the people he had met to try and formulate who was who.

Monica was standing next to him, that he knew for sure. He was also sure it was Jacob who was telling the story on stage, but he was basing that solely on the premise of recognizing the young man's shape from across the room after knowing him for less than twenty-four hours. Still, that deduction also led him to suspect it was the Cantwells standing in the wings watching Jacob speak.

He scanned the room to try to find another glint of the familiar and instead caught someone who wasn't emersed in darkness, someone who he assumed had to be Tracy Cantwell-Jackson.

She stared at him in confusion and wonder.

Zena moved through The Darker for countless days and countless nights that slowly accumulated into countless weeks, and those countless weeks became countless months.

She watched the gloomy shapes that she knew to be her parents as they moved through the house. The time without her had taken its toll, and while the disconnect of their worlds prevented her from deciphering the finer details, she had trained herself to read the body language of their shadows.

Even at her young age, which seemed to be holding fast against the passage of time in The Darker, she learned about how her parents were processing her disappearance. She read their grief, their anger, their frustration, and, eventually, their apathy. Wiser than the years she didn't know whether she'd get to experience, she didn't find herself hurt by that apathy; she understood and empathized with it. She understood because she was experiencing the same thing. It wasn't that she was accepting the situation, but she had grown bored of acknowledging it. She just existed in the ether, – like her parents who had grown exhausted with being so constantly sad and had transitioned into being constantly exhausted.

In the light, Ruby and Jasper were also in the dark. Zena's interpretations had been right. They had gone through the stages of grief but rather than settling on acceptance they had fallen into a state of apathy where they were both just so tired of hurting and found that ignoring the issue was the easiest way to exist. Of course, there was the semi-regular interference from local police who were never quite on the same page to just let the problem disappear. They were still intent on tying Jasper to it, even if they hadn't been able to figure out how.

Despite their attempts at burying their heads, Ruby and Jasper were still very aware that the anniversary of the disappearance was coming. How could they not? That's the thing about having tragic life events coincide with holidays; no one else cares that every simple celebratory gesture cuts into your heart. That the things that used to make it a special day—the traditions, the decorations, the curated pages of seasonal favourites on streaming services—all serve as a reminder of why that day will always be a bitter reminder of unwanted change.

Malcolm moved to Tracy. By his count she had about a nine-hour head start on figuring what the hell was going on and where they were, but by her expression, he wasn't expecting much insight.

"Tracy?" It was the first time he had heard himself speak in this world and was expecting it to sound as Jacob's had. Instead, he heard his true voice dampened and lacking the natural reverb the large ballroom should give to even a small, close conversation.

She couldn't answer. Her eyes just grew wider with the shock that not only was someone else in her world, but they knew who she was.

"I'm Malcolm, one of the authors here for the event," he continued. "You went missing last night and then this morning I walked into your office and then found myself here."

Watching him as he spoke, he could see her wheels turning.

He found that as someone who wrote horror stories his brain often went to weird places. Frightening places. That meant that his mind raced through worst-case scenarios whenever he was in big spooky houses, along quiet wooded paths at night, and when he got sucked into dark, ethereal worlds that seemed to run parallel to the normally perceived plane of existence. So, he grasped onto the tendrils of what the hell was happening a bit quicker than she did. As someone with a seemingly normal mind, she was still grappling with being sucked into this world. The idea that someone else was also experiencing this and was aware of her might take her a minute to truly grasp.

"Last night?" she finally asked.

"Yeah," he confirmed. "Does it seem like longer?"

"No." She looked around the room. "I just got here."

Zena knew she was alone in the house. She didn't know where her parents were gone, but from what she could tell her father had left the house last night and hadn't returned. Her mother left this morning.

She couldn't go with them. The Darker was her home. When she tried to exit the house, there wasn't a similar gloomy version of their yard waiting outside for her; it was just blackness.

Early, she had tried to wander into that space, but stepping outside the gloom and moving into the black *felt* different. Inside the house, in the gloom of The Darker, there was still an ambience that her eyes had adjusted to, but when she tried to move outside, that evaporated into a void that made her flesh tingle. The unknown of it all scared her even more than this twisted version of the home she had known her whole life.

She wandered through the empty house, waiting for the comfort of feeling her parents' presence, so when she heard the echoes of the door opening, she moved to the hallway to be near them.

Except it wasn't the shadows of her parents in the porch.

Standing in the threshold of the house with the low sunlight of a fading October day behind him stood a man with an outstretched hand and a top hat.

Malcolm, initially trying to give Tracy space and ease her into what he understood their reality to be, had since changed course and inundated her with questions.

From what the pair had discerned, she had met one of the writers last night in the lobby. She couldn't remember much about who it was, but they had read her a story, and somewhere during the story she lost consciousness. Well, not quite consciousness, it's not as though she had fallen asleep, but the world around her faded, and when she became lucid, she found herself in this strange darkened realm. She had wandered through the distorted version of the hotel until she found herself in the Matthias Room and face to face with Malcolm. All of which felt like roughly twenty minutes to her.

Malcolm's story wasn't all that different now that he really unpacked it. He remembered going to Tracy's office with Maggie, finding it in disarray with pages of a story covering the walls and then being here, in this darkness. He had tried his phone, found no signal and the flashlight would come on but did nothing to illuminate the world, just falling off into velvety blackness. He, too, wandered the building until he found his way to the Matthias and Tracy. By his calculation he had been in this world for about twenty minutes.

"What should we do?" She asked him, giving authority to his twisted mind, a place where until very recently was the only location they thought their current situation would play out in.

"I don't know," he answered, flummoxed by the reality. "Should we explore the place? I don't know if we'll find answers to any of this just standing here."

She nodded, accepting his proposition, and the pair made their way to the door. Their footfalls were cushioned by the mossy texture of the ground laying beneath a low hanging fog that, like so many unnatural things in this strange world, failed to dissipate as they moved through it.

Once in the hall, they both scanned as much as they could see but were met by the same darkness as inside the former ballroom, except for a shock of white that Malcolm could see at the far end of the building, past the lobby.

It would appear, like him and Tracy, the birch tree that the sunroom had been built around was also in this netherworld.

He motioned towards it, drawing her attention, and they slowly crossed the lobby and, still cautious of their darkened surroundings, made the trek slowly, peering around corners and opening doors.

They reached the front desk and Tracy put both hands on the far side and pulled herself over to look behind it. Malcolm kept watch and out of the corner of his eye caught a flash of movement by the birch. He broke into a sprint, feeling the ground squelch beneath his steps before bursting into the sunroom.

No light came in from the windows. None of the plants other than the tree had any sense of sharing this world with him. The only other thing in the room besides the towering tree that seemed to belong were the young woman and small child that held hands as they danced around the trunk.

There are two types of days in October. There are the gloomy days where everything is wet and the light of morning doesn't seem to penetrate the clouds until midday, only to retreat again a few hours later. Those are the days when Zena would stare out at the dreariness through a classroom window covered in construction paper jack-o'-lanterns and long for the warmth of her house and whichever Disney channel Halloween movie was next in her queue.

The other days were the ones where the sun stayed yellow and low, and you could close your eyes to feel the last of its warmth while inhaling deeply, taking in the sweet rot of the leaves as you listened to them skittering across the ground at your feet.

It was one of the latter days, and Zena, after spending the last year in The Darker, took in as much of that autumn sun as she could.

She had followed the man in the top hat out of her house and into a large double decker bus, the kind she had seen in movies set in England except this one was purple. He had led her through the lower deck, made out as a haunted house— much more elaborate that the makeshift one her dad had made the year prior—and up the stairs to the upper deck, which was made to look like an old-timey parlour.

She did all of this in a daze, aware that following this strange man onto this strange bus was against everything her parents had taught her, but he was also getting her out of The Darker and there was nothing that she could imagine now that could be worse than that.

She sat by one of the windows on the upper deck, with the faux-velvet curtain pulled back, and watched the sun as the bus raced toward it over the highway.

Towns and landmarks flicked by, quicker than she knew them to, and as they approached what she thought was the center of the island, the hatted man climbed the stairs and sat across from her in the makeshift booth. Until now, Zena had assumed he was the one driving, and the puzzlement showed on her face.

"I am sure that you have some questions, Zena," he said with an accent that sounded less like a Newfoundlander and more like an actor from a black and white movie. "And I promise you that you will have answers in due time. But for now, I recommend you sit back and enjoy the journey."

He watched her with a strange, empty smile.

"It's a lovely day," he continued. "I just adore this time of year, don't you?" He watched intently, waiting for her to take the bait and engage in the conversation. Instead, she wrapped herself into a ball and hardened her stare at the passing landscape. Outside, the late greens of the east were transitioning to the golden hues of the west coast, which Zena knew from family road trips welcomed fall weeks before the rest of the island and did so with a zest for autumn that was usually reserved for Ray Bradbury stories.

Finally, she broke the silence.

"Where was I?"

"Where did you think you were?" he answered, coyly.

"It was my house but darker. I called it The Darker."

"That sounds as fitting as any name I've heard for it. Let's just be happy you're clear of the place."

"Why was I there?"

"I couldn't rightly say why, just that you were and now you're not." His answers were infuriating to her.

"Where are my parents?"

"They're back in the city."

"Why are we going away from them?"

"Because there are other people I need to bring you to before you go to your parents." His voice, which had started playful through the beginning of her inquisition, turned cold and sinister. He immediately caught himself and corrected as he stood up and moved away from her. "But fret not, our chariot is spry and our journey shan't be long."

He tapped the tin roof of the bus with the head of his walking stick, which she first thought was a dog but quickly realized was a wolf based solely on the context of how creepy this all was, and quickly descended the stairs.

Out the window, the sun held its position just above the horizon.

Tracy hadn't seen the flash of movement that had caught Malcolm's eye, so she hadn't shared his fervour to reach the sunroom. But when she got there, she shared his shock.

"I have heard their story countless times, but it can't be them," she whispered to him.

"I only heard it once, but it must be," he answered.

The woman and child paused their celebratory dance, and the youngster, only now seeing the strangers in the doorway, latched on to the billowing dress the woman was wearing, using her as a shield.

"Who art thou?" she demanded.

Malcolm stepped forward, trying to mimic the woman's formality as a means of easing her fear.

"I am Malcolm Hennessey," he said, bowing. "Are you…"

Tracy didn't partake in the performative salutations.

"Are you Victoria Powers?" she blurted.

"Yes, I am she. And who are you?"

"I'm Tracy Cantwell." She looked to Malcolm to gauge his reaction to her dropped hyphenate, but there was none. He understood why she did it.

"Cantwell?" As Victoria asked, Elenore peaked around her.

"Ms. Powers, how long have you been here?" Malcolm inquired but she ignored his question.

Victoria wrapped her arm around Elenore, pulling the child closer to her.

"Too long. How have you joined us here?" she asked, voice quivering.

"I'm afraid Mr. Hennessey isn't able to answer that question for you, my dear."

They all spun to see the source of the voice and were shocked to find a young girl, no more than ten, standing in the door to the sunroom. Malcolm and Tracy shared puzzled glances at each other. The voice had been deep and booming, a man's voice, not this child's.

Then, like the showman he was, the man in the top hat stepped out of the darkness and made himself seen.

Malcolm's jaw dropped. It couldn't be. But it was. He supposed it was no stranger than this twisted world they found themselves in, but he knew that this was Simon, the mysterious host of the bus tour from his book. He had conjured this man who now stood before him—he had conjured him hadn't he?

Where had the idea really come from? Having the character invade whatever this reality was would be too much. The threads of his sanity were tenuous as it were and being confronted by what he knew to be a fictional character of his own creation could be the final straw that confirmed his descent into madness.

"Simon?" he asked in almost a whisper, unable to put any breath into his voice.

"That was never my name, was it? Just a game," the hatted man replied.

"Nathaniel!" Elenore tore herself from Victoria's side and ran to the man, jumping into his arms.

"Hello, pet, I've missed you." He kissed the girl on the forehead, hugging her tight.

"I've been here the whole time, Nathaniel. Why didn't you come?" the girl said.

"I wanted to, but I couldn't, and I've missed you for every moment." He kissed her head again and then turned to Victoria. "And you, as well."

She stepped to him and he lowered Elenore to the ground. He took Victoria into his arms and kissed her with the passion of missed centuries. As they parted, he held her face in is hands.

"It's been too long, my love," he told her.

"Nathaniel, what is happening? Who are these people?" she asked.

"You're Nathaniel Cantwell?" Malcolm inquired.

"He can't be, Nathaniel died in…" Tracy racked her brain to remember the date, and while she couldn't be sure of the exact year of his death, she knew that it was long enough ago for him to be considered an ancestor of her deceased wife, and "ancestor" wasn't a term thrown around for people who are still alive.

"Not died, m'dear," the supposed Nathaniel intercepted. "What you'll find if you dig through the history of the family is that Nathaniel," with this he doffed his top hat, "disappeared not long after his sister and her governess also ceased to be present."

Malcolm was impressed with how flawlessly the man chose his words, which he suspected came from lifetimes of practice. Based on the information gathered from the various placards of Cantwell history around the manor, he would estimate that Simon, or Nathaniel, would be every bit of 250 years old. Yet, this man claiming the persona appeared no more than 30.

"Vampire?" Malcolm asked.

"Goodness no," Nathaniel replied, "but Mr. Hennessey, I do appreciate your acceptance of the premise. I quite feared having to provide an exposition dump. I've become quite proud of my storytelling abilities and the idea of having to confirm the supernatural and my continued existence seemed bulky and pedestrian. I'm glad that you appreciate the conceit and that we can get into the nuts and bolts of it all.

"I'm just a merchant, Mr. Hennessey. Someone who has, through various dealings and arrangements, prospered and thrived. Sure, you wrote a book detailing one such deal."

"Detailing? I concocted a silly story about a sect of occultists making ritual sacrifices in the basement of my hometown theatre!" Malcolm spat back.

"You say you concocted it, and yet I stand here in front of you. So, I ask you, where did your story come from?"

Malcolm froze, his mind going through his back catalogue and fearing for what he had put his characters through.

"Am I...what...a prophet?"

"My goodness, Mr. Hennessy. Mere moments ago, you claimed you just concocted silly stories and now you believe yourself a prophet?" Nathaniel scoffed. "No, I would say it's slightly more complicated than some sort of divine enlightenment that you have been chosen for. After all, it's not just you, is it? My new friend, Ms. Jenkins, isn't even from one of your stories but of Jacob's, the bellhop."

Malcolm looked to the girl who had arrived with his character. She was watching this confrontation play out from the doorway. He then shot his eyes to Tracy, who stood next to him, mouth gaping as she tried to take it all in.

Nathaniel stepped between Victoria and Elenore, put his arms around them, and began ushering them towards the door.

"If you all don't mind joining us," he said, "we've got one last leg of our journey."

"No." Malcolm put himself between Nathaniel and the door, blocking him from leaving and from Tracy and the other child. "I need to know what's going on."

"And I will tell you," Nathaniel growled, before composing himself and adding: "just not here."

He snapped his fingers and instantly they were aboard a bus, the bus. Malcolm took it all in, the tiny details he thought he had imagined, conjured to the page, all there. He faced Tracy and the girl in one of the makeshift booths. The chain of the banker's lamp that populated the table between them swayed as the bus hurtled down the highway.

"If you'll all just show some patience..." Nathaniel was standing in the aisle with a hand on the shoulder of Victoria. She was seated next to him with a hand over his and her other arm hugging Elenore.

"...we've got one more stop."

ON SALE NOW FROM ENGEN BOOKS

"Dunne breathes life into a world of magic and lore that will draw the reader in right up to the epic conclusion. Ashes is a heroic tale not to be missed."
Amanda Labonté
bestselling author of Supenatural Causes

When fifteen-year-old Phoenix loses her caregiver, everyone that she has ever known inexplicably turn their backs on her. Given the impossible burden of repaying an unknown debt, Phoenix sets out on her own with her trusty donkey, Muler, as her only companion. A chance encounter with Malcourt, a mysterious traveller, not only saves her life, but sets it on a trajectory that she would have never thought possible.

Zombies have taken over!
#1 Bestseller!
Zombie hordes created by the evil Pharmakon company have taken over the world, including the one place that always thought it was safe from the calamities of the outside: the quiet, scenic shores of Newfoundland's west coast. In this horrifying first volume, the island of Newfoundland is besieged by zombies and are left unprepared for the massacres that follow, struggling to stay alive as the city of Corner Brook falls to the undead hordes...

Book One: Outbreak (Feb 2017)
Book Two: The Viking Trail (Dec 2017)
Book Thee: Republic of Newfoundland (Sept 2019)

Also from Carberry: Carcharodon (Sept 2020)

"[Carberry] draws in his readers from the first page, effortlessly providing the tension and fear necessary to create his terrifying apocalyptic tale."
— *Fiona Cooke Hogan, author of What Happened In Dingle*

"This is an astonishing first novel from Paul Carberry. I read it over the course of two days, and in those two days my time was divided thusly: reading it, and wishing I were still reading it."
— *Matthew LeDrew, author of Black Womb*

DARK SHORT STORIES FROM ENGEN

MORE CHILLING FICTION FROM ENGEN BOOKS

If you find yourself craving more of the craven short fiction of the Engen authors, you're not alone. Check out *Chillers from the Rock*, an incredible (and spooky) entry in the long-running bestselling From the Rock series edited by Ellen Curtis and Erin Vance.

Chillers from the Rock features not only short fiction from **Jon Dobbin** and **Paul Carberry**, but also two stories each from **Ali House** and **Kelley Power**. If you enjoyed *Terror Nova*, it's sure to make you feel the same way.

If that's not enough Ali House for you, she is the only author to be featured in every open-call book of short fiction Engen has produced, making her the natural first choice for a collection of her fiction - both new and old - to celebrate.

The Lightbulb Forest is available now wherever better books are sold!

DARK STORIES FROM ENGEN BOOKS

THE HOWL BECONS

Growing up without his father, Tyler had no way of knowing the horrible secret that has plagued his family for generations. To free himself and find the cure, he will have to look beyond himself and into his dark history.

"A very ambitious novel… the horrors of everyday life can be worse than anything in fiction. The idea of using werewolves as a metaphor – to me this pushes the book a bit above much of what is out there… Brad [Dunne] is a very good writer and obviously has a deep background."
— Andrew Peacock

WESTON'S WAR

Something evil grows in the heart of Colorado. Bill Weston was a man of the West. He knew it – its land, its people, its stories. It was where he plied his trade, hunting men for money. His life wasn't easy, but it was predictable. That all changed when he captured Faraway Sue and he was led on a trip through the Colorado forests

"Take a little Zane Grey. Add a little Penny Dreadful. Read with Sam Elliot's voice. Discover Jon Dobbin's masterful The Starving."
— Darrell Power,
Great Big Sea

TERROR NOVA
WRITERS RETREAT

In the year since the release of the bestselling TERROR NOVA, the author of the cult-classic has been roaming the countryside to promote the book, all while struggling with writer's block that is hindering its sequel.

When the invitation comes to spend Halloween weekend at a centuries-old merchant estate for a writer's retreat, he thinks it might be the solution to his problems.

He doesn't expect to find that some scary stories write themselves...

Featuring twelve terrifying short stories from Newfoundland's top talents, including USA Today Bestseller Tanith Frost (*Resurrection*), horror short-fiction master Kelley Power (*Tombstories*), the talented CH Newell, and many more!